THE SHOOTER

'What will you be doing?' [...] front of him. He turned the [...] contaminated. I knew Gru[...]

'Looking for a job. Any suggestions?'

'A few. But not in that line. What can you do?' He paused and added bitterly, 'Besides being an ex-cop.'

'I learned a few things in prison.'

'Everyone does,' Grundy said wearily. He reached back to his filing cabinet. As parole officer, he overseered my life.

'I've got to earn a living.'

'Who you kidding?' He flipped a page. 'I guess you were framed. Right?'

'Wrong.'

'You can actually tell the difference?'

'No. Cops can't tell the difference between right and wrong and good and bad. What's good one day is bad the next, what's wrong yesterday is right today. Believe me. A good guy, a bad guy, how do you tell the difference?'

'You were a bandit, Scott. You broke trust. You robbed, lied, cheated and destroyed . . .'

THE SHOOTER

T. N. Murari

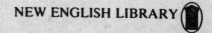
NEW ENGLISH LIBRARY

First published in Great Britain in 1984 by New English Library

First NEL Paperback Edition July 1985

NEL Books are published by
New English Library,
Mill Road, Dunton Green,
Sevenoaks, Kent.
Editorial office: 47 Bedford Square, London WC1B 3DP

British Library C.I.P.

Murari, Timeri
    The shooter – (NEL paperbacks)
    I. Title
    823′.914[F]   PR9499.3.M85

    ISBN 0-450-05813-1

Printed in Canada

For
Captain John Culley
and
Detective Andy Lugo
Extra-Ordinary Men

'Man grows used to everything,
the scoundrel.'
  He sank into thought.
  'And what if I am wrong. What if man
is not really a scoundrel, man in
general, I mean, the whole race of
mankind – then all the rest is
prejudice, simply artificial
terrors and there are no barriers
and it's all as it should be.'

Crime and Punishment
Fyodor Dostoyevsky

ONE

PRISON TEACHES patience. And police work. Cells and stake-outs. In both you're trapped. One by walls, the other by villains. I waited for Harry.

It was a white Christmas Eve. The suite in the Plaza Hotel overlooked Central Park. Snow blurred the lights and the sky. The view was as interesting as a cell wall. Below, on the opposite sidewalk the man waited. He wore a dark hat, a dark raincoat. Anonymous type. He'd been there three hours. I hoped he'd be frozen by dawn. I was warm. I had space in which to move around. Two rooms with attached bath. Better than an eight by six cell.

In the champagne bucket ice had turned to water. I opened a quart of Johnny Walker Red. It was two years, eight months and three hours since I'd tasted nectar. Harry wouldn't mind if I had a head start. Most probably he would have had a few on the way. One in the precinct, another in Rose's Garden. We'd tasted a few there, quite a few. Twelve years in the booths. Warm, dark, the odor of food and liquor. Harry would look at his watch: 'I gotta go, guys. I'm meeting my . . . '

What?

Friend? Too bland. Partner? Wrong. Ex-partner. He's out? Yeah. He's waiting in the Plaza. I promised to celebrate. I gotta go. I can't let him down.

Harry never let anyone down. The PD, partners, perps, victims, family. He'd come.

I poured three fingers of Red, dropped in two thin cubes and watched them melt. My palate awoke, kissed by alcohol.

The phone rang.

'Harry . . .'

'No. A friend asked me to phone.' It was an errand voice, bored, indifferent. 'You got everything?'

The envelope was on the desk. It contained five thousand dollars in hundreds.

'I don't want it.'

'Take it. You're gonna need favors now. He's just returning an old one.'

'It cost me a lot.'

'More than five?'

'My life.'

'For what it's worth. I'll tell him . . .'

'Nothing. I'll leave it where I found it. In reception.'

'Listen, if I were you I'd keep it.'

'You're not me.'

'No,' he admitted. 'I'm not an ex-con cop. It's your life.'

I drank and fixed another. Favors haunt, like alimony. You've forgotten the person and the place and the passion. It was past; I didn't want to think about it.

Midnight came. It was Christmas. I felt no different. The quart was quarter empty. Sometimes you drink with no effect. This was the some time. I heard them coming down the corridor – two men talking softly. They rang. I let them ring twice before opening the door. I knew the small one. Wide and broad, sparse hair neatly flattened, a trimmed moustache, a loud check jacket, patent leather shoes, gray eyes. He smelt, as usual, of deodorants.

'Paul, how are you?' Charlie Houldey was hearty. He pumped my hand, slapped me on the shoulder. 'This is

Marty Oakes. A new boy.' Oakes was thin, clean-shaven, balding, unsmiling. He looked as if he had a bad marriage.

'Great place you got here.' He strolled around.

'You got a warrant?'

Houldey was hurt.

'C'mon, we're old friends. I just wanted to say hi and welcome back.'

'We weren't friends.'

'We worked Homicide together,' Charlie smiled. He appeared not to have changed, yet he'd turned harder, the way a detective does without the smallest flicker in expression.

He remained superficially pleasant. 'How much this place cost? Couple of hundred?'

'Six.' Oakes remained at the door, arms folded, watchful. He didn't like me.

'A drink?'

'Sure.' Houldey swung the Scotch in his partner's direction, received a shake of the head. He poured a shot. 'Good to see you back.' He drank then sat. 'What was it like?'

I shrugged.

'Tough, I heard.' He stared pointedly at the scar. It began under my left ear and traveled down four and a half inches. It was not a neat one but jagged. It itched occasionally. 'They're out, you know.'

'I know.'

'Guess you did.' Charlie shook his head in wonder. 'Twenty to life for killing a cop, wounding you and they walk out in three. It's all shit. And you did almost your whole time.'

'What do you want, Charlie?'

'The same.'

'I did my time.'

'You could do more.'

'What for?'

'Oh, with-holding information. Taxes.' He changed abruptly, cruelly. 'You're a corrupt cop. We nailed you once, hard. We can do it again. We want the names of the others.'

'And the money?'

'Yes.' He returned to pleasantries. 'You hand over the money you made and the book will be wiped clean.'

'It'll never get clean. I made it. I'll keep it.'

'How you gonna spend it? Be reasonable. We'll stick the tax boys on you. They got Capone, you know.'

'They can try to get me.' I took Charlie's half-finished drink. 'I paid for what I did. Now, I'm going to enjoy it. Bye, bye, Charlie.'

Charlie didn't move. I hadn't expected to get rid of him that easily. Charlie and I had worked Homicide in the 48th precinct in the South Bronx. Charlie had been my sergeant. He also had a diploma from the FBI and a masters degree in criminal law from New York University. We'd not been friends, but we'd respected each other.

'Why IAD, Charlie?' Most detectives steered clear of Internal Affairs. The division, which investigated complaints against cops, had the stigma of betrayal. IAD men didn't mix with other cops.

'As a favor to a friend. Maybe I'll get a promotion after this.'

'Congratulations.'

I knew how it worked. A smart cop always had a 'rabbi' in the department, someone in a much higher position than him. It could be a lieutenant, a captain, even a chief. If you were truly lucky you had a rabbi downtown, an assistant commissioner, or two. Though they couldn't jump you from a sergeant to a lieutenant, or lieutenant to captain – those depended on civil service exams – they could ease a man through positions that depended on influence. It helped to have someone in your back pocket so that he helped you on the way up PD hierarchy. If you had no one you stayed where you were – for ever. I had had a rabbi. Once. Captain Ted Herlihy. I'd had a foot post in South Manhattan; Herlihy had been my sergeant. We were the same age, drank in the same bar, played on the precinct soft-ball team. As Herlihy rose through the ranks he'd helped me up. First he'd had me ride in the car, then he'd got me a gold shield. Then through the grades – third, second. I had nearly made first grade. You forget many things in prison. It was a self-imposed amnesia; a protective shell in which nothing could impinge. Simple things: a cold beer, a new shirt, an expensive meal, to sit on a sunlit beach. Major things: a woman, loving, playing with children, companionship. Life in prison was spare; longings were kept to a minimum, best forgotten. I'd never forgotten Herlihy. I remembered daily: a tall man with stooped shoulders, straight graying hair with a puff in front, thin-faced, gray eyes, smartly dressed in somewhat out-of-date suits. Herlihy had a courtly manner as if he belonged to another century. He would click his heels like a Prussian, even kiss a woman's hand. He liked to think all this sophisticated. I had too – now I thought him a clown. In prison I had had the time to examine a man's character in detail. Herlihy never looked you in the eye; he was a nervous man, his hands never still. He seldom made a decision without getting it cleared. This kept his ass out of the sling. He'd progressed by passing the buck.

'Where's Captain Herlihy?'

Charlie tilted his head, looking curiously like an ageing cockatoo.

'Didn't you hear? the captain's got God. He's a preachin' and sellin' Bibles.' He was pleased with his imitation of a Southern Baptist. 'He really dropped you in the shit, didn't he, boy?'

'I didn't say that.' I knew he'd have some answers.

'He travels around. We haven't heard from him since he quit the department just after you got sentenced. You're looking for him aren't you?'

'Just curious. He was my CO. I'd like to say hi. Nothing else.'

'Like hell. If you've got anything on Herlihy, you better tell me. Because if I ever do find out he was crooked, I'll break both your legs.'

I appeared bored. Not enough to fool Charlie. He'd given

his warnings, now he finally rose. He looked down regretfully at the glass of Scotch. 'What are you going to do now? Apply to NYPD for your old job?' He burst into laughter.

'I got time. I'll find something.'

'Tell me,' Charlie said standing by the window, glancing down. 'Why did you do it? You knew you'd get caught.'

'I didn't. A lot of guys didn't get caught.'

We watched a tourist couple, a young man and a pretty blonde-haired girl, climb into a hansom cab. The snow whirled around them and they looked happy. I imagined her face would be pink and cold when it was kissed, and if you slipped your arm under her coat and around her waist, you would feel only luxurious warm softness.

'So you went on the take only because you thought you wouldn't get caught?' Oakes sounded sad, weary too.

'Yes. I didn't have second thoughts. They offered money, I grabbed it with both hands.'

'Who's they?' It was slyly asked.

And ignored.

'Friends.' I sat down and for the first time felt weary, as if I'd traveled a great distance. 'Leave me alone, Charlie. I paid for what I did.'

'Because you were dumb. You kept your mouth shut during the whole trial – that's why you went up.' Charlie leaned forward, openly curious. 'Someone betrayed you. Your partners? Your buddies? Why didn't you betray them?'

'I couldn't – and live with myself. We all have things we can live with, or can't live with. Compromises, let's say. I couldn't live with betrayal.'

'Theirs?'

'My own. I saved my soul, Charlie.'

'Don't kid yourself. You never had one.'

He remained leaning, as if on a listing ship. He wanted to find a weakness and spoke carefully. 'Harry did.'

'Yeah . . . Did? What the hell you saying?' I couldn't breathe.

'I'm sorry.' Sadness settled changing his pallor. 'You were partners – the only good thing in your rotten life.'

'How? Goddammit. When . . . ?'

'Shot. Today.' He saw my face. 'Take a stiff drink.' He poured and I took a swallow but it tasted medicinal.

I rushed to the bathroom, gagging. Nothing came up. Only bile. I could not control the tears. I hadn't wept since a kid – not for myself, not for anyone. I washed my face. My eyes remained red. They waited with that familiar patience. We sat in awkward silence.

'Where?' My voice sounded dull and lifeless.

'He kept a small studio in Fordham.'

'Harry?'

'Yeah. We only learned about it when we got the call. Anonymous.'

Oakes moved away from the door.

'Where were you?'

'What the hell does that mean?'

'We're investigating. So far no suspects. Give us a rundown.'

I shrugged. 'No alibi – except I was in the halfway house downtown until noon. They opened the door, I took a cab here. I did some shopping, then waited for Harry.' I gestured at the champagne. It looked dispirited and neglected. 'We'd set to meet here at eight. What time was he killed?'

Neither replied.

'Aw come on. Harry and I grew up as kids together. We joined the PD the same time and always worked as partners. We even live . . . lived . . . in the same town.'

They remained expressionless. I read them wrong though. There was something else. They held it inside them tightly.

'You can check with your partner outside. He's been there since six – and knows I haven't left here. You guys are crazy.'

They glanced at each other. Both rose and peered out of the window. The man had gone.

'We didn't have anyone watching you.'

'How did you find me?'

Houldey sighed, his patience at an end. 'We're cops. We find people when we want to.'

'Okay then – there's something else you're holding back. What is it?'

'Nothing.' They rose. 'You're not a cop any more. We don't have to tell you anything. You were a good cop. Once. Now you got guys like Ventura running you.'

'I run myself.'

'Yah.'

The Ventura family controlled south-east Manhattan and Queens. The elder Ventura had been in the same prison as me. Charlie had put him there. It had been a lengthy operation. Charlie had run one of his men into the Ventura family. It had been a dangerous job, and he'd chosen a young detective, Bob Mark. Charlie had changed Mark's identity, invented a yellow sheet, controlled him alone. Big Mafia families had pipelines into the Department; and the less who knew about Mark the better. It had taken over two years to get all the information strong enough for a case against the elder Ventura. The price had been high for Mark, too. His wife divorced him. She could not take the strain of his double life.

'He paid this hotel bill.'

'So they owe me a favor.'

'I heard it was the other way.' He stared at the scar. 'If it hadn't been for Ventura, they'd have finished that job.'

'We all live off favors,' I said. 'Do me one.'

'I'm leaving.'

'That too. Who was Harry's partner?'

'Tony Mascali.' He went out, then stuck his head back in. He didn't speak a moment, but let his eyes roam the large, expensive, empty room. 'Merry Christmas.'

TWO

CHRISTMAS DAY! I woke early, from prison habit. I had a
suitcase of new clothes: two St Laurent suits, cotton shirts,
Bally shoes, silk ties, underwear. I had blown my savings.
Once I'd dressed well and expensively and I could not forgo
the pleasure. I shaved, showered and changed, and then
realized there was nowhere I wished to go; no one I wished
to call – yet I felt an unbearable loneliness.

I ordered breakfast and pulled a chair to the window.
Central Park was white, the trees starkly black, the street
below slushy and gray. It had snowed all night. The
wreckage of the night before remained. Two empty glasses,
half the quart, an overflowing ashtray, the stale pall of
cigarettes. An unsmoked cigar lay crushed and broken on a
table. It was all so little: a sad farewell. I had imagined my
first night of release to be an extravaganza. Money no object:
music, laughter, drinking, dinner and a good friend. We'd
planned it together over the years. I had kept my part of the
bargain: a wake for Harry.

In the distance I saw the kids on their toboggans: small,
silent figures, sliding down, trudging up. I could only

imagine their pleasure. Closer, the city appeared deserted. Traffic was sparse and only a few people moved along the slushy sidewalks. The man who had staked me out could not be seen. Maybe he had been a cop. Cops deceive from practise – it's like a religion.

I ate breakfast by the window.

It had snowed the day Harry had arrested me. The weatherman had predicted snow and heavy flakes had begun to drift down. Across the street a couple of cars were having trouble starting, and kids bundled in down jackets were drifting towards school. It was a shabby street. Most of the cars were old, beaten up. The buildings needed a coat of paint and major repairs. The room I'd rented had been small and sparsely furnished – a cot, a chair, a stained washbasin. I'd used it as an ashtray and it had filled with butts. I'd rung Harry and told him where I was. I'd seen the car turn on to the street, drive slowly, and stop at the entrance. Harry stepped out. He'd worn a white raincoat, a felt hat. He'd glanced up – a cop reflex – to scan the roof then bent to speak to someone in the car. I didn't know Harry's partner and was grateful the man remained in the car. I'd picked up my jacket and slipped it on. Sat and waited for the knock. I couldn't deny I'd been afraid. I was terrified. I'd perspired and trembled. It was the awful nightmare of every cop – to be arrested. To bring upon himself what he brought to others.

Harry had entered shlyly. He was embarrassed and sad. I wished then I'd given up to a stranger rather than my old friend. But it was done. We'd exchanged hallos, then an awkward silence followed before Harry had become the professional. He'd read me my rights. He didn't cuff me. We'd walked down, still silent, and into the street. The snow was heavy then and had clung to our clothes. Harry opened the back door and I slid in awkwardly. I'd nodded to Dan Callaghan, Harry's partner, a big, red-faced Irishman with a neat, thick moustache. He played the bagpipes for the Emerald Society.

The *News* and the *Post* gave Harry the front page: Cop shot. The *Times* slid him in on page fifteen. The reports were spare. Too spare. Shot dead, period. Awards for bravery. Wounded twice in the line of duty. A nineteen-year veteran detective. Police were investigating. Period. No one was quoted: 'He was a good cop.' It disturbed me. I felt the unease of the night before. Harry had been the best. The PC, the mayor, the commander were conspicuous by their silence. I hated their betrayal. I re-read in disbelief. Not even an honor funeral planned. What the hell happened?

Christmas is a bad day for condolences. I could not just ring his widow. I'd known Sandra as long as he had: since childhood. She was the new girl on the block. Small, shy, pert. Not a beauty, more an abandoned waif. Her parents had split and she'd moved in with her grandparents. We'd been sitting outside the candy store when she'd walked past. Harry had fallen in love. So he claimed. He never made out with her. He was too much of a gentleman even then. He seldom made out. I figured he married her because she was lonely. Harry did things like that.

I picked up a hire car and drove out over the 59th Street bridge. Traffic was light; the road glassy. The Long Island expressway swept past small, familiar towns, tucked behind the turnoffs. I could drive it with my eyes closed. There were some changes, not many, since I'd been away. A factory here, a gas station there. I'd not wanted to make the trip for a while. Chatsworth was forty miles up and I turned off. Almost reflexively I began to make a right at the first traffic light. Home was four blocks south, two west. Harry lived the other side, a five-minute drive. I turned into the crescent and halfway round I pulled into the kerb. The house was two-storeyed, white, with a small porch running its width. It looked as neat and trim as the others but it did not have the air of busyness. It was as if life had passed it by. No toys lay on the porch and there was a faint air of neglect.

I rang and waited. I thought at first no one was home and peered into the garage. The car was in. I rang again and heard the muffled movement of someone approaching. The door opened. The woman was tall, pleasantly attractive, weary. She wore a dressing gown.

'I'm sorry, Sandra. I truly am. I loved Harry.'

19

'Paul.' She put out her arms spontaneously and hugged me. 'Don't. I know. Oh Paul, it's so good to see you.' She wept and clung to me, nearly reducing me to tears once more. Finally she let go.

The interior smelt of cigarette smoke trapped too long. I kept an arm around her waist. She had a strong, supple body. In profile she had only a small indentation between brow and nose and this gave the impression, if you looked her full in the face, that her eyes were wide apart. They were red now and suffocated by rage.

'When did you get out?'

'Yesterday.' I looked around. It was familiar: the leather armchairs, the massive ashtrays, the leather-topped bar, the orange pile carpet. It was all simple and inexpensive. Shabby in contrast to my own home. 'I wake you?'

'Just had a Valium siesta,' Sandra said. 'A drink?'

'Sure.'

'You know where it is, I'll just slip something on.'

Barefoot, she went upstairs. I heard her moving around, imagined whispers but thought little of it. Hung behind the bar were photographs of Harry: certificates, medals. We'd led similar lives up to a point. One or two were new: bravery awards. Sandra came back down. She wore a brown wrap-around skirt with a wide leather belt, a flowered blouse. She'd brushed her hair and touched up her face.

'What happened?'

'Only what I read in the papers. We were going to have a drink. To celebrate. Harry didn't show. Two cops did. They told me nothing. What did they tell you?'

'Nothing. Just that he's dead.' She fixed a drink and sat. ' . . . God I'm going to miss him.' Her eyes glistened and she turned away. Her profile reminded me of an Egyptian queen. She shook herself, trying to throw off the melancholy of Harry's death. 'What'll you be doing now?'

'Nothing much. I'm on parole, so have to behave myself. I'm looking for a job.'

'How's Lauren?'

'Fine, I guess. I haven't seen her or the kids yet. I can't just walk back in as if I'd been on vacation.'

'Oh. She came over this morning when she heard.'

Talking was difficult. It was as if we were both short of breath. Gradually we fell silent, suffocated by Harry's invisible presence. He was gone and we no longer had that bond. I knew I'd not see much of her again. She had her life. We would drift apart and eventually lose touch.

'I'm going to investigate Harry's case,' I said abruptly.

'What difference does it make now, Paul?' Then gently, 'Let the cops do it, for my sake.'

'I can't. You know that.'

She shrugged, and appeared too tired to respond. Finally she repeated, 'It makes no difference now. He's dead. So you find the perp and he gets three years. My Harry's not going to come alive.' Her eyes shone again. 'I miss him so much.'

I held and comforted her, breathing in the sweet rich perfume of her skin and hair. She cried a while, then sniffled and stopped. 'Thanks,' she whispered and I returned to my chair. We said nothing. I finished my drink, the feeling of strangeness creeping up on me. Nothing seemed familiar now: all was different, even his leather chair in which I'd spent nights talking and drinking.

'Did Harry have anyone else, Sandra?'

'Not that I know of. We were happy together. Not ecstatic, but comfortable. Why?'

'One of the detectives said he kept an apartment in Fordham. You know about it?'

She looked bewildered. 'No. How long did he have it?'

'I don't know.'

'We never had enough money for ourselves.' She sniffled. 'He was a good cop I'm told. What do we wives ever really know about our men? Maybe like you he needed to get laid by someone now and then. I'd rather not go on any more.'

'I better get going.' She walked me to the door. 'If you need anything . . .'

'I'll call.'

The door closed with such finality behind me, like a lid slamming down on a coffin. I sat in the car smoking. Home was five minutes down the road. I'd open the door, walk in

21

and say . . . 'Sorry.' Too inadequate. I drove back to the city.

The chief medical examiner's office for New York City is in a modern building on the corner of 32nd Street and 1st Avenue. It is as ordinary as any office building. I knocked on a door before entering the wood-paneled offices of the ME. Pierre Fanon was young, in his early thirties. He was French and dressed elegantly. His suits were expensive and form-fitting as if sprayed to his body. He was small, not more than five foot seven, and his brown hair was cut close. He had a flat, sleepy face, like a cat purring. His appearance was deceptive though. Behind the languor lay a sharp, probing mind. From a fragment of bone, I had seen him build a whole body, and give every detail about the victim except his name and that of the perp.

'Paul Scott!' Fanon said after a moment's hesitation.

'You remembered.'

'You were a good detective. Like me.' He hesitated then shook hands. He spoke with an exaggerated American accent. 'Merry Christmas.'

'Same to you.'

The office hadn't changed. It was spacious with comfortable leather armchairs. The curtains were half-drawn. The lights were harsh and sharp as a morgue's.

'I need a favor.'

'You're not a cop still?'

'No.'

Fanon shrugged, an eloquent shift of his shoulders.

'A special favor. A friend was killed. I'd like to see the report.'

Fanon tugged an ear lobe, considering. 'Who?'

'Harry Margolis. He was my partner. Shot.'

'Twice.' He stood abruptly having decided. He left the office and returned with a file. 'Both times in the heart.'

He flicked through the neatly written pages. 'The bullets came in at a low trajectory as if the killer was crouching, or sitting, three feet away.'

'Not on the same level?'

'No. The first one killed him. Through the heart. It broke the right ventricle. The other was a half-inch to the left. Not bad.' He saw my face. The professional enthusiasm froze. 'Not good either.'

'Can I see him?'

I had forgotten the smell. It was strong, sickening, familiar. Half my life had been spent here worrying at death. Shot, stabbed, butchered, hanged, poisoned, gassed, drowned. The human expressed an eloquent creativity in his killing of another. A girl lay on a trolley, naked. She was serene and pretty, her beauty intact except for the 'Y' cut into her body and crudely stitched.

Harry lay on the table, beneath lights. He had been a stocky, powerful man. Five foot ten, around a hundred and eighty pounds, blond curly hair, a strong handsome face with a day's growth. In death, as in life, he was neat. You learn detachment early. Even a loved one is another corpse. His 'Y' too had been stitched.

'They were twenty-fives. He was a great guy. Good detective. Many aren't, you know. Harry had instinct. He knew how someone had died long before we did. He would come here just to confirm his guess.'

I touched his face. The skin was cold and stiff.

Busily Fanon removed a sheet and covered Harry up. It was a final gesture. His work was over.

'I just can't figure it out.'

'You said two bullets.'

'That was easy. No, that he was a corrupt cop. Shows how wrong I can be in judging a man.'

'Harry? You're out of your mind. He never took even a thin dime in his life. I know that man better than myself.'

'You don't. They found half a kilo of coke hidden in his apartment, my friend. And two thousand dollars in cash.'

THREE

THE ROOM had grown dark and the sky was clear and brittle as crystal. I must have sat for hours, frozen in disbelief. I still couldn't comprehend the enormity of Fanon's information. It had that kind of weight that suffocated your breath.

'I don't believe it.' I spoke aloud.

Harry loved his work too much. He took the good with the shit. All he ever wanted was to be a cop, a good cop. He had no rabbi, he never rose above third grade. He couldn't pass exams. And he never took a dime. Half a kilo. Two grand. That was a fortune. He'd lived poor, died rich. It made no sense. Sandra had said they never had money. The apartment then? I didn't know. In the Bronx they come cheap, unlike Manhattan. The coke and the money explained the silence of the PC, the mayor and the commanding officer. They were embarrassed. A no-good cop dead. They figured it a narcotics hit.

'I don't believe it. Harry hated drugs.'

No one replied. In my cell I'd kept silent. Here, I was

talking out aloud. It was crazy. I wanted good thoughts.
There were many.

We had been rookies back then. A call had come over the
radio to investigate a disturbance. Harry and I had responded and walked into a plush Upper East Side apartment. A
man and a woman awaited us calmly. She was red-headed
with everything that God could give a woman: great legs, a
beautiful body, a lovely face, only her eyes betrayed an
anger. The man was older and had that sleek look only the
rich can cultivate: arrogance, pampered hair, tanned face, a
Japanese silk kimono. The woman wore one too and nothing
underneath. The man had taken Harry into another room; I
had remained with the woman. She sat showing pussy and
ignoring me and all I could think of was getting into her. I
was hard as a night stick looking at her. Harry returned a
minute later, his face tightly solemn. He was trying not to
crack up. He jerked his head towards the room and I went
in. The man stood with his kimono open: his penis had been
glued to his thigh. Its head was also glued shut. It was an
instant glue that held steel girders together. We called an
ambulance and listened to the story: he'd been playing
around with another chick and then, tiring, called back
his red-head. She'd forgiven him. They'd dined, drunk
champagne, screwed. While he'd slept she'd glued his
cock.

I laughed out loud. Harry told the story so well, over and
over. Briefly I felt lightened. People did crazy things. At
least she'd not shot the son-of-a-bitch. I'd seen enough of
that for a lifetime.

The doorbell rang. It started me from my memories like a
wind through dust. It was night and I switched on the table
lamp. A woman stood in the brightly lit corridor. She smelt
the whiskey and recoiled. She looked in her late twenties and
vaguely familiar. Blonde hair, an alert, attractive face,
clear gray eyes. The kind models have. There was a small
break in her nose, indistinct at a distance.

Behind her in the corridor were two more people. One a
small, pert woman with short hair. Her down jacket made
her look wider and chunkier than she really was. The other

was a tall, ageless black man. The woman carried a mini-cam tucked under her right arm and pointing straight at me; the man babied a tape-recorder on his belly. Both stared at me in boredom. A mike hung down from the man's left hand.

'Paul Scott?' She had an attractive, soft voice. It was meant to calm.

'Who's asking?'

'I'm Christine Breelander. Channel Three.' She looked past my shoulder. 'I'd like to come in.'

'What the hell for?'

'Harry said you bit. He was right.'

I stood back and she strolled past me as if it had been right all along. The other two followed her. They were used to passing people planted at doorways. Breelander sat primly but at ease and as she removed her top coat she sniffed loudly. I could smell nothing except her perfume. She wore a modest blue dress and the color complemented her eyes.

'Why don't you open a window?'

'I like the smell. You knew Harry?'

'A little.' She wrinkled her nose. It was an affectation meant to soften me and make me sit by her side in confidence. I had seen her reporting a few times, mostly cop stories. She and her colleagues had voracious appetites for the horrendous: child murders, disembowelments, family extinctions. They were paid by every second of air-time and made more a week than a cop did a year: 'We were friends.'

'The only expensive-looking chicks cops know are hookers.'

'I'm not one.' She was calm and unflurried and used to the difficult. She rose, found the bathroom and when she returned a couple of minutes later there was an additional polish in her hair and on her face. She also carried a glass and poured herself a couple of fingers of Scotch. 'I was very sorry to hear about Harry.'

'You came here to say that.'

'No. But I did like him.' She sipped solemnly, like a child testing a strange soda. This time her nose didn't wrinkle. I swung the bottle in the direction of her crew. They ignored me and sat whispering conspiratorially in a corner. They too had learnt patience.

'What do you want?'

'A story.' She pulled a notebook from her purse, then searched for and found a pen. I took it away from her and saw surprise for the first time.

'What kind?'

'A profile of Harry. When a cop gets killed all we ever do is report the facts on the killing and then show footage on the funeral and a close-up of the weeping widow. I want to do something in depth. At least five minutes of air time.'

'Is that all he's worth?'

She ignored me. 'What kind of a man he was. What kind of a cop. Why he became one. What his friends thought of him.'

'I'm not in the mood to talk to a stranger about my friend.'

She met my stare unwinkingly and snapped her book shut. It sounded like a snap of the fingers and drew the attention of her crew. They noted the finality and stood up, drifting to the door.

'I reported your case. Detective Paul Scott taking kickbacks. How much did you make?'

'You from the IRS as well?'

'I heard the number was around twenty, thirty grand. There were others involved too but you wouldn't give up their names. Someone set you up.'

'I know that.'

'That someone knew exactly where and when you were to be paid off. And the cops were waiting. They'd been tipped off.'

'What are you trying to do? Change my mind?'

'Just remembering your story.'

'Go remember elsewhere. Okay.'

'I will.' She leant back and sipped her whiskey. I didn't scare her. I'd lost my charm. 'I heard a whisper about narcotics. Was Harry corrupt?'

'No.'

'You're pretty sure. He could have changed over the last ... three, four years?'

'Harry never changed. He couldn't. He was stuck with being what he is ... was. A good cop.'

'Then how do you explain it?' She smiled gently. 'Presuming the whisper I heard was right of course.'

'Yeah. And like a sucker I just confirmed it. This an interview?'

I glanced towards the two by the door. They stared into space, and their equipment showed no telltale lights.

'Just research. Harry always helped me on any of his cases. Of course he gave the information in confidence.'

'In confidence then: it was planted.'

'My whisperer also told me it was around half a kilo. You know the street value of that? At least thirty thousand. Who's going to leave so much coke lying around? They shot him. Wasn't that enough? They would have taken the coke.'

'That's why it's a flake. No one leaves something like that behind. The shooter wanted to hurt Harry beyond the grave. He knew how as well. By destroying what Harry cared for the most: his name and his reputation.'

She shrugged. It meant she wanted facts not speculation. She studied me gravely as if seeing me for the first time. Her face was a mirror. She noticed the bone pallor of my skin and the scar on my throat.

'Prison does that.'

'You should do a circus act.' She swallowed her drink and it didn't flush her. I heard the door open and watched her companions step out. They knew it was over. She opened her handbag, returned her notebook and pulled out a visiting card. 'If you change your mind, call me. I want to do this story and even if I don't get you to talk, others will.'

'Because of the narcotics?'

'Because he's a dead cop.'

She slid from the sofa revealing the inside of her thigh. She knew it showed and deliberately took her time in adjusting her clothes before standing.

28

'You want to get laid?'

'No thanks. Harry had more style than you.'

'I know. You lay him?'

'None of your business.' I didn't shake her poise. She stared down at me. Her height was no advantage. She dropped to the scar.

'I don't like your eyes either.'

'Most people don't.' She walked to the door nicely. No exaggeration. A healthy beast with coiled buttocks. 'How'd you find me?'

'Sergeant Houldey.' She turned at the door. 'You related to James Scott Prescott?' Her crew moved off down the corridor.

I didn't reply. Success clung to her like a sheen of perspiration on a champion runner.

'You know the one? Couple of seats on the Stock Exchange, house in the Hamptons, apartment in Sutton Place. Old money.'

'Distantly.'

'So I heard.' She was framed in the light. 'Don't bother to get up.'

She went quietly. Another woman would have slammed the door. It was an elegant card, too. At least she hadn't wished me a Merry Christmas. I waited an hour, and called. She answered.

'Scott! How about dinner one evening?'

'Why not? Can you wait till New Year's Eve?'

'Won't you have a ball in the Waldorf?'

'I'll skip it this year.'

I checked out at noon. The celebration was over. I took the five thousand. It was too big a tip for the help. I caught a cab up to Bruckner Boulevard, promising the driver a round-trip fare. The South Bronx was unloved and rooms went cheap. I found one and took it for a month. I caught Harry's last partner, Tony Mascali, starting tour, and set up a meeting at midnight.

CJ's was new, elegant as a Manhattan restaurant. There

was gold lettering on the smoked plate glass, elaborate oak doors, and inside, mirrors and plants in profusion. The bar ran the length of the room and beyond was a small oval dance floor. The mirrors were sprayed white and plastic holly wreaths hung on the walls. It was cool and quiet. A few men sat at the bar. I recognized one or two and wished I'd not agreed to Mascali's choice. The men in turn glanced, then stared. They appeared wary, then one smiled.

'How are you Paul?' He shook hands. Dick Lester had been a sergeant in Homicide. He was small and frail with graying hair and a friendly, round face. 'A drink?'

'Thanks no. I'm meeting a detective, Tony Mascali. You know him?'

'Sure. At the end of the bar.' Dick paused. 'I'm sorry, Paul.' He knew it was inadequate. 'That was a real son-of-a-bitch.'

'Yah. You're looking well.'

'You too,' he answered, though he glanced at the scar, then away. Everyone knew.

Mascali sat hunched, a glass of beer on the bar. From the stoop of his shoulders he appeared preoccupied, burdened, and to be sitting alone when other cops were at the other end of the bar was strange. He looked a young man though his hair was thinning.

'Tony Mascali?'

Mascali had a broad, strong face. He stood, and looked fit and powerful. He wore a blue suit, well cut except for the slight bulge of his shoulder holster. He was about my height, and his hands were strong and thick, with powerful fingers.

'Yah. Scott? How are you? Listen, why don't we take a booth over there.' He gestured. 'What'll you have?'

'Red Label.'

'How can I help you?' Mascali sat opposite. He was nervous. He had slot-machine eyes: whirling. How in hell could Harry have worked with this crazy?

'I knew you when I was a kid,' he said suddenly.

'Where?'

'I lived on 114th and Lexington. I'd seen you around

30

with Harry. You guys were always having a great time. I was only a kid then.'

'So was I.'

'An older one but,' he added apologetically. 'Harry always talked about you. You were . . . had been his hero.'

'I know.' I wished he'd not pursued the subject. 'You were his last partner?'

'We been partners three . . . four weeks,' Mascali sounded defensive.

'I'd been in Theft working out of the four-six, and got transferred to Homicide. He didn't remember me.' Mascali fell silent as if wondering why Harry had not recalled his presence on the streets as a kid.

'What happened?'

'We were on the day shift. It was one-fifteen, just when we were going to lunch when he got a call. It didn't come over the radio. Someone called into the office.'

'You mean they called the four-eight?'

'No. Homicide. They asked for him.'

'You took the call?' I took out a steno book and wrote carefully and deliberately.

'No.'

'Then why do you keep saying "they"?'

'It's a figure of speech. Harry took the call. He seemed . . . ' Mascali hesitated as if he'd thought often of the moment. ' . . . pleased by it. I don't know. It made him happy, let's say. Like it was Christmas.'

'It was nearly.'

'He said he'd grab a bite to eat and catch me later. That's the last I saw him alive. Then we got an anonymous call and found Harry.'

'What time was the call?'

'Two-oh-three. We responded immediately.'

'The caller say where.'

'Exact address. The door had a deadlock. We went down the fire-escape. The window was locked and had a guard. We smashed it and got in. Harry lay in a corner.'

'What else?'

31

'Nothing else. Except the narcotics in a flight bag. The cash was in a brown paper bag.'

'His gun?'

'It was in his holster.' Then he added, almost apologetically, 'His jacket was buttoned. He didn't expect to go for his gun when he got chopped.'

Silence settled. Mascali played with his glass. I leant back, imagining the call. The response from every cop in the area. The catcher examining the victim. Detectives combing the apartment. Finger-printing. The canvass of the building and the neighborhood by countless detectives asking questions, taking notes, returning. What did you see? What did you hear? Anything at all. The crowds that materialize from nowhere to gawk at the death of a fellow human, their faces blank and incurious as if they were watching another television program. Possibly in the South Bronx reality and illusion were indistinguishable.

'You the catcher?'

'No. It was Johnny Johnstone.'

'Why not you? You were his partner?'

Mascali turned away, eyes flicking to each arrival in the bar. My silence unsettled him. The question wasn't repeated but a reply was expected. Mascali had not been Harry's partner long. I guessed that Harry had been forced to take him.

'You'll only get it from someone else,' Mascali whispered. 'I'm not a bad cop. I'm . . . hot-headed. I act before thinking and often get myself into trouble. I'd been on the verge of losing my gold shield, when I got transferred to Homicide. Lieutenant Dwyer, the commanding officer of the 7th Homicide zone, looked through my file then sent for Harry. I was kind of flattered to be working with him, I guess. I was asked to leave the lieut's office. When I was recalled ten minutes later I was Harry's partner. Harry himself stayed silent. His face was pink as if he'd been blushing. Or angry.'

I wasn't sure who I felt sorrier for. Him or Harry.

'When I first saw Harry dead,' Mascali continued, ' . . . lying there like a discarded doll, I thought, he's going to be mad, getting his clothes all mussed up like that. I wanted to pick him up, dust him, wipe off the ugly red stain and apologize, as if it were my fault the jacket was all fouled up.'

'No weapon?'

'No weapon. The bullets were from a .25. Fired at a close range.'

'No leads.'

'Zilch.' He hesitated. 'The department doesn't know how to handle this one.'

'Fuck the department. Everyone in the building questioned?'

'Yes.'

'What about the canvass?'

'Nobody saw nothing. It was lunchtime, Christmas Eve – people got other things on their minds.'

'How long had Harry had that apartment?'

'Eighteen months.' He spread his hands. 'I didn't know about it.'

'Any description from the super?'

'From the wino? He couldn't describe himself standing in front of a mirror. He's got a permanent blur.'

I wrote. He turned restless and fidgety, then suddenly jumped up. 'Another Red?'

'Sit down.' He wanted to refuse, then sat reluctantly. 'You scared of me?'

'No.' He shook his head to reinforce his answer. He glanced at the scar and away. 'I knew you'd be asking questions. I've been waiting. You and Harry were like that.' He entwined two fingers. 'Maybe you'll find out who chopped your friend. I liked Harry, believe me, I liked him. He was a lovely guy, a great cop . . .'

'You trying to tell me something?'

He held my eye a second. A long time for him. 'Was Harry crooked? You knew him better than anyone?'

'No.'

'His prints were on the coke bag – all over. No one else's.' He sighed. 'If someone had put a gun to my head and said Harry was crooked, I would have taken the bullet. Now, I don't know.'

'What do you figure?'

'Maybe he was moonlighting. Giving protection.'

'You never knew Harry then.'

'I know.'

He rose, mopping the sweat. 'I've got to go.' He put out his hand. I ignored it. It hovered before dropping.

'Where do you live?'

Mascali hesitated: 'On Westchester. I used to live on the Island. My family still does,' he added unnecessarily.

I wasn't surprised. How many of my cop friends were divorced or separated. I couldn't count. At first they moved to Long Island, upstate New York, with brand-new families, brand-new houses, brand-new lawns, brand-new pools. Four, five, sometimes ten years later they would return alone. Solitary men missing their families, sharing untidy apartments in and around the Bronx or Queens or Brooklyn with other divorced cops.

'You got a phone?' Mascali scribbled out a number on a napkin and slid it across. 'Talk to you later,' I said and watched Mascali move to the exit. He reminded me of a bee in his progress. Stopping, starting, darting from person to person, booth to booth. Finally he reached the door.

I waited five minutes before following. More off-duty cops were propping up the bar. Some recognized me and shook hands, others deliberately turned their backs. I had a drink with Lester. We talked of the old times and as I finished asked: 'What's Mascali like as a cop?'

'Okay, but off the wall. Aren't we all?'

I left, feeling a stranger. I no longer belonged to them. I belonged to no one. Though it was dark the street was filled with people. Blacks, Hispanics, here and there a few whites. A black man stood in a doorway. He was neatly dressed, buoyant.

'Hey, mister,' he called, 'I'm an alcoholic. Got a quarter?'

I flipped a coin. It was deftly caught. 'Hey, aren't you The Man?' He came up and peered at me, then laughed in delight. 'I know you. Paul Scott.'

'Yes.'

He put out his hand, palm up. I gave him skin. I didn't recognize him. Too many faces passed through a detective's life. Some remained, others faded into obscurity or early graves. I bought a *Post* at the subway entrance and hailed a gypsy cab to take me back to my rooming-house. When I reached the building the street was gloomy. The lights were on, washy and fuzzy still. Night dimmed their brilliance. The streets here were empty. I reached the front door when the bullet hit me.

FOUR

I FELL back and upset a garbage can; its contents spilt over me like a covering. I rolled once, and struck my head against the bottom step. I fell into dark silence.

It was a long, narrow corridor I moved down. A bare bulb lit the stained walls, the creaking floors. I crept along the edge, mesmerized by the closed door. I wished I would never reach it. It seemed to race towards me. I sensed the men behind me: Harry and four patrolmen. The light gleamed dully on their guns. Like me they crept, inching up the corridor as if it were a mountain we scaled. A man stepped out, saw us, silently stepped back and locked his door. Sounds: children talking, music, television. Warm and comforting. The door was on me too quickly. It was blurred then. I kicked it in. A man, Caucasian, young, by the window, stared in astonishment and then his hand moved. I wasn't sure why or for what. I fired, then Harry. Our bullets hurled the man half out of the window, shattering the glass. I'd just started to turn when I was hit in the side. I'd fallen and Washington Clay came to stand over me, firing down. I'd rolled, twisted, curled, thrashed. The bullets

36

gouged and splintered wood. Harry stood at his head, firing at Washington. It was weird, hallucinatory: they both kept missing. Harry fired five rounds, missing Washington; Washington eight, all around me. My head filled with the boom of weapons and my own harsh screams. The guns suddenly silenced and my screams were loud and afraid.

My first clear thought was: too long in prison. I'd lost my cop instincts. I'd not watched the streets the way a cop does. Cops' eyes are different. They flick constantly, catching people's signals: a man loitering, a girl standing in a doorway, two men arguing, a face turning away suddenly, another frozen, reflected in plate glass, a parked car with a single occupant. I'd seen the car, double parked, engine running. Green? Gray? I wasn't sure. License plate? I'd not seen it. Once it would have all registered automatically. Driver? Black? White? Hispanic? Male? Female? Only a shaded silhouette wearing a hat, low. That should've warned me. Too long in prison.

I managed to stand, leaning heavily against the wall. My right side was bloodied; my suit soiled. Breathing hurt, but my head throbbed as well. I stumbled slowly to the corner. I waited a while, blood trickling through my fingers. My teeth ached from clenching them. A gypsy cab rolled to a stop. The driver had second thoughts but my face scared him.

'Don't mess the seat.'

'Brook and 145th.'

'You want the hospital?'

'No.'

'It's your life. Just don't mess up the seat.'

There was no elevator in the tenement. I climbed slowly, sadly, holding tightly to the railing. It seemed to have become colder and I felt I should rest in the darkness to regain my strength before climbing further. It looked the same corridor: smells, walls, the floor, even the bare bulb from my dream. I knew it was different but I wasn't sure. A door had to be reached and I scraped along the wall, wishing it were not that distant. I pressed the bell finally, not letting go until it opened. The man was small and elderly with graying hair and a calm face. He looked out of place surrounded by such poverty but it didn't appear to disturb him. He looked down at the blood and then at my face and stepped back. It was bright and warm in the corridor and there was the comfort of carpets and books. The small room was spare: a couch, a glass cabinet with instruments, the odor of cleanliness. He helped me off with my jacket and shirt and peered at the wound.

'It's only a flesh wound but it bleeds badly. You're lucky.' He spoke slowly with a heavy accent, unused to the English language. 'It's been some years, Detective . . . '

'No longer.'

'Like me. No longer.' He chuckled and delicately cleaned the wound. Then he examined my head bump. I winced at his touch.

'But it wasn't your fault,' I said. 'Don't you miss it, Doc? Don't you get angry?'

'I'm an old man. I no longer have the passion for anger. Yes, sometimes I miss it.' He spread his hands. They were stubby and strong. 'A clerk's hands. They can distinguish one form from another, unerringly file and find it again.' He shrugged: 'I made the choice to leave Cuba. I was old then and I did not have the ability to study again to get my license here. I settled for peace after the years of storm.'

'You were a big-shot surgeon and now you're a hospital clerk.'

'Those are the surprises of life. I practice a bit on friends like you who have nowhere else to go.' He lifted an eyebrow, half in question, not wishing for an answer. He covered the wound with plaster and dabbed an antiseptic ointment on my head. 'There, rest it and take some aspirins. You are fit. It will heal.' He moved to the cabinet, brought out a bottle and poured a shot. 'You have lost your fire. This will help.'

'I'm going to need more than that.' I gulped it. 'Thanks.' I took out money.

'No thank you. I did it *por favore*. Okay? You treated me kindly, my friend. That is rare here.' He looked at the scar. 'That can be removed with plastic surgery.'

'Someone's got to pay for it before I let it disappear.'

The room I returned to was bare as a cell. It contained a bed, a whitewood dresser, a battered cupboard, an armchair of hazy colors, a washbasin and a hotplate. A threadbare carpet, which could have been valuable once, covered a part of the floor. The ceiling was low and the air smelt of lilac deodorizer. It clung to my nostrils, barely camouflaging the musty odor of neglect.

This simplicity was comforting after the day of splendor in the Plaza. My years in prison had shorn needs to a minimum. Life was spare, as to a desert dweller, and luxury only made me uneasy. Even freedom, the choice to wander, to eat irregularly, to be routineless, unnerved me.

I lay back carefully, too tired to undress. Who had shot me? Why? Washington Clay? He had been the darling of the liberal movement back then until he killed a cop. Harry and I had tracked him down. What had been that white kid's name? Charles Hyslop. He had been going for a .38. Rich kid too.

I drifted towards sleep, puzzling the bitter irony of being sent to the same penitentiary as Washington Clay. That was the nightmare: not the confinement but to be cheek to jowl with your villains. I'd not been afraid when I'd seen Washington across the dining hall. I'd felt a heavy sense of inevitability. Clay was a tall, strong man with an Afro, a small neat beard and slanted eyes. The sum of his features, his presence, was the essence of anger, an unrestrainable savagery. I had immediately requested an interview with the warden. The warden was an unmistakable bureaucrat: soft-skinned, pleasant bulging eyes and a sense of fussy unease. He listened with pursed, disapproving lips.

'Are you sure he threatened to kill you? They boast often.'

'Clay doesn't boast.'

'You frightened?' And he leant forward curious, partly excited.

'No. Prison's no different from the streets. It may be more confining but no different. I can take care of him and that means I'll have to kill him. I can't afford to do that. It would mean life in this place.'

'Okay,' the warden said reluctantly, sighing at the

paperwork. 'We'll transfer you. I've first got to check your story.'

Nothing was secret in that confined world. While I waited I had a summons from Sonny Ventura, a Capo who ran the south-east side of Manhattan from within the prison walls. He was a thin, scholarly-looking man with a long record of violence applied by his minions. He'd made one mistake – to be seen at an execution – and was sent up for five years. He was attended to, like an emperor in exile, by three attendants. Hard, surly protectors.

'I hear you got trouble?'

'I can live with it.'

'You don't have your cop friends around, Scott. Here you survive with a little help. You treated me fair once. Maybe you remember?'

'Yes.' His son had been caught in a drug raid and I had delivered him to the Ventura home in New Jersey without pressing charges. It had been a calculated move to gain a favor for an unseeable future.

'I will protect you while you remain here.' He nodded to two of his men. 'I have also had the word sent out but men like Clay can be hard of hearing. They aren't afraid of dying.'

I had accepted the protection, knowing that without it I would have had to kill Washington. Ventura didn't scare him. He had his black brothers. They jumped me and Ventura's protection in the exercise yard and stuck the sharpened fork handle in my throat. I chopped him between the legs and after the infirmary did my time in solitary.

I spent the morning in bed. By noon my head had cleared, while the graze in my side only slightly stiffened. I had to report to my parole officer.

The nameplate read: Bob Grundy. It was white on black plastic. The desk was in a corner by a chipped and hissing radiator. Behind it was a noticeboard with papers pinned to it. Grundy's chair creaked. My chair was upright, hard. I sat carefully, controlling pain. Grundy was black. He had a neat moustache, horn-rimmed spectacles, weary, reddened eyes, as if he'd spent too much time reading the papers piled on his desk. On his right pinky he wore a class ring. On his left third finger a wedding band. There were pockmark scars on his cheek. A file lay open in front of him. He turned the pages daintily as if they were contaminated. I knew Grundy disliked me.

'What will you be doing?'

'Looking for a job. Any suggestions?'

'A few. But not in that line. What can you do?' He paused and added bitterly, 'Besides being an ex-cop.'

'I learnt a few things in prison.'

'Everyone does,' Grundy said wearily. 'I mean legit.'

'I got a degree in law.'

'This town's full of lawyers.' Grundy reached back to his filing cabinet. As parole officer, he overseered my life.

'I've got to earn a living.'

'Who you kidding? You take a room in the Plaza . . . '

'A suite. And I know: it's your week's salary.' I knew I'd antagonized him further. 'How else would you celebrate?'

'With a McDonald's.' He flipped a page. 'With an extra of fries. I guess you were framed. Right?'

'Wrong.'

A semblance of remorse, the illusion of a lie would have satisfied Grundy. A straw, not for them, for me. They wanted me to clutch at it to save myself from their contempt. A weaker man would have held it: blaming the system, the injustice of his imprisonment, absolving himself of blame. Lying could not save me or them. What else to do? Forget what I had once been? A good detective: a bad cop. The juxtaposition of those words – good/bad – had long mesmerised me. I'd had the best arrest record, in grand theft, narcotics, homicide. The youngest man to make first-grade detective. It was not only Herlihy's patronage but also my own abilities. I had the natural instincts of a hunter: when a man lied, when he told the truth, a scrap of cloth, a broken glass, a scrawled sentence, anything. I remembered and put together the puzzles until I got a collar. For some I'd waited years. I'd learnt patience from Harry. To build and build until it was watertight and no DA could plea bargain a guilty verdict into a three-year suspended sentence.

'You can actually tell the difference?'

'No. Cops don't know the difference between right and wrong and good and bad. Believe me. What's good one day is bad the next, what's wrong yesterday is right today. To get a collar you cut a few corners. What's wrong with that? The guy's a killer and the only way to nail him is to cut the corner, to lean on some guy so heavily he breaks in two.'

'And what happens to the guy that's innocent?' Grundy asked bitterly. 'A black kid who gets himself killed for doing nothing.'

'That again. You think the cop who shot him really thinks he's done wrong? No way. He might be sorry, but at the time he knows he's doing his job. A bad guy, a good guy . . . how do you tell the difference? A little shift in the law, infinitesimal, a ruling from the court, and a good guy becomes bad, and a bad guy good. The codes of behaviour aren't the ten commandments. Those were simple, clear cut. Thou shalt not kill. You can say the same today, except you can plead insanity at the time, extenuating circumstances, and a high-priced defense lawyer.'

'Good, bad, wrong and right. You were a bandit, Scott. You broke trust. You robbed, lied, cheated, destroyed.' He spoke without heat. His compassion was too precious to be poured on me. 'Do you have any remorse?'

'Remorse implies a conscience. And conscience implies a discipline and a punishment. I stopped going to church when I became a cop. I couldn't pray to a monster; I couldn't condone his cruelty. Oh, some cops are fervent Christians. It's a blind panic. They are trying to cling to God and to ask him not to abandon them in the world that only they see daily. He's gone, Grundy, and our inheritance is the streets. You take what you can and if you're lucky you get away with it. If you're not, you pay. I paid.'

'And you're free.'

'Yes. Prison erases all remorse, all guilt, all conscience.'

'That's if you had any in the beginning,' Grundy said bleakly. He looked at the file then glanced up. 'An expensive school.'

'A rich father. Don't you have one too?'

42

'Fuck off. Mother?'

'Dead. Long back. And I've got no father either.'

'An orphan?'

'Self-made.'

The page was turned over slowly. I puzzled him. It was the least he could live with. There was silence between us but not in the room. Telephones rang, boys, girls, men and women sat with equal sullenness before the desk of their officers. Impatient to escape back to the streets.

'Why don't you go home, Scott?' he asked finally. 'You've got a wife, two kids, a house in Long Island. You ashamed?' And for once there was a faint note of sympathy.

'I can't just walk back in as if I've done the day's commute from the IBM office in New York, and say "hallo".' I stared flatly at Grundy. 'I'm an exile. There is no safe corner for me.'

'Why don't you try it? She visit you in prison?'

'Yes.'

'Then you stopped her?'

'Yes.' My stare remained flat, unwelcoming. Grundy shrugged and visibly withdrew.

'You know the rules. You report in once a week, don't move out of the area, no weapons, no moving with known felons.' It was a monotone like the reading of rights.

I took the stairs down. The old building echoed with footsteps, voices, the almost subdued cries of forgotten pain. There was a phone in the foyer. I checked my book and rang a number. A sleepy voice answered.

'Sammy Rollins?'

'Who's that?'

'Paul Scott.'

'Hey, Detective, how are you? You out?'

'No. I'm calling from the federal pen. You alone?'

'Yah.'

'You're a compulsive womanizer, Sammy. You can't be alone. Get her to make you a coffee.' The phone went silent for a long time. 'You didn't have to screw her again.'

'You gotta be gentle,' Sammy said. 'What can I do for you?'

'I want a piece. A .38. New, untraceable.'

'Give me a couple of hours,' Sammy said. 'Where will we meet?'

'You know the Nedicks near Yankee Stadium?'

'Yup.'

The stadium was in a different country: an island enclosed in itself, dormant, dreaming of the sunny days of baseball games. Even its silence seemed deceptive. Under the cruel rumble of the overhead subway you heard the prolonged whispers of the vast crowds, like an echo that had no place to fade.

Nedicks was on the corner by the bus stop. I bought a coffee and took an empty booth. I faced the doorway, watching passers-by. None were familiar. Sammy came in fifteen minutes later with a Florsheim shoe box under his arm. He was an undernourished, tall black man of indeterminate age who permanently wore a black leather jacket, cord trousers a size too small and an open-neck lumber shirt. His hair was just graying, and if his face bore the marks of weariness his eyes were alert and good-humored. For a daily living he drove an eight-seater van. It could be hired for the hour or the day or the month. If business was slow Sammy worked the airports. If it was at a standstill he would take a run south to the Carolinas, buy hand-guns, and sell them in New York. It was a lucrative, if dangerous business, and Sammy didn't like danger much. Most of his energy and money was spent in the endless pursuit of women. He didn't smoke or drink and owned little. He mainlined on sex.

'I thought of a Gucci bag,' Sammy said. 'But this ain't the neighborhood for it. How are you, Detective?' We shook hands.

'Ex. Fine. It's clean?'

'Brand new. Still in its wrapping.' His head resembled a lighthouse: ceaselessly revolving. If he saw an attractive woman he was momentarily still, appreciative, hungry. If she was with a man a sadness settled in his eyes and then they brightened at the challenge.

'I need some information, Sammy. Where can I find Washington Clay?'

The name distracted him. He looked pained. 'Sheet, Mr Scott. I'm no informer. That mutha could tear my head off. I don't even want to know if he's breathing.'

'Who'd know? Try and concentrate, Sammy. She can wait.'

He turned to look at a pretty black girl who leant against the counter pensively staring out of the window.

'You can try Cisco. He knows everything.'

'That kid?'

'You've been away a long time, Mr Scott. The Cisco kid is gettin' to be *numero uno* supplier.'

'Where'll I find him?'

Sammy waved generally. 'In Harlem. I don't know where. Don't want to either.' He slid over the shoe box anxiously. The girl was buttoning her jacket. 'Four hundred.'

He met my stare and flinched but remained stubborn.

'Fuck you, Sammy, a piece sells for under a hundred.'

'That's with a shield. You're out on the street now and you gotta pay street prices.'

'Make it three hundred.'

'Three-fifty.'

'Okay, you're on.'

I slid the money across and gathered the box. Sammy gave me skin and hurried out into the cold after the girl.

I sat low in the car. It was a cheap hire job which stank of cigar smoke and perfume. Two hours had passed; the street glistened with melting snow. Neon flickered crazy patterns, hallucinogenic colors streaked and ran. For a white man, 133rd and Lennox was a lonely outpost. I watched the ebb and flow of people; movement never ceased. I listened to the music from half a dozen bars – the Yard Bird, the Third Planet, Dunbars – and watched the patrons spill in and out. Some stood half hidden in the doorways watching the street. I knew I'd been made, though no one gave an indication. A couple of Mercs and a Lincoln cruised by. I looked up 133rd. The kids were out. I watched one, wearing a gold lamé bomber jacket, Gucci shoes, designer jeans and a heavy gold identity bracelet, saunter up to the corner, peer deliberately towards me and saunter back. The kid couldn't have been more than thirteen or fourteen. He probably made more money than half the men on Wall Street. Across from him two men approached each other, awkwardly shook hands and moved on. An exchange had been made.

Harry and I had worked Harlem together once. Way back in the sixties when they had riots the way they showed theater: matinées and evening shows. As a cop one felt the hatred on the streets, in waves, and physically: stones, bottles and cans. I'd sat like this with Harry on many nights, watching the streets. Nothing much had changed. Harlem looked seedier, harsher. Once it had been a beautiful, regal place. I'd seen photographs taken in the old days and was saddened by the changes in the place and the people.

It was the corruption of the innocent I hated most. Kids were not involved with narcotics in my childhood. They went to school, played stick-ball, wore neatly patched clothes. Drugs were a dark, bloody stain that seeped through all their lives now. They pushed them, because they'd been hired by the adults to do so. An adult got fifteen years if caught in possession; a juvenile was put on probation. So they now were the pushers, quarter kids named after the amount – less than one eighth of an ounce – that they pushed, in glassine bags.

A cop van cruised by; no one paid attention. They knew uniforms were too busy with ordinary crime to bust the pushers. Even if they did the case would get thrown out of court. A cop had to have photographs, spend days on surveillance, before a court would admit the case. No one could be bothered so the kids became rich. And dead.

A man rapped on the window. I lowered it an inch. He wore a leather jacket and dark glasses, a gold chain dangled from his neck.

'You're not a cop.' It wasn't a question.

'No.' I wound it up. The man rapped again.

'You a buyer?'

'No. I'm waiting for Cisco. My name's Paul Scott. He still around?'

'Sure, man. He'll be by sometime.'

I timed it. Fifteen minutes later a Cadillac pulled up alongside. A haughty, beautiful black girl dressed in a mink uniform stepped out from the driver's seat.

I wound down the window.

'You lookin' for Cisco?' The contempt wasn't veiled.

'Yes.' I closed the window and waited. The woman returned to the car, spoke to someone, then beckoned me with a long manicured finger. I got out and peered into the car. In the back seat sat a youth. He was twenty, sullenly handsome. He wore a black cowboy hat with a silver band, a silver-threaded sports jacket and an open-neck silk shirt. The tips of the collar were encased in arrow-shaped silver. I wondered what those were called.

'Hello, Scott,' Cisco said. 'Long time no see. What was it like inside? Home away from home!' He laughed.

I showed my teeth. 'Listen, you were a punk then, you still are. A few years older, but no different.'

'You ain't a cop now.'

'That makes it worse for you, Cisco. No one's holding me back and you must've heard the kind of connections I have.'

'I heard. They don't scare me none. Those Guineas don't come up here anymore. We run it all.'

'Small time.'

'Step in,' Cisco said after a moment's thought. 'Drive around,' he told the fox at the wheel. 'Drink?' There was a bar with silver tumblers. I helped myself. 'What do you want?'

'Where's Washington Clay?'

'Why should I tell you where a brother is?'

'Cut the shit, Cisco. He's no brother.'

'What do you want him for?'

'Someone's been trying to kill me. I'd like to stop that. It could become a nasty habit.'

'I heard he already tried.' He leaned over and deliberately pulled down the collar of my coat.

I jerked away. 'Don't touch.'

'Another inch,' Cisco said. He considered as the car drove around the block: 'You did me a favor once and it cost me. But you didn't press charges. I'll ask around.'

'I want the exact address, the times, who's with him. I don't want to walk into a reception.'

'Okay.' The car stopped. I finished the drink, crunching the ice.

'I'm sorry about Harry Margolis. He was a good cop. Straight.'

'You hear anything?'

'Not a thing.'

'Well start listening. Hard. I want to know where that supply found in his apartment came from. Names. Dates. Price.'

'How the hell can I find that out? The Bronx is run by those crazy Columbians.'

'Find out. Or I'll jam your head in the fan belt of this fancy car.'

'You were always a mutha.'

'That was nothing. My friend's dead and someone flaked it to make him small. I'm mad now. Crazy. You know what I mean.'

'Sure, man.'

The girl slid a paper across to me. On it was a telephone number, written in her hand.

'Ring me there,' Cisco said. 'Tomorrow.'

I got out. The Cadillac slipped away softly as lava flowing down a slope.

FIVE

I DIDN'T return to my room. I abandoned it with a month's rent and a suitcase of new clothes. It took me a few hours to find a furnished studio in a large block near Fordham. The furniture was new and cheap but adequate for me. A sofa-bed, a desk and chair, an armchair, and some plates and saucepans in the kitchen. I shopped for necessities: liquor, coffee, a couple of changes of clothes. I made sure I wasn't followed, parked three blocks away, and walked slowly. The old disciplines, like a sculptor remembering the familiar feel of his tools, began to return. I saw the streets with height-ened awareness: a gesture, a glance, a bulge, a hesitation, all were quickly absorbed, sorted, discarded.

I poured a drink and sat at the desk, staring out of the window. It was mid-afternoon but the light resembled the twilight of a fine summer's day. Faintly gray, pleasurable. The silence was unsettling, an electrode that made me restless and I wished for the familiar noise of a prison: bells, voices, cries, commands. It wasn't easy to discipline thought, to force my mind to follow a narrow line of reasoning. In prison thoughts bounced around inside the head like reflections in a hall of mirrors, tantalizing, confusing, illusions that slipped away.

A thought escaped. One I'd not wanted to confront. I sighed. Escape wasn't possible. I prided myself as a man who accepted his responsibilities. It was the bargain with life; others were the compromises. I took out a faded photograph from my wallet and stared at the photograph of my wife and two girls. They would have grown over the last two years and eight months, like butterflies metamorphosed into beautiful replicas of Lauren.

There was a telephone-booth on the corner. I dialed and waited, scanning the street, feeling vulnerable.

'Lauren Scott please. Her husband.' I listened to the music on hold. Three years back there had been only silence. Fractionally, inconsequentially, things changed.

'Paul! Where are you? We waited for you on Christmas Day and when you didn't come I got worried and I rang the prison. They said you'd been released. The children were so disappointed.' Her tone had begun with warmth. She had a pleasing voice too, husky with a catch in it, and she sounded breathless. I sensed her pleasure too at the beginning, to hear me again so close, but then as she continued the irritation, the frustration of disappointment surfaced, beyond her control. 'You could have rung, at least . . . '

'I'm calling. I needed time.'

'You had time. You had . . . so much . . . time.'

'It wasn't enough.'

'Where are you?'

'In the Bronx.' I heard her sigh, a whisper of heartbreak as if I'd said I was in the old bar.

'What did you do Christmas Day?'

'Nothing much.'

'Your presents are still under the tree. Are you coming home?'

'In a day or two.'

Her silence was angry. I couldn't blame her. Then she remembered. 'Paul, I'm sorry about Harry.' Her voice thickened. 'I saw Sandra. We just cried. When I got home I thought I cried for him and for you. Oh God,' she sniffled. 'What happened? They won't tell her.'

'I'll tell you when I see you. How about lunch tomorrow?'

'One moment.' I heard the flick of her diary. 'I'll cancel the one I have. Tavern on the Green at one.'

'Fine.' I hesitated. 'Lauren, how've you been? How are the kids?'

'They missed you,' she said, avoiding her personal feelings. 'I'll see you tomorrow.'

I returned to the studio, prowled and drank, avoiding the images of Lauren and the two girls. The comfort, the companionship which I wished to deny as a further punishment. I'd paid. Yet it continued, embedded too deep in my soul to be erased by a stretch in prison. I had to escape.

I drove around, checking the mirror constantly. No one followed. No car was ahead. I drove through empty streets with only razed rubble on either side. It was like crossing a man-made plain.

Events returned with clarity. There: a woman had been raped and killed on the rooftop. She'd had a dog leash around her throat, her legs tied wide open with wire. The perps had been her ex-boyfriend and two companions. I passed a recently abandoned building. Three men had been murdered in the basement. They had been tied and two had had their limbs cut off with a chainsaw. The third had died of fright. The unremitting cruelty of people towards each other haunted my memories as I drove to Webster Avenue. My life had been the sum total of such events; I remembered days, months, years by the horror, and I had picked through the debris of flesh and bone and brains, wondering why it had happened. What rage had driven them to such extremes, what fires lay in those frail bodies I caught, cuffed and jailed? There were other memories but I avoided looking at them, turning my head away as if they would be exorcised by the mere gesture.

I turned on to Webster. The road was better and there was more traffic. At the Cross–Bronx expressway I took a one-way street. Through the chain-link fence and the shadows of the expressway I saw the 48th precinct. It was two storeys, cast out of gray, granite slabs, and its second-storey windows were eye-level with the expressway. The expressway ran straight towards the squad room, then at the last moment, curved and passed it by a few feet.

When I went in it felt as if I'd entered another dimension. It was still, quiet, secretive. No exterior sounds penetrated and it was as if the outside world had vanished. It felt strangely church-like. Here too was practiced a religion, a special calling. At deep night, when a handful remained, the whispers of questioners and confessions could sometimes be heard. There was a sense here, not of transience, but eternal permanence.

It was achingly familiar. The pale green walls, the toilet-like corridors felt more like home than my own. I took the stairs. To the right was the desk. On the second floor I hesitantly pushed open a door. The squad room hadn't changed. Lined along the walls were the dark green filing cabinets, and two rows of desks. In all six desks for forty men. On the ceiling were stuck pinups from *Penthouse* and *Playboy*. To the left were the holding cell, the interrogation rooms and the commanding officer's office.

'Hey, Paul. Jesus, how are you?' Nicky Robespierre, a first-grade detective, came across and shook my hand.

'Fine, how are you?'

'Okay. Still dealing with the same shit.' Nicky was a neatly dressed man, warm, with a bristling moustache and a huge enjoyment of jokes. He'd sat for his sergeant's exam three times, passed them, but never made the list.

'How long you been out?'

'Couple of days.'

'Good to see you. You know most of the others.'

I did. Many came and shook my hand. I'd been popular when I'd worked with them and now, in spite of my disgrace, they still had an affection for me because I'd not betrayed anyone. I'd fallen in silence.

Johnny Johnstone came over to embrace me. Johnny was a child's simple drawing of a fat man. He had a spherical head balanced on a vast spherical body. There was geometric perfection in his shape. Below were two short legs.

He was black, and in spite of his girth undeniably handsome. His arms could just grasp me by the shoulder and pull me in against his huge belly.

'You still on your diet?'

'He's always on a diet,' Bobby Rath said, giving me skin.

'Sure am,' Johnny said. 'I'm down five pounds. Can't you see, man? Look.' He turned, like a ship maneuvering. 'I'm gettin' slimmer by the day.'

Johnny hadn't changed. He looked the same weight but I agreed. The others laughed. I slapped many palms. A few were new faces, and the unit was no longer 7th Homicide zone. The department had disbanded the specialist unit.

'The lieut in?'

'Yah. You got a few minutes to spare later?'

'Sure, Johnny.'

The office was small. It was crowded with three desks, and four filing cabinets. A man had to maneuver delicately between the spaces to reach Lieutenant Mike Dwyer's desk by the window. The room hadn't changed. On the wall was a large chart, breaking down the methods of murders over the past year: gun, knife, strangulation, others. Only the figures in square boxes changed. On another wall a row of portable radios was being recharged. Three men inhabited the room. Two sergeants. One I knew: Willi Brand. The other a stranger. The lieutenant was a big man – brick wall size – with a distinctly Irish face and gray chips for eyes. They could turn warm or chill in a fraction of a second. He was a straight cop, third generation, with a powerful rabbi downtown.

'Hi, Lieut.' I remained standing. Hierarchy was deeply instilled in me. I couldn't escape the formality still.

The lieutenant studied me, then leant back in his chair. From old times I knew this was his sign of informality.

'Hi, Paul. How are you?'

'Fine. I wanted to thank you for getting me transferred out of that prison.'

'Not fast enough, eh.' He stared at the scar. 'They rang me only after that happened. Dumb shits. What are you doing?'

'This and that, Lieut. How's the family?'

I had never met them. On the cabinet was a silver-framed photograph of a blonde, extremely pretty woman.

'Fine.' Silence settled. The lieut wasn't a man of words. He used silences to pry information out of suspects – and friends. He watched me, waiting to discover the reason for the visit.

'It's about Harry's murder,' I began. The lieutenant leaned forward, elbows propped on the desk, staring intently as if listening to a confession. 'I'm running my own investigation.' Silence remained. 'I'd like to get a look at his files.'

The lieut smiled. He looked a boy suddenly.

'No. You're not a cop any more, Paul. You're a felon. You got no rights here.' Then softening. 'I'm sorry.'

I had expected the refusal. The lieut was a political man. Nor could he openly do a favor for me. Too many eyes watched him, and like most ambitious cops, he had too many enemies. Favoring a fallen cop like me would be noted in his records, or one day remembered, and held against him. The lieut's favorite saying was: 'Position is everything.'

'Sure, lieut.'

He continued staring. I'd worked for him when he was a sergeant. I knew his mind. It was full of razors. I couldn't leave. I hadn't been dismissed.

'Since you want to help and you're here . . . ' He went to the door and shouted for Johnny Johnstone. Johnstone rolled in, squeezing through the narrow lane. 'You got some questions for Paul?'

'Yeah.' He opened his folder and looked at me. Friendship was over. I didn't know what the hell they had but I knew the formality. Two of them. One a witness to the questioning. Someone shut the door. There was a feeling of finality in that gesture for here priest and sinner were alone and face to face. How many hours and days had we all sweated it out here? Questioning, cross-questioning, listening to thoughts unspoken, slipping in between the silences. Except now I was the target.

54

'What's this about?'

The lieut and Johnny ignored the question. The file was passed to the lieut.

'You were a good friend of Harry's?'

'Yes.'

'When did you last see him alive?'

'Three, four months back. He came to visit me.'

'He visit often?'

'Every three . . . four months.'

'A real good friend.' I ignored the crack. 'He was supposed to see you Christmas Eve?'

'Yes.'

'In the Plaza?'

'Yes.' Let them work for what they wanted. And they wanted it bad.

'To celebrate?'

'Yes.'

'Nothing else?'

'No.'

'Where were you between one-thirty and two that afternoon?'

'Checking in. Shopping.' I touched my clothes. He studied them as if searching for a bad stitch.

'Witnesses?'

'Reception clerks, store assistants.' You itch to shoot your mouth off. What the hell's this about? I knew patience. They'll tell you when it's time. I couldn't help it though. 'He was my best friend.'

'Sure.' He didn't disguise disbelief. Why? Everyone knew. He deliberately studied the file. Waiting. I stared over his shoulder. The window framed ruins. 'When you were sentenced you told the court you'd get whoever betrayed you.'

'Spur of the moment.'

'Yah?' His stare called me a lying bastard. 'Any ideas?'

'None.'

'How about this one?' He tapped his pen on the desk: 'Harry.'

'Bullshit.' I began to laugh.

'Harry.' He was harsh, implacable. I writhed. He hit again: 'Harry.'

'He'd never do that to me. Never.'

'He knew you were crooked. Right?'

'No. I never told him. He wouldn't want to hear.'

'Because he was a good cop. He loved his work.'

'You bet. And he wouldn't touch those drugs. They were planted.'

'Maybe he learnt from you.' He looked at the file. 'Let's see. On July 19th you met Capezzio in Van Cortland Park to receive your kickback. It was around 4 p.m. Right?'

'Yes.'

'At 3.30 p.m. Homicide got a call. There was a body in Van Cortland Park near where those guys play . . . what's the game, Johnny?'

'Cricket,' Johnnny said softly. He looked away.

'Yah. Cricket. Harry was the catcher. A pusher got whacked out. He was there the same time you were. He made you. He made Capezzio. He put two and two together. He made the call and we picked you up with the two grand.'

It was midsummer. A battalion of guys in white were playing cricket. I watched them, uncomprehending. Weird. Capezzio drove up, dropped the money and took off. I waited, then started up. The detectives were waiting. They searched, charged me, released me on bail. Where the hell had Harry been? I didn't make any homicide activity in or around Van Cortland.

'He wasn't there.'

The lieut carefully removed a complaint report and delicately slid it across the desk. July 19th. 3.30 p.m. Harry had caught a homicide.

'Who else knew you'd be there?'

'No one.'

I pushed the paper back. It was damp from sweat. Sadness, not anger, suffocated me. How long ago had we met? I had been eight and he nearly ten. His father used to chauffeur mine and I was a punk, hanging out in a rich school. I needled him, the privilege of wealth and arrogance.

56

Money awed and crushed. Not Harry. We fought, long and bloody. He beat the shit out of me. Twenty-six years back. Was the total, if love can be calculated, only betrayal?

'No. Not Harry. He would have talked to me, warned me.'

'He arrested you.'

'Because I asked him to. It was cruel.' They'd been watching me. I had been too absorbed in sadness to note their eyes. They looked speculative. I knew the conclusion. 'So you figure I got out and whacked Harry?'

'Yah.' He tapped his pen. 'You want to tell us?'

'You can stuff that report up until it comes out of your nose. I had to know it was him and you can't prove that. You just told me. And I don't believe you.'

'Yah,' he looked mournful.

I stood up. 'You holding me?'

'Not yet. But don't go too far.' He paused, hardening. 'When we find the murder weapon we'll nail you.'

'Keep looking then.'

Johnny held up his hand. He looked to the lieut and received permission. He went through the file, and pulled out the December 24th front page of the *Post*.

'What do you make of that?'

'The headline?' It was about Poland.

'No . . . that.' He pointed to a scrawl along the top.

I looked: ' . . . 4 . . . 4 . . . s . . . e . . . I don't. Where was it found?'

'Beside Harry. It looks hurriedly written.'

'Looks like Harry's writing.'

We stared at the figures and letter in silence – 44se – they made no sense, yet we couldn't turn away. Those were his last words. They made us feel stupid. Sighing, Johnny took it back.

'Anything else?'

'We're checking.'

'Maybe someone else threatened to chop Harry? He put a lot of bad guys away.'

'Like you,' the lieut snapped. 'Don't tell us our job, Scott. Johnny's going through them all.'

'Nothing as yet,' Johnny said softly.

The pain was insufferable. It welled from my heart. I couldn't staunch it. God: please don't let it be Harry. All I have left is dear memory and now that too is being destroyed. I drank some more. Red-on-the-rocks. I'd laughed in there but now it hurt.. He had been there. Maybe he had made me but he never said a word. All these years he'd kept silent. In prison his visits were my only gift. We'd reminisced. Telling each other war stories, the way all cops do. Without him I would have gone crazy inside. And he never said a word. He didn't even ask why. He knew. He did remark once: I miss you, brother. His love was encompassing. Or was it guilt that brought him to visit? The past does get distorted.

329 Monterey was a yellow-brick, twelve-storey apartment building. A fire-escape zigzagged down the front. The building was old but still had a semblance of dignity. Given a year or two I knew it could become another derelict building: pipes ripped out, doors removed, charred here and there with arson attempts. Families still lived here but for how much longer? The front door was broken, the mail boxes were smashed.

I took the stairs down to the basement. No lights worked and the hall was dark. It was as if I'd entered a tunnel which had no end. I flicked my lighter and the weak glow threw wavering shadows that were dark as the brown walls. A broken sign: 'Supere . . . ' I rang and waited. I rang again and kept my finger on the buzzer. Finally I heard a thump, as if someone had fallen off a bed, then the dragging footsteps that expressed a weary hopelessness. A door opened. A small man, stinking of Midnight Express, plump, unshaven, a grubby T-shirt, baggy jeans, peered at me.

'Hello, Angel,' I pushed the door. It resisted briefly, then Angel fell back a step. Even at the best of times he appeared incapable of keeping his balance. I shut the door. Angel stood, swaying: indifferent to my presence.

The room was small. It stank worse than Angel's breath.

The air was a hundred years old; decomposing food, spilt liquor, sweat. It contained an unmade bed with graying sheets, a black and white television, an icebox, a desk and chair. Clothing lay scattered all over. In a corner was a stove and by it a sink stacked with unwashed dishes.

Angel sat on the bed and stared at the television. It had a fuzzy picture, no sound. It mesmerized him.

'You remember me?'

With an effort Angel turned to locate my voice above him. He squinted. It took a long time for him to answer, as if the use of language was a strange magic.

'Yes.'

I picked up a photograph by the bedside. There was a pretty woman, plumpish, warm-looking, with four children and Angel. They were dressed clean and smart.

'Where's your wife?'

It took time. Talking to him was like communicating with a distant star. I waited for an answer to echo across that universe of melancholy.

'Home. Puerto Rico.'

I pulled up a chair, shaking off the dirty clothes, and sat near Angel. I cleaned the dust off the photograph. A boy stood to Angel's right. He was about the same height and wore a shirt and tie. He looked bright and happy. The whole family did.

A sixteen-year-old boy, Paco Rodriguez, had shoved a bread knife through the boy's throat. All for a transistor radio and a few bills. That needless death had destroyed Angel and the family.

The boy should have been at school, but feeling ill he'd been sent home. He'd surprised Rodriguez ransacking the three-bedroom apartment. Rodriguez had tied him to the bed and as a casual afterthought had driven the knife into him. Harry and I had picked him up at his mother's home seven hours later.

We had known Angel when he'd been a proud and successful man. That was four years back.

'Angel, can you remember the day Harry Margolis died?'

'Detective Harry? Yes. He was a good man. A good, good man.' Tears formed in Angel's eyes, slid down his unwashed cheek leaving a glistening scar.

'I told him he should kill Rodriguez, like a dog.' Then bewildered: 'But he didn't.'

'He put him in jail. Where he belongs.'

'And where do I belong?' Angel looked around as if noticing for the first time the filth and decay. 'Where? I will kill him.'

'Sure. What happened that day?'

Angel groped under the bed. He pulled out a dark green pint bottle of Midnight Express. An inch lay in the bottom. He swigged and passed it to me. I pushed it back. It was a chemical wine, bottled specially for winos.

'Did he have any visitors?'

'I tell the police.'

'Tell me.'

'No.' The silence was interminable.

'He use it often?'

'No.' It was like pulling teeth out of a man stuck in a deep well.

'How regular?'

'Now and then. I don't know.' Angel peered into my face, his breath a furnace of stench: 'You're Harry's friend.'

'Would he come alone then?'

'I don't know. It was always dark.' He looked sly, secretive.

I pulled out a ten and shoved it in Angel's hand: 'It was still dark.' Then he tapped the inside of his head and I knew it was hopeless. I would have stood but Angel grabbed my hand. There was an urgency in the grip. 'One moment.' He stood, lifted the mattress and felt underneath. His fist emerged, clutching bills. He pressed them, crumpled and dirty, in my hand. There couldn't have been more than fifty. 'You will kill Rodriguez.' The tears came faster. Dripping and dribbling like saliva, staining his T-shirt. It looked as if he wept often.

'I can't.' I placed the money by the photograph. 'He's in prison.'

'He will be out soon. I have heard. How can they do that to that animal? He kills my child and they let him free. Why can't they kill him too?'

'That's the system. Can I see Harry's apartment?'

'Kill him.' Angel fell to his knees and held my legs. He cried, yet the look of cunning remained in the way it does in all those people teetering on the edge of madness, of death. 'They sent you to prison.'

'Not for killing a man, Angel.' I wasn't surprised that out of the sodden mind a memory somehow functioned.

'You have killed men?'

'Yes.'

'Kill Rodriguez.'

'I can't.' I removed Angel's hands and sat him back on the bed. 'You have a key for the apartment?'

Angel pointed to a bunch. I took it, knowing it wouldn't be worth while getting Angel to pick the key. I left him slumped on the bed. I took the elevator up and got off on the fourth floor. The building was still beautiful. The ceilings wer ornate with intricate scroll work and the beams were of oak. I moved down the hall. From either side I heard voices, the blast of salsa music, the whine of televisions. Apartment 412 was at the far end. I tried the keys patiently. A man came out, saw me, abruptly looked the other way and hurried down the corridor.

A key fitted. I stepped in and closed the door. There were a few pieces of furniture. Drawn in the pile carpet was the chalked outline of a body. Faded but discernible. Overwhelmed by sadness I sat and stared at the silhouette of my friend. An arm remained outflung, a leg stayed crooked, another straight. The head angled down, hidden against the shoulder.

'Watch this,' Harry had said one afternoon, when half a dozen of us were in the squad room: it had been hot and sticky, and sweat glued shirts to our bellies and backs. A new detective, Johnny Kane, had joined the squad that day. He was young with sleek black hair and had the air of a boy wishing only to please and be accepted by the veterans. Harry was good at voices: he could imitate anyone, especially

61

Sergeant O'Reilly. Harry went next door into the lieutenant's office, and called through over the phone. He asked
for Detective Kane. When Kane came on the line Harry
said, 'Kane, my boy', in the same way Sergeant O'Reilly
would say: I've got a suspect but he won't talk. I'm bringing
him in right now.'Is there anyone in the holding cell?'

'No, Sarge,' Kane said.

'Well,' said O'Reilly's voice, 'can you get one of the men
to lock you in the cell, then I'll put my suspect in with you
and maybe you can get him to talk. And Kane,' he went on,
'don't tell anyone what you are doing.'

Kane turned to me and said, 'Will you lock me in?'

I did so, taking Kane's gun and cuffs and shoelaces.
When the rest of the squad drifted in they saw Kane sitting
locked in the cell and no one said a word.

The lieut came in, saw Kane inside and said, 'What the
fuck you doing inside?'

'O'Reilly told me to lock myself in,' Kane said.

'Oh, O'Reilly did, did he?' the lieut said and went into
his office so Kane wouldn't see him breaking a gut laughing.
Kane sat in the cell for an hour until the squad couldn't take
it any longer. First one began to laugh, then all the others.
They let him out and told him Harry had imitated
O'Reilly's voice.

Dust drifted down a shaft of sunlight and settled on the
carpet. It was cold. I shivered. I pulled out the sofa, the bed
still had sheets. Lilac. Not Harry's colors. There were a few
books on the shelves, mostly thrillers. I switched on the television. It still worked. On the carpet below were four indentations – something heavy had been there. What? I'd ask
Johnny. Maybe they took it. I ran my hand around the
corners. They came up gray with dust. The bathroom was
bare. The sink had thin brown scum from a dripping tap. I
checked the tiny kitchen; nothing except two cups and
saucers, two shot glasses and a bottle of wine – Burgundy.

I went to the window. It looked out on to the street. The
building opposite was abandoned. I looked down: first the
fire-escape, then up; broken bits of furniture cluttered some
of the levels. Half a block east was a phone booth. Whoever

had called 911 had made the call from there. There was little else to see.

I slammed the door shut and went downstairs to return the key.

Angel stood on the other side of the bed with a gun in his hand, pointing straight at my head.

SIX

I STEPPED out and checked the street. Children were playing in the rubble, hurling stones at bottles with satisfying violence. Over the years, as they aged, the violence would expand to fill their whole horizon. On patrol at nights I'd seen them roaming the streets in packs, or else huddled around blazing drums on cold winter evenings in the company of addicts, pushers, thieves, winos. From children they evolved into the monsters that glided through the dark streets, killing, stealing, incapable of understanding their evil.

I waited and it came: an uncontrollable tremor as if I were an addict experiencing withdrawal. It was the backwash of fear and I was soaked in sweat. I tried to light a cigarette. It fell from my hands.

Angel had held the .44 Ruger Blackhawk with two hands. Not police fashion one hand gripping the other wrist, but like a child. It looked a cannon. I knew wherever it hit it would take out a fist-sized chunk. I thought of stepping back into the hall but I'd shut the door. The gun wavered. It had a big kick; with luck Angel would miss. I judged the distance. It wasn't close enough to grab.

'Here are the keys, Angel,' I tossed them on the bed.

Angel nodded as if he'd had a whispered conversation with himself and lowered the gun. He held it out, butt first. I leaned across the bed and took it.

'You will kill Rodriguez with that. I bought it when they sent him to prison.'

It never changed; you never got used to it. At the time no thoughts – apart from how to escape the death, how to dominate it – went through the mind. I emptied the chambers: magnum shells, soft nose. One would have blown me in half.

'I told you, Angel. I won't.' I weighed the gun. It had a nice balance. 'Go home to your wife and children.'

'I cannot. When she sees me she cries, and I think, What kind of a man am I that lets that animal live?'

'You will be a stupid man if you kill him. They'll put you in prison.'

'It will be worth it. It will be better than this. I will sleep then.'

I tossed the gun on the bed. If I took it Angel would buy another. Maybe the killing would be best, to escape the nightmares, to drain the vengeance. Angel was beyond salvation; Rodriguez wasn't worth it.

I scribbled my Long Island number on a scrap of paper and placed it under the photograph.

'Ring there if you remember anything.'

'If I do . . . ?'

'I still won't kill Rodriguez for you.'

There was a tavern a block away. I went in, ordered a large shot of Red, downed it and felt the return of self-control. I made a call from the tavern to Cisco's number. The Fox answered.

'He's no longer Washington Clay. Calls himself Mohammed Abdul Khan. He's at 381 West 133rd. Top floor, back.'

'Any brothers with him?'

'No. He parties till nine, ten in the morning. Go in after when he's asleep, Cisco said.' If it was her, she would have told me nothing.

'What about the other information I wanted?'

'He tried but that's not his territory. He said to ask Yolande, 12 Davidson Avenue.'

'Thanks.' She missed the thanks.

The sky was gray, the light muted. I turned off Central Park West and pulled into the parking lot of the Tavern on the Green. The earth was layered with gray snow; the trees were bare. I left the keys in the car and strolled towards the entrance.

'Hey, Mister.' I turned. A uniformed attendant laconically gestured to the car. 'There's a garage on 65th. Park it there.'

I didn't move. My hands remained in my pockets. 'You move it.'

'That's not my job.' The attendant strolled over, cocky. He stopped, looked into my eyes. 'Okay, Mister.' Sullenly he tore off a stub and handed it to me.

It was warm inside. I glanced around: wood and glass, and the sparkle of light made it look pretty, a fragile kind of toy. Lauren had booked a table and I followed the *maître d'*. I ordered a drink and she came in fifteen minutes later. She wore a neat gray suit with a pale lemon blouse. Her hair was swept up and back. Make-up was minimal, only highlighting her natural beauty. She radiated the impression of a confident, independent woman. At times she reminded me of an expensive racehorse. Her long, fine legs apparently began at her shoulders.

'Hi, legs.' I half rose. We kissed fleetingly, not as strangers would but with the brushing hesitation of people unsure of their emotions.

'You look well, Paul.' She studied me anxiously as if she only dimly remembered how I looked and now searched for a transformation. Her nostrils flared at the scar, an anger at those who'd inflicted it. 'Where are you staying?'

'I told you.'

'I forgot. I guess I'm nervous.' She ordered a Perrier.

'It's been some time.'

'A year.'

'Why did you stop me visiting? You refused to answer in your letters.'

'It was so . . . futile. And a long journey.'

'Not for me. I mean the futility and the traveling.'

'Maybe for me then. How's Sandy? How's Paula?'

'Very well. They want to know when they'll be seeing you. What about New Year's Eve? They want to stay up.'

'Maybe.' I guessed I could cancel Breelander.

'No maybes,' Lauren said fiercely. 'Yes or no? I have to face your children. Not you.' The anger heightened her color.

'Yes.'

'I don't understand your reluctance to see us. God, how long we waited on Christmas Day. It was as if those two years and eight months were repeated in one day. The seconds – days, the minutes – months, the hours – years. I'd cooked and cleaned and in the morning we'd been so excited. The joy seeped away: draining patience, love, forgiveness. I felt a bitter anger at your betrayal. I put the children to bed and drank a whole bottle of wine and fell asleep on the sofa.'

'I'm sorry. My best friend was killed and I didn't feel like Christmas.'

She grew calm. We sat in silence, looking not at each other but at the people around. They had the holiday spirit. It was all joy for them. We ordered. Lamb cutlets for me, snapper for her.

'How's work?'

'I'm a VP now. I wrote and told you.'

'I remember. Congratulations.'

'Thank you. Why did you stop me from visiting you in prison?'

'It seemed futile watching you walk away each week. You had your own life to lead.'

'What does that mean?'

'Why didn't you find someone else?' It hurt me to say that.

'Do you want me to?' And it hurt her to hear it.

'Yes. I've caused you enough pain.'

She flinched.

'Another, if you pardon me, cop out.'

She met my stare unwaveringly. She was one of the few who could. Harry had been another. What could I offer her more than freedom? The silence was broken only when the food was served.

'What do the children think about me?'

'You ask them. I'm not their mouthpiece. I told them the truth about you. It isn't worth lying to children. They only remember when they become adults and then end up hating you. Paula couldn't understand how a policeman can go to jail. She thought only bad people did.'

'And?'

'I told her you'd done wrong.' Then in a burst of outrage: 'You come and explain. I can't. You're their father.'

'I'm sorry.'

She looked in surprise first, then suspicion. Humility wasn't one of my characteristics.

'Who for? Them? Me. You?'

'All.'

'Christ.' She ate little and watched me. My movements were minimal, hurried, as if the food would be removed at the sound of a bell. 'What are you going to do?'

'What can I do? I was a detective. A good one. I'm not a pickpocket or a safe-cracker or a corporate executive. I've spent my life at one trade. I don't know any other. I studied law inside. It was something to do.' I finished and sat back. I couldn't remember the taste. 'I have a case: Harry.'

'I'm sorry.' Instinctively she placed her hand on mine. 'He'd come and see me once a month to make sure I was okay. Most probably you miss him more than you will ever miss us. Hasn't the PD any leads?'

'So far no. They're playing it soft because they found drugs in the apartment. They figure Harry was mixed up with a pusher.'

'Oh God, no.'

'They're not sure, let's say. How's Sandra?'

'I saw her yesterday. She has some friends across. I wish she had a family. Are you making any progress?'

'Some,' I said. Then out of old habit, as I once used to, I told her what I'd found out. Sometimes we would talk at dawn, as she awoke and I came to bed after night duty. At others in the evening. There was no pattern. If it grew in my mind I unburdened the case. Sometimes, even then, I stayed silent so as not to frighten her. The horror, the sheer horror of the streets frightened me at times. I didn't tell her I was now a suspect. It was only another horror.

'What about his old cases? Someone he sent away?'

'They're checking them out.'

The check came and she took it before I could.

'It's my treat – our celebration.' She smiled but her voice held regret.

'It didn't feel it, did it?'

'No. I hoped it would be. You'll come and see the girls?'

'Yes.'

'Be careful, Paul.' It was all she could counsel. I sensed her unhappiness. Mine too and the unspoken wish we'd been braver.

It was cold and bracing. I walked her to a cab and after a momentary hesitation she bravely tucked her hand into mine. It comforted. It felt small and frail.

'New Year's Eve then?'

'Yes.' We kissed again lightly and I handed her into the cab.

I sat smoking, staring across the flat expanse of the park at the silhouetted buildings along Fifth Avenue. Like cells they were a barrier to vision. I could not see beyond to the East River, the limitless horizon beyond. I thought Lauren had not changed much: she matched memory, possibly an added crease around the mouth, not age but sadness. It had been so long. Like everything else I'd suppressed memories, so that now, when I needed them, they were too hidden to be instantly recalled.

I drove to 133rd and sat awhile in the car, checking the mirror, checking the street ahead. Finally I stepped out. 381

West 133rd Street was an old brownstone. In the crisp winter light it had a dignity that years of neglect and abuse couldn't dull. A few thousands and some care could restore its grandeur. The steps were cracked and garbage spilled down them. It was a working day and only a few people eddied around. By nightfall the streets would be crowded. I climbed the steps nonchalantly, hoping those who noticed me took me at face value: as The Man. I wore a three-piece suit, patent leather shoes and a loud tie. I walked arrogantly, not trying to hide my presence.

The door lock was broken. The scars in the wood looked old. The hallway was dim, and I could smell the overcrowding, the spare existence of people surviving. I tapped the familiar comfort of the gun, tucked into my waistband. I'd taped the butt so no prints could be lifted. The stairs were steep and dark, with the sunlight muted through unwashed windows.

On the top floor I eased the gun out and peered around the corner of the wall. The rear apartment was twenty yards down. It was to be a dark walk. I sweated, feeling the nightmare starting to repeat itself. This time I was alone. I listened. A man snored in one apartment, in another a television played softly, in a third, a woman spoke to a child. The floors creaked. I stopped at the door. I heard nothing. Either Washington slept, or he waited. I had chosen my own time. I didn't want to be set up and trusted Cisco as far as I could throw the Cadillac. I stood a full five minutes, wishing I had the company of Harry, and a back-up team. My back was vulnerable. The nightmare of guns haunted me, hammering to be let in. The door had only one lock.

I took a step back and kicked at it hard. The wood splintered and the door swung open. I ran in. The room was empty. I hit the door into the next room. Washington was coming out of bed, untangling himself from the sheets and the woman and scrambling for the bedside table. I reached him before his hand touched the gun and hit him with the barrel across the head. Washington yelled and fell back, flecks of blood staining the pillow. I scooped up Washington's gun, a Mauser, and shoved mine into Washington's mouth. I broke a tooth and split the top lip. Blood dribbled on to the barrel.

'You. Get into the closet. Shut the door. Fast.'

The woman rolled over. She was a cute brunette with scared eyes. She ran into the closet and shut it. I stepped back, pointing my gun at Washington, and jammed a chair against the closet. Washington began to pull himself upright. I slammed the gun down on his ankle and heard the bone crack. Washington yelled again. I yanked the sheets and pillows off the bed. Nothing was hidden.

'Spread your arms and legs.' Washington complied. He was a big man, a big butt, well muscled. His profile, facing me, was raging.

'Mutha fucka.'

I backed out. I looked quickly to the front door. A small crowd had gathered in the hallway. They saw the gun and drifted silently back to their rooms. I shut the door and stepped back into the bedroom. Washington lay still, but his head had turned away as if he were looking for a line of hope. I wedged him against the wall, facing the door and closet and window. The room was barely furnished; a bed, a dresser and a rocking chair. I shoved the Mauser hard into Washington's face by the edge of his right eye. The eye bulged. I pointed my .38 at the door – in case.

'Where's your brother, Troy?'

'Fuck off.'

I hit Washington across the mouth with the barrel. I knelt and whispered: 'Listen, mutha fucker. I'm as bad and mean as you are, and you know what that means. I'm no cop and I don't have to read you Miranda or any other shit. I'll just blow your balls off. You and me, we got no civil rights, and that means when I finish blowin' off your balls, I blow off your head.'

'I should've finished you inside.'

'Sure. The blood bothering you?' I brought the gun down on his nose, splitting it. 'Where's Troy?'

Washington spat. It didn't go far. A tooth and blood and saliva trickled down the side of his mouth on to the sheets.

'He went south.'

'Visiting family, huh? He's a good boy.'

'What do you want, mutha fucka?'

'You.' I lifted the gun, Washington flinched and tried to turn away. His eyes were shut tight, braced. I waited. An eye opened. I brought the gun down on the bridge of his nose. Washington screamed and tried to pull away. I pushed the gun hard against his throat and pulled back the hammer. Washington froze.

'You took a shot at me the other day.'

'Who you shitting, man? I ain't been near you. I swear. I never been near you. I got other . . . ' I hit him across the throat. The blood bubbled out and Washington struggled for breath. 'I swear . . . ' His voice rose two octaves. 'I didn't even know you were out. When were you hit?'

'Two days back. Evening.'

'I hit a bank in Garden City. You can check it out. A mutha fucka described me.'

'Try then?'

'He's been away weeks, man. I ain't seen him at all.' I pressed harder, remaining silent. The face on the bed was bloody, the eyes slid up to look at me, away, back again.

'You can check your sources, man.' The silence was only disturbed by the rasping, bubbling breathing, and the faint scuffle from the closet.

'What kind of a car do you drive?'

'TransAm. I'll get you one day, mutha fucka.'

'Color?'

'Red.' The same as his eyes, his passion. We were ancient enemies.

I had seen it outside. I sighed. Washington was telling the truth. Someone else was trying to kill me. I felt the high, that sense of elation at danger, draining out of me. I slowly let the hammer fall, reversed the gun and hit Washington hard on the back of the head, before retreating from the apartment. I left the girl in the closet. I drove a block, stopped at a phone and rang 911. I told the operator where to find Washington.

SEVEN

I HAD a new enemy and I didn't know who. He frightened me more than Clay ever would.

I drove over to the East Side, parked and found a bar opposite the Channel Three building. The six o'clock news was over a half hour back. A dumb game show, punctuated by screams as fake as a hooker's orgasm, played on the television.

Christine Breelander came out and turned west towards Third Avenue. She wore a fur coat and a fur hat with style. She looked invigorating and the street light spun a halo on her gold hair. I followed for half a block. The heels of her boots struck the pavement crisply. At the lights I caught up with her.

'Hey lady, you for real?'

She stiffened, glanced, then smiled.

'Is it New Year's Eve already?'

'That depends on you. We can make it feel like one. Dinner?'

'Make it a drink. Is it off?'

'A prior commitment.' We crossed and stood on the

opposite corner. 'Just when you want a bar you can't find one.' I looked back to the one I'd waited in.

'No. Too many familiar faces. I'm down in the village.'

She stepped back on to the street, put her fingers to her mouth and whistled. It blew my ears out. A cab skidded in the slush towards her like a faithful hound. I waved it away.

'I've got my car. That's if it hasn't been towed.' We walked to it. 'Where did you learn to do that?'

'My brother. He taught me quite a lot. It's strange. Little girls learn things from brothers. Never the other way around.'

'Like what?'

She shrugged: 'Play stick-ball. Marbles. Ride a bike. Take a leak standing up. I could never master that. I envied boys for that.'

'Quite a guy.' I opened my door. She went around. 'Where is he?'

'In New York.' She stared at me over the roof. There was something indistinct about the gaze, as if her thoughts flew to him. 'I must meet him.'

She slid in. The perfume was subtle like a good chilled wine. Her fur coat felt cold but radiated the warmth of her body.

'We'll see.' It sounded like it depended on my good behavior. 'I'm down on 8th Street. Corner of Fifth Avenue.'

When we got down there it took nearly a week to park. She was amused by my impatience and watched me quietly. The heat in the car made me perspire.

She took out a small handkerchief decorated with rosebuds and smelling of lilacs and dabbed my forehead. It was comforting. It was a small kind gesture and I wasn't used to it. I found a hydrant and didn't care if I was towed. There were plenty of bars. I wanted a quiet one. She chose a crowded noisy one, as if the anonymity comforted her.

'How did you get that?' I touched the break in her nose. She didn't shy away.

'I was learning boxing from my brother. It was a lucky punch. I was winning on points in that round, way back.'

'You could get it fixed.'

74

'Why? There should always be some imperfection in beauty. Perfection is boring, even sterile.' She spoke simply without boasting. 'My brother told me that in India the ancient sculptors would always make one small deliberate error in their carvings. Only God is permitted perfection. Not man.' She chuckled. 'Besides, it's a good conversation piece.'

It felt good sitting with her in a warm bar, surrounded by young people. Reality began to return. Life was meant to be like this: companionship, Red, laughter. It is, I thought, easy to talk to strangers. They don't know the darkness in you and gladly want to be friends for a while. Wives know too much, want too much. If not perfection, an approximation. Strangers expect nothing.

After her spritzer she was hungry. The meal was simple, hamburgers, and it made me glad to watch her eat. For the first time since getting out, I tasted the food.

'What made you become a cop?'

'Harry. Since a kid he'd always wanted to be one. I couldn't think of anything better so I followed him.'

'You could have gone to Harvard. Yale. Taken a seat on the Stock Exchange.'

'You know too much,' I said quietly.

'I'm sorry. We'll talk about other things.'

'No. How did you find out?'

'Researching my special on Harry. James Scott Prescott is your father?'

'Was.' We ate in silence. She showed no unease. I felt it. How long since I'd discussed my past? Years. It was a faded memory. 'The rich live fragile lives. They get disillusioned young. I did anyway when I discovered money has no philosophy. Descartes, Sartre wrote no essays on money. It's only true philosophy is numbers. The bigger, the better, the more powerful. I also belonged to the only generation in America which questioned the values of money. We asked questions even though we had no idea of their meaning and when you don't know that you can't understand the answers.'

'So you quit.'

'My father never forgave. I'd not wronged him. I'd wronged money, and that enraged him. Hell, half the time I never ever saw him. He was too busy.'

'Why did you become corrupt?'

'Genes. Not the wrangler type. I couldn't shake heritage. I was an over-achiever. Smart, quick, and things came too easily. I was only doing what my father did. Taking a commission. At least it's called that in his world. In mine it was a kickback.' I wiped my mouth, sat back. 'I didn't have the moral strength to resist.'

She looked away and it seemed she was staring at something distant, shrouded in the past and she struggled to pierce the gauze. I waited for her to speak but she only shook her head to clear her thoughts and smiled.

'We'll have coffee at my place.'

Her living room looked north through huge windows. Wintery Manhattan was clear, glittering, stretched beyond the PanAm building and RCA. To the east, Queens lay flat and featureless, as if we were looking down from a plane. The apartment was high fashion. It wouldn't make *House and Garden*. It was comfortable, lived in, crammed with books and a couple of good paintings. And a cat. It peered and retreated back to the bedroom.

She didn't try to play music to fill the silence, to set a mood. For what? I wasn't sure. She was in the kitchen and I smelt the beginnings of coffee. A friendly drink? A seduction? I'd forgotten how. Once, like everything, it had come easily. She brought the coffee and stood by me, sipping.

'It's been a long time since I've been alone in a room with a woman.'

She looked at my reflection in the window steadily: 'I prefer you uncertain. The other way, you're too difficult to handle.' She curled her legs under her and sat on the sofa. She'd loosened her hair and it fell below her shoulders. 'Do you think of women often when you're in prison?'

'No. You forget. It's surprising but without seeing them your need fades.'

'Then you turn gay?'

'No.'

76

'No one made a pass at you?'

'Not in solitary. Cops spend most of their time there. Protection.'

'It sounds monastic.'

'It's meant to be.'

'What about your wife?'

'What about her?'

She shrugged: 'It was an idle question. You in prison. She out. Was she faithful?' She laughed. 'What an old-fashioned word.'

'I don't know. Sometimes it's best not to know these things. I couldn't blame her, yet I would. It was tough on her.'

'And the kids.'

'You know a lot.'

'Not much. Just bits and pieces from Harry. In half an hour you can learn unimportant things about people.'

'And important. But it sounds more than half an hour.'

'Sure I saw Harry now and then. We'd have a drink. He'd tell me a case. Then we'd talk generally.' She reached out and took my hand. 'Come to bed.'

I used her mouthwash and showered. At least in prison the body didn't turn to fat. Mine was lean, muscled. I'd had all the time to exercise. It kept craziness at bay.

She had a four-poster bed, and rose-patterned sheets. Like her handkerchief the bed smelt of lilacs and her perfume. The cat spat, glared, then retreated into the closet. There was a television and a video. It was strange – no photographs. A book was on the table. Dickens' *A Tale of Two Cities*. 'It was the best of times, it was the worst of times, it was the age of wisdom.' I dropped it back.

'Like a man who doesn't like books,' she said.

'I read a lot in prison.' She was naked. Her body glowed in the shadows, pink from the shower, still moist. She had pear-shaped breasts with large nipples, and the pubes were the same color as her hair. My greed registered only the salient parts. 'It's nice not to have to.'

She pulled back the sheets and looked down at my erection. 'At least you've not completely forgotten.' Calmly

77

she examined me. Her finger touched the fresh wound, like a spot of rust in my side. 'Bullet?'

'Yes.'

Her lips brushed it. 'You shoot back?'

'I didn't have a gun.'

'Now you do. I saw it. Are you allowed to have one?'

'No.'

'What if they find it on you?'

'It's back inside to finish my term. I'm on parole.'

Her body was incredibly smooth and firm. As I stroked it it felt like some erotic metal. I wanted to devour her: the sweet taste of her nipples, the flesh of her breasts against my face. Her stomach was flat and the perfume from her pubes was familiar.

I wanted to wallow in her body, roll in it, drown in such perfect flesh. Her pussy tasted of honey with the faint and bitter special aroma of some exotic strain. Like a child with ice cream, I thought, getting it all over my face because there wasn't enough and had to be prolonged. I'd missed having a woman. But the ache had had to be suppressed and now I felt myself nearly exploding. I rose to enter her, hurriedly.

'No.'

She slid down as I lay on my back. Her mouth felt hot, her tongue hard and quick. I watched. She took delight in her act and looked up at me as she rolled me with her lips. Then, seeing I wasn't far, she rose and lowered herself carefully on to me. I called out, thrusted upwards, wanting to tear into her. It had been too long and I came too swiftly to prolong my need.

'Better?'

'Yes. Thank you.' I kissed her and took out a cigarette. 'It feels as good just lying beside you.'

She murmured softly and her eyes remained closed. She looked a child, sated, settling into slumber.

'Did Harry . . . ?'

'I told you it was none of your – '

'Not that. Let me finish. Did Harry ever talk to you about the day I was busted?'

She didn't reply but seemed to doze. I knew she had heard me. Finally, she whispered: 'He said he saw you in the park. It hurt him terribly.'

'Anything else?'

'Like what?'

'He didn't say he did . . . anything . . . when he saw me?'

'He didn't tell me. Should he have?'

I was too tired to reply.

When I woke, it was snowing lightly. The sky was gray like a solid pearl. The cat slept at her feet. I found my clothes neatly hung on the chair. I thought I'd dropped them on the floor. I didn't leave a note. 'Thanks' was trite. In sleep the nose was even more attractive. Vulnerable.

It wasn't a good day for sadness. No day is but the sky and slush made it worse. I was emotionally askew, stranded in a mental, slushy street. Not once, these past years, had Harry mentioned he was in the park. Now, twice in twenty-four hours he was made there. He told her he'd seen me. And worse, knew the reason for my presence. 'It hurt him terribly.' Yes, it would have. I had betrayed him. Not the Department. Him. Harry had the moral standards of a European peasant in a feudal world. Loyalty was important, the cornerstone of his values. But eventually in which direction did it lie? In mine? The Department's? Would he have called to tip them?

I managed a coffee and a donut. The cigarette helped. Who else had known of the meeting? Captain Herlihy. I'd not told him but he was the team leader. Capezzio would have passed him the information. I had to find the captain and I was no longer sure I wanted to. One more confirmation and I fell into an abyss. Now I clung to hope, wanting to believe they were all wrong that Harry had tipped them.

I drove to Davidson Avenue in University Heights and parked outside an apartment block. It was twenty storeys with a neat, clean lawn outside. I was surprised Yolande still lived in the building. People moved rapidly in the Bronx. I remember cases in which the witnesses, even after a couple of weeks, had gone. So many cases then fell apart. A conscientious detective kept in touch with every witness to make sure that, in the months it took to get to court, he could still reach out to them.

The doorman watched me cross the empty foyer. He wore no uniform, only jeans and an open-neck shirt.

'Yolande?'

'Yah?' The doorman looked me up and down; amused and curious.

'You know which floor?'

'Sixth isn't it?'

'Sixteenth. I'd buzz you up, except it don't work.'

I remembered the apartment. It had a brass knocker; a lion with a ring in its mouth. I knocked, heard soft voices, movement, and felt myself studied. The door opened.

'Paul, how are you, darling?' The voice was husky and slim, braceleted arms, the fingers ringed, reached out to embrace me. I took a step back.

'You macho bastards are all the same. Come on in.'

The door closed. Not much had changed. The living room was still in red. Red carpets, floors, ceilings. The other color was gold. Gold masks of pharaohs on the walls, gold-based lamps, gold and glass chandeliers, gold and glass table. The chairs and sofas were one color or the other as if the occupant couldn't decide. Against one wall was an enter-tainment unit: stereo, speakers, television. I'd never seen the bedroom; it couldn't possibly be worse. The lighting was subdued and I had to peer to notice the figure in the chair.

'That's August,' Yolande said. 'It's such a pretty name. I thought after the years inside you would have switched, darling?'

'No way.'

'Well, come into the kitchen and talk. I'm washing.'

The kitchen was a glare of neon. I took a chair. Yolande was smaller than me, slimmer and shaped like a woman. In this light he'd aged and there was a day's stubble showing through the make-up. It made him unappetizing. He had a small bust. His face was round, faintly oriental, and the mouth permanently pursed as if puckered to kiss. His eyelids were bluish. It wasn't illness, only make-up. The flesh had a porcelain texture and looked fragile. He wore a long red négligé. Yolande saw the scar.

'Inside?'

'Yes.'

'*Madre Dios.* If you want a drink, help yourself,' Yolande nodded to a bottle of Jack Daniels. It was too early. I saw what Yolande was washing: panties and bras. I felt uneasy as the strong manicured hands rinsed the delicate material.

'You got to do that now?'

'Does it bother you?'

'Yes. Do it later.' Yolande shrugged prettily with one shoulder and sat opposite. He took out a cigarette and waited for a light. I tossed over the lighter. 'You get your operation?'

'Yes, thanks to you. You were so sweet.'

'The State paid for it.'

Yolande had been a witness to a murder six years back. The only sure one in a weak case. Harry and I had found him, holed up in lower Manhatten, frightened and shivering. We'd given Yolande protection, set him up in an apartment on the West Side, and got the DA to promise financial help for him to have a sex-change operation. Yolande had testified. The perp got twenty-five to life.

'Ahhh, my life is so much fuller now. I've got this guy. He's so beautiful and he gets very jealous. God, I hope that bitch August won't tell him you visited.' He called out, 'August.' Then in a whisper, 'I'll tell her who you are, otherwise she will make up some dumb story.'

August was young and much prettier than Yolande. He had a delicate face with good bones, gray sullen eyes and a wide mouth. His nose too had been changed. It had a pert bump at the end of it. August's hair was short and glistened in the light. He looked as ethnic as Yolande: Hispanic.

'This is Scott,' Yolande said. 'He's a cop, remember, the one I told you about, the real sexy one.' He laughed at my discomfort. 'He helped with the op. I keep forgetting. He's an ex-cop. The poor thing was put away for . . . ?'

'Cut it.'

'But how marvellous! All those men! We would have had a ball, wouldn't we, August?'

August made a face: the nose wrinkled up and his eyes closed in a weary distaste at Yolande's exuberance.

'Listen, I want to ask you something.'

'I knew it wasn't a social visit.'

'You remember Harry Margolis?'

'Poor, dear man. He was a good man.'

'Someone planted coke in the apartment. What do you know? Talk to me.'

Their faces closed tight, the glance between them was quick. August rose abruptly and left; Yolande shrank into his corner. His hands clenched each other trying to wring blood, but they only whitened.

'So you know something?'

'I don't. I swear, Paul.'

'You owe me a favor.'

'You want me dead?'

I shrugged. I kicked the door shut, turned the key and dropped it in my pocket.

'Talk to me.'

'Paul, I swear . . . '

'Your face won't look good.'

'Oh God.' And Yolande hid his face in his hands.

Deliberately I removed my jacket and hung it on the back of the chair. I turned on the tap; the water splashed in the bucket noisily. I opened drawers, found the cutlery and carefully chose a knife. I shut the drawer with a bang. Yolande stared, saw what I held and cried, 'Oh Jesus.'

Tears streamed down his fingers. I took his long, pale hair in my hands, wrapping my fingers into it, and tugged gently.

'I'll tell you what I know,' Yolande said.

I stopped.

'I was contacted by a young pusher five, six months back. He had a good customer who needed half a K of coke. Good-quality stuff. I was to deliver the bag to an apartment and collect the money direct. I didn't like the smell of it but it was big money. I only dealt in dime bags. So I went ahead –

with some protection. I handed the coke through the door and got the money. I made four deliveries in all because I couldn't finance half a K all at once.'

'So what's it got to do with my question?'

'You're not going to like this. Promise you won't hurt me.'

'Come on, Yolande. Give.'

'The address was 329 Monterey.'

I tightened my grip. Yolande yelped.

'Apartment?'

'Four-twelve.'

'You're lying.' I put the knife at his throat. The apple bobbed like a yo-yo.

'I swear on my mother.'

I let go his hair and stared at Yolande in silence. The eye make-up had run, the eyes were red, and he sniffled into a Kleenex. He reminded me of the time we'd first met: the same shivering fear. I felt sorry for him; sorry, I'd frightened him, reduced him to this wreck. I wouldn't have touched Yolande. It was worse than hitting a woman. Like violating some creature which was neither here nor there; confused, worried, always running. I had used the threat of unimaginable violence. Sometimes it worked, if the act were good enough, if the person thought he was dealing with an uncontrollable force. At times, it didn't; then you roughed them up a bit. Harry and I worked the old act; good guy, bad guy. Harry always played the good.

'Oh shit.' It was a true day for pain. 'The cops been here?'

'Not yet.' He sweated. 'Will they?'

'You bet your ass. Listen now, did Harry himself give you the money?'

'No. I never saw who did. The door opened, a gloved hand took the coke, checked it, gave me the money. It was always dark inside.'

'What kind of glove?'

'Man's.'

'Did Harry make the connection with your pusher?'

'He never said who it was.' The tears had dried but left

their mark. His growth more noticeable in the bare patches. He was getting cocky. The heat was off him.

I sat silent. I looked resolutely patient, infinitely tired. You always played roles. Implacable.

'My friend's dead. I want answers. I'll take your fucking nose off. Who was the connection?'

Yolande looked disgusted. I knew his thought. Bastard.

'He made it in Manhattan – some big posh party. You know, where the rich hang out. He specialized in supplying those poor rich folk.'

'Get him. I want to talk.'

'I've got to dig deep for that.' He looked satisfied, suddenly, as if he'd won a point. 'He got chopped – two and a half weeks back. He double-crossed someone, I hear. He was a cute kid, lovely blond hair, blue eyes. His father was a lawyer.'

'Can you find out where this party was thrown?'

'No.' Yolande stood up, angry. 'I start asking questions and I'll end up the same way as him.'

'C'mon, your contacts can tell you.' I wrote down my number: 'I want it, Yolande. Otherwise . . . ' I played with the knife.

'You cops are all bastards. Even when you're an ex-one. Look what happened to Harry.'

'Harry?'

'Yes. He was investigating this kid's death. Nick Silver was his name.'

'You tell him about you supplying his apartment.'

'What for? I figured he knew.' The tears returned like a faucet. 'Now I'll get killed.'

'Tough. Call me if you get any threats.' I put on my jacket. 'I'll say I picked it up off the street. No name. Okay?'

Yolande nodded half-heartedly. We shook hands and I went out. August was watching a video-taped movie.

'What about him?'

'She's my best friend. She won't talk.'

The snowfall was heavier. It blew across the street obscuring vision. Traffic crawled. I sat in the car. Once the cops found the connection they'd nail Harry shut and drop him in a pauper's grave. His life would have passed wasted. I knew the lieut had doubts but, as I said, he was a political guy. The case already smelled. Once it stank, period.

Or maybe I didn't know Harry well. Who knew anyone well? Thirty years of marriage and you wake up to find your wife hated you from day one. A father you've loved a lifetime suddenly says drop dead and takes off to the Canary Islands with your girlfriend. Chasms yawn around us. We walk on air half the time, sustained by hope and by keeping our eyes shut tight. Otherwise we'd bounce on the rocks. The way I did now.

I felt hungry for a pastrami and rye with a cold beer. There was a kosher deli on 163rd. It was filled with the lunchtime crowd but I was served fast. They thought I still had the badge.

There was a small, damp mark in the carpet outside my door. It felt warm. My footmarks were cold from the snow. I backed off. The door was still locked and I saw no damage. No scratch marks. Someone had used a key. I listened. Silence. Only the building creaked with the cold and heat. I pressed against the wall, shoved in the key, turned and pushed open the door. I waited. Nothing. I peered around the jamb. It was empty. As soon as I stepped in I smelt the cordite. It was harsh and strong, still fresh.

The sofa had been opened out. My shirt was neatly laid out. It had a bullet hole in its pocket. I now wore the only remaining good shirt. I sniffed the pocket. Cordite. The bullet had passed into the bed. There was something in the pocket. I slid out a photograph and took it to the window. It was an Instamatic picture taken four years back. The suit looked of that era. The building behind the 48th precinct. The Man wore a blazer and I recognized it. It was me. I had no face. It hadn't been cut out but shot out. I turned it over. A date had been stenciled in red ink on the back: January 15th.

EIGHT

I HAD other trouble. The lieut was climbing out of a car. He wore a jacket only. Commanding officers don't wear overcoats. They sit in warm offices, ride in warm cars. They only get into the cold when it's important.

I opened the window as soon as he'd entered the building with his two detectives. I flapped the shirt to drive out the smell of cordite. The photograph had been in the pocket when the shot was fired. I dropped my gun on the window ledge, bundled the shirt into the closet and fell on to the bed.

I lay rigid. I guessed I was meant to die on January 15th. Why?

The doorbell rang. Twice. I stumbled out of bed and opened the door. The lieut filled the space. Behind him were Johnny Johnstone and a detective I didn't know. They drifted in. The lieut had an unlit cigar in his mouth. The room shrank.

'Well, hallo, Scott.' He spoke from the middle of the room as if he'd just noticed me. 'Mind if we look around?'

'You have a warrant?'

He looked hurt. An act. Johnny dropped it on the bed. I

read it. They were investigating a homicide and it authorized them to search my premises.

'You're not still on about me chopping Harry?'

'Nope. Someone else.'

'Who?'

'Angel. We found him a couple of hours back.'

I felt sorry for the little man. Dying was the best thing that had happened to him.

'How?'

'A bullet in his head. He was holding this . . . ' The lieut had pulled out an envelope and carefully extracted a slip of paper. He held it up to me. It was my writing – the telephone number. 'He call you? Or leave a message?'

'I don't know.'

'What did you see him about?'

'Harry.'

The lieut's eyes narrowed. 'We're investigating that,' he said.

'So I heard.'

Silence. The lieut used it the way a surgeon did a knife. He let it probe, cut, poke, spill confessions. He knew men shunned silence. Life was noise, chaos, radios, televisions. Here it was reduced to the breathing of four men. His eyes never left my face, even a blink was to be read, absorbed, interpreted. I had seen him work hard men who finally talked. Anything, crazy things, to keep it at bay. I returned the stare. Johnny and the detective searched. They tossed the shirt aside. It didn't take them long to find nothing. The lieut lit his cigar and gestured. The two men left the room, Johnny with an apologetic smile.

'You were a good detective,' the lieut finally spoke.

'I know.'

'Once. Why you went bad is your business. I suppose the money was too much and too easy. Maybe you needed it. Most probably you didn't. It was lying there and you thought of all the things you could buy and didn't need. We're all conditioned to want things we don't need. Once you got hooked you had to do other things. Breaking the law, blackmailing, lying. It was a habit you had to feed. As I said, it's your business. You went to jail. Harry worked two years under me. He was worth ten of you. I liked him a lot.' He sighed. I was meant to bleed. 'The Department wants this case closed fast. I don't. But I'm getting heat. They didn't know Harry like I did. They figure he was bad and not worth the trouble. I'm gonna keep working but I'm getting my hands tied. Maybe you'll some luck. You're a bad bastard and you got nothing to lose. Probably we'll fish you out of the Hudson one day, or dig you up out of a garbage dump.' The cigar had gone out. He lit it from a matchbook. The hands were huge, scarred. 'Angel was killed around midnight, give an hour or two. We're waiting for the ME's report. He knew his killer; he let him in. He shot him and left. No prints, no witness, no mourners. Period.'

The lieut rose and stretched. His fists nearly touched the ceiling. His brown, worn blazer fell open revealing the gun on his waist.

'There won't be anyone there soon. Maybe you'll find something we didn't. He was ringing you for some reason or other.'

He moved to the door and stopped a foot from me. We were nearly eye-level.

'Now, I've not told you anything, have I?'

'No, Lieut . . . And while we're not telling each other anything, Lieut, did any of your guys take a shot at me a couple of days back?'

'No.'

'A "yes" would have surprised me.'

'Maybe it was Washington?'

'No. He'd do it face to face, just so I could watch him.'

'As a cop you didn't win any Dale Carnegie medals.'

'Not as a con either. Why do you want me to break Harry's case?'

'Justice,' he said as he went out, knowing neither believed it to be the truth.

I heard them drift down the hallway. For big men they walked quietly. I fixed a drink. It was neat, precise and infinitely subtle. The lieut always surprised me. A big man, a simple face, a guillotine mind. If I broke the case and cleared Harry's name he got the medal. If I didn't - no sweat. I had a free hand until someone up there gave an order, then I'd be chopped. I doubted they'd dish me out of the river or dig me up. I'd lie where I'd fallen. They'd dust their hands and walk away.

I looked at my watch. I'd give the lieut an hour to pull his men out. I smelled a trap but I doubted it would be sprung immediately. Maybe another day, when I became inconvenient.

I understood the lieut. Men functioned to convenience; they weaved, ducked or stood still depending on the breeze. In the beginning, with a badge and gun, came an ideal. Halfway, you cared little. Somewhere the dream got lost and you could not be precise in remembering where, when or why. It became a matter of a half-pay pension and just holding in. At the end, you just emptied your locker, returned your badge and wondered what had happened to your life.

But I had other worries. I looked at the photograph again. It was only half a one. I couldn't place the time. It looked like summer - nor could I remember whom I'd been with. The other half. January 15th? What had happened on that day and which year?

I dug the bullet out of the mattress. It was a .25. A good hit gun for close-range work. Harry had been killed with a .25 - and a million other guys.

Angel's room had been turned over. There was powder on every surface that could hold a print. I stood by the door, there was a chalk mark by the telephone. Angel had lain, arms spread out, legs together as if crucified. Dried blood stained the center of the head. The mattress had slid off the bed, the drawers were open, spilling their grimy contents, the clothes in the closet lay in a heap on the floor, papers were scattered by the table. When men like Angel died, they had pathetic little to sift through. They hoarded shoddy things: cigarette lighters, a couple of prints of Christ, a badly stitched jacket, an old camera, a plastic wallet. I picked it up. It was empty. I tossed it back into the junk heap on the floor. The fistful of money had gone.

I looked for the photograph. It wasn't on the bedside table. I poked through the mess of bed sheets, then through the dump on the floor. Finally I went down and peered under the bed. I caught a reflection: it had fallen behind the bedside table. I pulled it out. The glass had broken; the crack gruesomely cut across Angel's face, distorting it.

What had the poor bastard ever done to deserve a lonely death? He had been a gentle family man. He'd committed no crime, harmed no one; all he'd wanted was to raise his family, eat three squares, live with some comforts promised by the great society. It was little. Men asked for much much more: untold riches, beautiful women, fast cars, power. He'd not wanted them; not even dreamt of them. Yet his life had gone crazy and wrong.

I placed the photograph carefully back on the bedside table. His wife would be informed. She would come to collect two packages: possessions and a body. That was his children's inheritance.

Harry had hated the inequality of justice. It was a farce; a sleight of hand, a rich hand. I remember investigating a sad little case of a youth killed on his birthday. Someone leant on his cake. He got mad. He got shot dead. Period. We'd caught the perp and Harry had read him Miranda and asked him if he understood. The man had said Yes and he was sent up for twelve years. 'If only they knew that if you had the money and got an expensive lawyer, you'd be out smoking cigars and laying rich chicks.' Harry had said it stank. 'Sure the guy did the killing, but sometimes I want to tell them, don't confess, don't talk, get a rich lawyer and the judge will kiss your ass. But then they don't have the bread. All the poor got is time and they might as well spend it inside as out.'

There was some re-addressed mail lying by the door. Angel had made some effort to be conscientious. Mostly junk stuff. One was a letter from Colombia to a Mrs. N. Diaz. She'd lived in 413, next to Harry's apartment. I jotted down the new address.

Ma Bell hadn't cut the phone yet. I rang Lauren. The 'Yes' was snapped. I knew she was angry. What the hell can one do about a wife's rage? Not even a good detective ever really discovered what made a woman mad.

'Did a man called Angel ring you?'

'Someone rang. He didn't give a name.' She stopped for control and was incapable. 'He rang at midnight and I don't want to know what it's about. God, how I hated you for being a cop. Calls at night, at dinner, on birthdays – and you would disappear, God knows where – for days. I can't take it again. Give them some other number. Leave us out of it.' Her voice trembled and I heard her suck breath. I had no answer. 'You still there?'

'Yes. What did Angel say?'

'I don't know Spanish. He gabbled. Then the lieutenant called too – wanting to know.'

'What did you tell him?'

'Nothing. I said I'd had no call. I lied for you. Again. Oh shit.' She fell silent. 'I got only one word – Rodriguez. What happened to the man? No, don't tell me.'

'He's dead.'

'What do I say? "I'm sorry." Why? He was a complete stranger. Besides, as I told him, I don't know where the hell you are. And you can stay there too.'

She slammed the phone down.

I took a last look around the sad little room and left.

Across the street was a bodega. The lights were bright and it was crowded with men and women like a private club. I went in, browsing the shelves, feeling the glances in my direction. They made me. I hoped there were no forgotten enemies in the crowd. The owner caught my eye. He came over and we stood in a corner far from the others. He reached my shoulder and in the harsh light was not a prepossessing man. He had a round face and a round body, the two rounds divided by a column of neck. His skin was pale and yellow and sagged. He had tired eyes. He looked a man who worked too long for too little and spent all his life afraid.

'You remember me?'

'Si . . . yes.' He turned to look at the others grouped by

the cash register. They looked joyless and uninterested, yet alert to any move. 'You were Detective Harry's partner, long time ago. He is dead. It is sad and he was a very good man. I gave him lots-a credit because he didn't have much money but he would always repay when he got paid.'

'I know. You hear anything?' The man shrugged. 'About his killing? About Angel's?'

'Ahh Angel. Life was not good for him. I knew him when he was so happy.' He paused and thought out aloud: 'I speak of more and more people in the past. In my country I would still know them all. They would grow old with me and they would die when I too would die. Here it is quick. Boom-boom.'

'Harry. Angel.'

'Harry, I only know what Angel tells me when he comes. He shop here. Just for beer. As much beer as he can carry. No food. I tell him, Angel, compadre, you must eat. What for? he say. My son is dead, my family gone. Angel tells me Harry take the apartment. He pay cash.'

'Harry have any visitors?'

'A woman, Angel say. A woman. I don't know what woman. She is dressed as if a man – but all women do that now.'

'He didn't tell me that. He didn't tell the cops.'

'Don't blame Angel. He drink too much and cannot remember. He come in here just after. He hadn't drunk then. He buy beer then buy liquor from the store. After that he will have forgotten everything.'

'What did the woman look like?'

He shrugged: 'Angel only say a woman. He was waiting for the elevator when she step out and go to Harry's apartment. She wait for him to leave. He say she was small, dark; maybe Hispanic.'

Yolande making his delivery. It checked.

'When he go out there is a man standing. But he never remember what he look like. It was time for Angel's drink.'

In court this would be hearsay; easily dismissed. I wasn't taking anyone to court. I thought only now of what I would do when I found Harry's killers. What? Turn them over to the Department? But what if I had nothing to stand up in court? Kill Harry's shooter myself? At this moment I felt I would. In court, with a clever lawyer, everyone walked. In front of my gun they wouldn't.

'You are not a detective anymore?' the bodega owner asked uneasily.

My eyes frightened him. Sweat broke on his forehead.

'No. What about Angel's killing?'

The man shrugged expressively, as if slowly he was growing less afraid. The aura had faded and he was considering that possibly he'd spoken too much. I could not do anything for him, if and when the time came. Information always had its price.

'Don't take chances, my friend,' I spoke gently. The man held my eye only a moment, a sad kind of defiance quickly extinguished, then they flicked away. He was afraid once more, a return to his natural state.

'Jesus,' he turned and called to the crowd. A tall, thin man wearing a dark, stained felt hat came reluctantly towards us. He looked as if he ate little. His face was thin too and only his moustache appeared to have any life. It curled upwards. He held a can of beer in his hand.

'You tell him what you saw.'

He inspected me. 'When? I see a lot.'

'When Angel was killed.' I turned to the bodega owner. 'Many thanks, my friend. I won't forget your help.' I flicked out my notebook. 'What's your name?'

'Jesus Seaga.' He eyed me up and down, sipped the beer, noting the elegant clothes. 'How much?'

'I'll see what it's worth.' He leaned against a shelf stacked with beans and rice. 'That's if you know anything.'

'I was standing outside . . .'

'Where? This bodega?'

'I haven't finished. Outside the next building, the empty one. I see a car pull up outside Angel's place. A new model Ford. Two men get out and go in. They come out maybe five, ten minutes later and drive away.' He fell silent, looking expectantly at me.

'That all?'

'Yeah. It happen the time Angel got blown away. They wear coats and hats and boots.' He paused. 'They're small.'

'How small?'

He shrugged: 'Not tall. It is difficult to tell.'

'What's the color of the car? You get the plate?'

'Some dark color. It is difficult in the light.' He shook his head regretfully to the second question.

'You talk to the cops?' The man's glance was answer enough: it eloquently conveyed his dislike.

The information was worth a sawbuck. I returned to the car. I sat awhile watching the men in the bodega. They were friends, laughing and gossiping. Now and then they looked out but were no longer afraid of me. Jesus's information was worth more than a buck. Not for its content but for the lack of it. The detectives hadn't done much of a canvass. Angel sure wasn't important. Just another one of their eighteen hundred homicides in the city.

I cruised awhile. The streets were familiar, I drove almost reflexively, watching the life that spilled out on to the pavements. I felt a bitter loss, a loneliness. I knew why I drove so randomly. I had no place to go. The apartment suffocated me. I belonged to the streets. I'd lived on them for so long, knowing the bars, the bodegas, the people. I wanted a drink. Three bars came to mind. They were cop bars but I didn't want to meet any more familiar faces, shake more hands, feel the mute sympathy or even the open dislike. I didn't want to laugh and joke and make believe the world was fine for me. I was lost.

It was past midnight by the time I reached the 48th precinct. I found a vacant spot under the expressway and parked the car. The front door of the precinct was locked and I went in by the side entrance. It was peaceful and silent; I felt I was ghost-haunting my only place of happiness. A couple of uniformed men were behind the desk. One was Sergeant Lynch. He'd worked the 52nd when Harry and I had been there. We shook hands. Lynch was a big man, ruddy-faced with pale blue eyes and sandy-haired. He carried a big gut. We talked, enquiring about each other, the past we'd once spent together, men we'd known, villains past and present, and the usual threat of early retirement with half pension and a boat in Florida.

The squad room was empty. The shades were drawn and it was brightly lit. The desks were clear of papers and the phones quiet. It resembled any other office at night and yet I always felt a sense of expectancy even at the midnight hour. I knew men were not too distant. If a phone rang it would be answered. If a man died violently his manner of dying would be investigated. It was this sense that nothing stopped here, that there was a continuity that ran around the clock, that made rooms like this so different from other offices.

I peered into the lieutenant's office. It too was empty. I heard the subdued hum of voices and went down the corridor. There was a small room past the washroom. In it was a couch, a couple of chairs and an old television set. Detective Sergeant David sat staring at an old Bette Davis movie. David always looked tired. It was the length of his face, the set of his mouth that gave the impression of weariness. He always had a dead cigar in his mouth; its butt dark with saliva. He was near retirement and all through his career had been a man who didn't cause waves. He took life easy. To him being a cop was a job. At the end of the shift you went home and closed the door. He was not a man of great ambition, nor particularly brave nor dedicated. He was a decent and ordinary man.

'Paul!' He removed the cigar from his mouth, hesitated, then slowly stuck out his hand. 'I heard you were out.' He was embarrassed and stopped, not knowing what to say. It was not an illness for which congratulations for recovery could be offered. 'What are you doing?'

'Looking around.'

'Yeah?' There was disbelief, scarcely veiled. 'What can I do for you?'

'I need a trace on a villain Harry and I locked up. His name's Rodriguez, Paco. He got ten to life. Is he still locked up?'

David looked around uncertainly as if there were others in the tiny room. He wished there were to help him make up his mind. He chewed on the cigar thinking about the favor, then, remembering he'd liked me once, nodded. He made a note on Rodriguez and went out to make a call. I sat and watched Bette in *Now Voyager*. It was still good. The guy had just lit two cigarettes when David returned.

'He's out. Parole. A couple of weeks back.'

'Shit.'

NINE

COPS GET threats often. It comes with the territory. You don't ignore them; you don't let them nail you down sweating. Rodriguez had sworn on his mother's Bible – she carried it to court daily, an evil woman – that he'd get us. Harry. Angel. Me. What did January 15th have to do with him? I couldn't get a fix on that one; it was only seventeen days away.

I woke early and rang Christine. Her voice was husky from sleep. I almost smelt the sensuality over the phone.

'How about letting me cook you brunch today?'

'Can you cook?'

'Can I! I make the best spaghetti bolognese in town – and a special sauce.'

'Well . . . ' She hesitated. I didn't want her to give me a raincheck. I needed her comfort. 'Okay, make it around twelve.'

It was the best way I could think of to start the day – expectantly.

I checked my mirrors constantly as I drove slowly to Bedford Boulevard. I went north on the Bronx River Parkway and kept in the slow lane. No car stayed behind me for long and when I got to Moshulu Parkway and came off only a dark blue Ford came off with me. It turned west, I went east. I checked Mrs Diaz's address. She lived at 18 Briggs Avenue. I vaguely remembered the church. It was an old red-brick building, nearly in ruin. Its parishioners were poor and could barely manage its upkeep. I spent half an hour weaving in and out, squeezing my memory to remember the exact street. I found it finally off 199th Street.

It was a sad little church, huddled against a crumbling apartment block. Its windows were boarded against vandalism. The sign board outside was faded and barely decipherable. The door had a huge lock on it and the small yard was overgrown and neglected. Yet it still had an air of use, a feeling of being alive, just.

The apartment building was neat and clean inside and the hallways well lit. The door at the back had three locks and a peephole. I rang the bell and heard the shuffling of an old woman. I felt myself studied through the peephole.

'I'm a friend of Harry's.'

There was some hesitation, then very slowly the locks began to click and open. There was also a bolt at the bottom. I could hear her heavy breath as she bent to pull it back. The door opened six inches, the chain taut.

'I haven't seen him for some time.'

She was a small, dark woman, who appeared to be no higher than my waist. Her eyes were bright, button brown, but wary. She wore a shapeless dressing-gown, and worn carpet slippers on her feet. I guessed her age at fifty.

'I know. I just want to talk to you about him.'

'Has anything happened to him?'

'Yes. He's dead. You lived next to him in Fordham.'

She closed the door softly. I waited unsure, then heard the chain being removed. On the walls were many paintings and I studied them in some surprise. The Bronx wasn't an artistic neighborhood. They were all oils of television people. Johnny Carson, Larry Hagman, the Fonz. Maybe she thought they were all real people. Jesus.

'I'm sorry about Harry,' she whispered. 'He was always kind to me. I didn't see him often.'

The apartment was small and comfortable. The shades were drawn and the table lamps gave off a soft glow. Most of the room was in shadow but the walls here too held many more paintings. They were all by the same artist. 'They are mine,' she said. She sat in a comfortable armchair, well worn and shabby, in front of the television set. I couldn't imagine her elsewhere. 'I like painting. It keeps me occupied. Otherwise the day is too long and I get tired of watching the television.'

'They're good.' No Cézanne. So his reality was different. What the hell?

'I think so too. Sometimes I think I should sell them but I love them all too much, so I want them around me, like children. I look at one and I think, there I felt in a good mood, I was happy when I did you. Another, I see my sadness, and I recognize it each time I look. Do you wish for a drink? I have only coffee. No, I also have some beer. It is in the kitchen.'

The kitchen was tiny. There was just space for a stove and a small icebox. The worktop was clean and the sink was empty. The washed dishes were neatly back in their cupboards. There was little food in the icebox. A head of lettuce, half a cooked steak in plastic wrap, a couple of beers, a carton of milk. I took the Bud back to the living room.

'If you were a friend of Harry's, you're a detective.'

'I was.' I hesitated. 'No longer.'

'I shall light a candle for Harry. He was a very good man. I saw him only as kind and gentle, and happy. It's a good way to remember a person.'

'Yes.'

We sat in sad yet comfortable silence. Our memories of Harry were the same, though she knew only a part of him. She studied me. In this light she saw the half-hidden scar and then my face.

'You are troubled?'

'No,' I said, then, not understanding, changed my mind. 'Yes. I'm a bad man.'

'Who told you?'

'Everyone. I was sent to prison. I was released last week. I

99

did a number of things, taking money, hurting people, using the law to benefit me. Not us. You had to do things at times that were illegal to put bad people away.'

'At least you are aware of it,' she remarked drily. 'Most people aren't. How can you be that bad if you have a love for Harry?'

'I've known evil men who love dogs.'

'In which case they can't be truly evil. There is a drop of sunlight in their souls. Harry loved you?'

'Yes.' Of that I was certain. It was the very foundation of my belief in man.

'Then you cannot be that bad.'

'But he never told me about the apartment and the woman. You ever see her?'

'No. Some things don't have to be told. He was married, wasn't he?'

'Yes.'

'I suspected that though he didn't mention it. Maybe that is why he didn't tell you.'

'Maybe.'

'I had a postcard from him once, a few months back. I had moved away but he still remembered me. Most people like to disappear, it is an escape from pain, from the people they've loved once.' She got up and went to a desk. She opened a drawer and shuffled through some papers. 'Here.' She handed me the postcard.

It was a picture of Niagara Falls. It was postmarked Windham and dated July 18th. The writing was neat. Harry's. 'Dear Mrs Diaz: Spent two days at Niagara. Never seen it before – would you believe it! Hope you're keeping well. Harry.' She watched me jot down a note.

'What will you do?'

'I'm investigating his murder. I want vengeance.'

'Let it be. Get on with your life.'

'I have none. This is something I have to do. Harry and I worked together many years. He was patient, methodical, careful. I was quick, slick and not too careful how I got someone. We balanced each other out. Once Harry sent a man to jail for a murder. Everything pointed to that guy and

100

I was happy. Harry wasn't. He felt uneasy about it and even when the man was sent up, Harry kept working away. He did it in his own time. The guy we sent away was a bad guy, he'd been in before, but to Harry this wasn't a good enough reason. Do you know what he found out? That two of the witnesses were related. It took him months to find that out, but when he did the case became totally different. He sprung the guy who was sent up and one of the witnesses was tried and sentenced. Right now some son-of-a-bitch is walking around laughing because he got away with killing my friend and destroying all Harry stood for. I'm going to get him. Then, I'll figure out what to do with my life.'

'I will light candles for you.'

'Do it for Harry.'

'I did. His soul is in good keeping. Yours is restless and dark. You cannot face your own life, which is why you pre-occupy yourself with Harry's death.'

'My mother used to be like you. Believing in souls and God as if they were real, as if they could be touched. It got her nowhere.'

'She is alive?'

'She died when I was three. I guess I was kind of brought up by Harry's family.'

'Is that why you became a policeman?'

'No. Because Harry did. I wanted to do what he did. I wanted to be by his side. What did it get him? Face down in some apartment, and the Department thinking him crooked. He was always broke. Day before pay day, all he would have on him was two bits. Jesus, how many times I used to loan him money. I figured out the system. I made the money and I'm alive. He didn't. He died.'

'But you went to prison.'

'Everything's got a price, Mrs Diaz.'

I didn't like the compassion on her face; I'd seen it on too many priests. A righteous understanding. Except hers was not smug.

'Thanks for the beer. If you should remember anything, give me a ring.' I went over to shake her hand and stood on

101

four indentations. They looked the same as the ones in front of Harry's television.

'What's that?'

She peered down, frowned and began to shrug. 'Ahh. I had a machine, for the TV, it plays tapes. My daughter gave it to me, but I never learn how to use it, so she took it back. There's enough for me to watch.' She got up and came to the door with me. 'If you need comfort I have the keys to the church.'

'Thank you.'

I gave her Lauren's number and heard her carefully lock the door. God and locks, I thought, were not compatible.

I made a call to Johnny Johnstone from a coffee shop. It took some time for him to come to the phone. Maybe he'd rushed home. Three years back Johnny and his wife Susan were trying to make a baby. The timing had to be just right the doctor told them and so did her body temperature. She would take her temperature every fifteen minutes and when it hit the right number she'd call Johnny at the office. 'She's hot. I gotta run.' He'd take off like a sprinter and the whole squad would give the Bronx yell each time.

'Paul, where are you? I'm kind of busy. Can I ring you back?'

He sounded off-hand, not busy.

'Sure. Say, you ever make that baby?'

'Twins. Would you believe that! What's the number?'

I gave it and asked, 'You figure out what was standing in front of the television set in Harry's apartment?'

'Sure, we did. A video-recorder. But we didn't find it. Maybe he rented one and gave it back. Where are you?'

His persistence suddenly made me uneasy. It didn't help to have him suddenly cover the phone with his hand.

'Yankee Stadium. Near the subway station. You know Rodriguez is out?'

He relaxed and became chatty. 'Sergeant David told me. That was smart of you. I was going back over Harry's cases and hadn't yet reached that one. You worked with him on it, didn't you, Paul? Great detective work. We've put out an APB for him.'

'You read the file?'

'Sure.'

'Can you refresh my memory. Is there anything in it dated January 15th?'

'I'll check it. Hang on.'

I hung. The phone cut off. I put in another dime and dialed. This time it took five minutes to find him again.

'I've got it here. January 15th?'

'That's right.'

He hummed, leisurely turning pages. Harry had done the filing on our cases. He had been meticulous.

'I've got something. Why do you want it?'

'Just curiosity. Give, Johnny. It's urgent.'

'He went to trial on that date.'

'When was he sentenced?'

'April 23rd. That's when he said he'd get you and Harry? Right? You figure he's gunning for you too?'

'I don't know. Trial dates aren't dramatic highlights for a punk like Rodriguez.' His hand muffled the phone again. 'Johnny?' I heard indistinct voices.

'Paul, where the hell are you?' He sounded mad.

'Couple of miles from Yankee Stadium. You sending someone to pick me up? So long, Johnny.'

I drifted through flesh. Dreamlike. If only we could prolong our vigor, life would be ecstasy. A permanent state of physical union in which we never let go. If our first effort had been swiftly over, now intimate with each other's bodies, Christine and I caressed, kissed, smelt, licked. We were like explorers, wallowing in sensual discoveries.

She lit my cigarette, inhaled, passed it over. We lay in twilight slumber.

'Why did they want to pick you up?'

'God knows. Maybe I'm still their number one suspect. It's never any good asking. Cops lie and cops tell the truth strictly to convenience. Theirs.'

She moved to lie against my shoulder. How swiftly we'd moved to familiarity, like habitual lovers. I touched her nose, bent to kiss it. I felt such tenderness. She gave me comfort when I hurt the most. I did not know as yet why. Sometimes you don't want to when a good thing happens.

Christine touched the wound. The skin was still raw but the pain had lessened.

'You find out who shot you?'

'Not yet. Maybe it was Rodriguez. When I find him I'll tell you. But it's an odd date to choose for a killing. A trial day.'

'It got fixed in his mind.' She sat up suddenly, laughing. How her breasts sprang from her body. Like delicious fruit. I kissed them. 'I know how to shoot!'

'You're kidding.'

She ran out of the room, laughing and returned with a small box, palm-sized. It was a medal. She was a crack shot.

'Where the hell you learn this?'

'At home. We used to shoot duck. My father and brother did, so I'd go along. Then they taught me and I just continued. My brother was the best.'

'He doesn't shoot any more?'

'No. Think I'd make a good cop?'

'Shooting isn't enough. Besides the pay's lousy compared to yours. How many hours a day you put in at the TV station?'

'Six. It used to be much longer when I was reporting. Some of the anchor people come in a half hour before we transmit. I like to do most of my own writing. I hate reading out someone else's words. What about brunch?'

'You expect me to cook too?'

She pushed me out of bed. It was a small efficient kitchen with hanging plants in the window. There was a Picasso poster framed on one wall.

'You expect me to cook naked?'

'As long as you don't burn the important parts. I'm going to shower.'

I poured myself a Scotch and by the time I'd made the meat sauce and got it simmering, she returned. She wore no makeup and with that scrubbed, shining look resembled a child. She also wore pajamas. Silk. I took the drink into the

104

bathroom. When I got out the table was set with tall red candles and gleaming silverware.

'Screwing always makes me famished.' She tasted the sauce and considered solemnly. There were two sides to her constantly present. The child and the woman. Pajamas and screwing. 'It's good.'

As I ate, I savored too the contentment of the surroundings. 'Cops always exist in two realities. The one like this: home-life, kids, a woman, good food. Things other people take for granted and do daily.'

'And the other?'

'The streets. I guess that's why we get schizophrenic. You have to totally alter your behaviour for the streets. The cop is one person at home; another with his badge.'

'But doesn't everyone have the same difference in identities?'

'The division isn't as harsh as a cop's. The guy who works in the office I'm sure is different to the guy who goes home, but he doesn't constantly deal with violence, pain, death in one reality, love and gentleness in another.'

'What did your wife think of it? I mean when you were a cop.'

'She didn't want to know. Very few cops tell their wives exactly what's happening. We lie. We just stay silent. We drink. Most wives don't want to hear either. It frightens them.'

She cleared the plates away and poured more wine. The cat came to peer at me as she set out its food. It seemed to think me wretched.

'Have you seen her?'

'We had lunch.'

'You don't want to talk about her?'

'Yah.' My abrupt silence didn't unsettle her. She sat back, eyes half closed, daydreaming. Of what wondrous things? Her calm wasn't placid, rather that of one satisfied with the order of the world. Like a journey ended. I waited. She made no effort to break the silence.

'I . . . ' She turned her head fractionally but didn't open her eyes. She listened. 'I guess we're heading for a divorce.'

'Whose fault?'

'Mine of course. I let her down. I let the kids down.'

'You're the heroic type. You can't figure out another role. That's why you became a cop. It gave you an escape . . . from all this. It was your daydream. Like Harry's.' She chuckled, 'Down these mean streets a man must go.'

'It's not streets you walk out there. You're on the edge. You're between the garden and the chasm. And you get to look down into the faces of men there and you know the fall isn't far.' She was beyond arms' reach. 'Come closer.'

She stretched out and lay with her head on my lap. It seemed natural, not a pose. Her eyes remained closed, her breathing steady.

'You still love her, don't you?' she whispered. Only when I didn't reply did she twist around and open her eyes. They reminded me of the shiny new marbles I bought as a kid. 'You do too. The hero. He tells her to sue for divorce because he's hurt her enough.'

'And what do you think I feel about you?'

She frowned. 'You're attracted to me. Not just physically. That's there too. But also emotionally. I'm the new possibility, the future for you. If it works out.'

'Will it?'

'Who knows? It may. I like you.' She gathered herself and embraced her knees to look into my eyes. 'You haven't denied you're still in love with her.'

'I don't know,' I said evasively, wanting to avoid her stare. 'How's the special on Harry?'

She laughed. 'Fine. I've interviewed Patterson, Epler and Inspector Murphy. I'm still waiting for you. You knew him the best.'

'I need more time. Want me to stay?'

She shook her head. 'When you've figured out whether you love your wife still.'

TEN

I RETURNED to my own room dismayed by love. It was pain and exhilaration. The pain was more. I had ruined it. How swiftly women cut to heart with their intuition. Had my face been so openly obvious, like a dreaming adolescent.

I couldn't deny it.

I remembered the precise moment. Last spring. The sun shone in the exercise yard; I lounged against the wall feeling its warmth and strange sense of peace. I was called in for Lauren's visit. She'd been wearing a pale gray silk blouse, a cream skirt, her hair fell shoulder-length. In that harsh artificial light, even through the glazed reflection of the plexi-glass divider, I fell in love with her again. I was tongue-tied; I'd received a hammer blow, a fatal wound. I could scarcely speak or breathe, and wanted to break through the glass and touch her: caress her face, her body, curl the cool hair through my fingers. The rediscovery of loving her, fiercely, unwaveringly, sustained me more than the thoughts of the children and eventual freedom. It was after that visit that I'd stopped her coming. To punish myself? To save her?

I heard them coming down the corridor. Two men. One walked softly; the other was heavy-footed. I let them ring and ring and then moved to the door. As I unlocked it a shoulder was slammed into the door, sending me flying back. Oakes burst in, a gun in his fist.

'Freeze.'

Houldey strolled in, glanced at Oakes and walked over to the window. He opened it, spat out his chewing gum and shut it. He unwrapped a new stick and popped it in his mouth. He was a man who believed every bad-breath commercial.

'Tell your monkey to put his toy away or I'll take his teeth out.'

'He grew up on Kojak. I keep him happy by letting him kick down doors and yell "freeze". Put it away.' Charlie carefully hitched his trousers and sat down. His vest strained and the gold-plated watch chain stretched tightly across his gut.

'You've got a warrant?'

'Show him.'

Oakes reluctantly put away his gun and pulled out the warrant. He threw it across to me. Another. It was for possessing an illegal weapon. I tossed it back and gestured expansively. Houldey gave him a nod and took out his notebook. Oakes gleefully emptied the icebox, opened the toilet tank and began unscrewing vents.

'If he finds it you've broken parole and it's back inside.'

'If he finds it. Who tipped you?'

'You tell me.'

If I'd said Abe Lincoln, he would have agreed. I knew it couldn't have been Sammy. Washington? He saw it. He smiled, looking like a friendly rabbit. 'Why don't you talk to me?'

'Names?'

'Dates, places . . .'

'Come on, Charlie. I could have spilled the names when I was arrested. Why should I do it now?' I turned to watch

Oakes. He had his head in the oven. 'You forgot to turn it on.'

'Because you know what a dumb bastard you've been and you've had time to think about it.'

'You don't get educated in prison. All you do is wait it out.'

Charlie stared at me, placidly chewing. The names he wanted were of my partners, superiors, friends. Some in the PD, others long gone. As a cop I believed in loyalty more than I did in justice. Justice was a shell game.

'I found it,' Oakes was cruelly triumphant. Charlie didn't flicker an eye. I only half glanced. Oakes delicately held up an automatic.

'Put it away,' Charlie said and rose sighing.

'But, Sarge.'

'Shut up,' he said conversationally. Oakes sullenly slipped the weapon into his overcoat pocket. He looked like a boy whose game had been spoiled. 'We'll be seeing you, Paul.' And as he passed, he punched gently, yet deliberately, at my right side. I winced. 'Bump into some furniture?'

'Fell down the stairs.'

'Yah. So I heard. Next time you could break your neck.'

'Say, Sarge. You remember Headache Bayer?'

'Sure.'

'Where's she now?'

'She's a detective now, working in the two-oh. Why?'

'A good looker.'

He eyed me curiously, shrugged and took his boy with him. They didn't think of searching my mail box downstairs for the .38.

Detective Bayer lived in a small town house in Brooklyn Heights. I parked on Montague Street. I'd checked Bayer was still on duty. It was dusk and I strolled down the Promenade. North stretched Manhattan. The buildings stood clear and distinct. It was like looking at the tops of mountains with the sun dazzling on the glass slopes. No shadow destroyed the symmetry of their solitude; each alone and splendid. It was when the eye moved further that they tumbled against each other and one shape and line blurred into the next so that it was hard to distinguish where one began and the other ended. Distinct peaks could be identified. It was hard to imagine that beneath that solitude, the still serenity imposed against a clear blue sky, was darkness. Gloom remained for ever, shifting imperceptibly from one sidewalk to the other, a distance of mere feet, instead of miles. Shadows climbed one building, down another, trapped until it was all one day flattened.

A father and son, holding hands, were approaching. A dog jumped with delight by their side. A group of half a dozen kids also drifted along. One, fooling, hurled an empty coke can at the dog. It hit, the dog yelped. The kids were expectant. The father turned away swiftly, pulling his son and the dog away. He was afraid and the small boy knew that. The kids burst out laughing and drifted on.

Fear replaces innocence. Fear not only of violence, pain, death, humiliation, but of other things too: age, loneliness, failure, sadness, poverty. It was contagious, an element in the city air to be breathed in, along with the souls of those who'd died violently on the city's streets.

The boy kept looking back. He had been diminished by his father's fear. If he had thought once that his father was a hero, he no longer could. Even the dog was subdued.

I returned to Montague Street. How could the man have been brave? It was a foolish quality, like innocence, like honesty. It brought you nothing.

From the shadow of a doorway I saw Bayer coming towards me. She wore a gray overcoat and boots, her dark shoulder-length hair swayed and bobbed as she walked. She held her handbag in her left hand; her right was across resting on the clasp. She carried her gun in her handbag. She'd not changed much. She still had a nice, easy walk, loose-hipped, straight-backed. She held her head high, giving the appearance of height and authority. When she'd passed the Greek restaurant her features were clearer. A straight slim nose, a small mouth, an oval face, delicately curved eyebrows. I remember she had pale blue eyes. At first glance they were attractive, even warm. The longer you studied them the more you saw the frost around the edges.

It was by chance I'd discovered Captain Herlihy was laying Bayer. I had been on a stake-out on the Upper East Side. It was a new apartment with a doorman who had more braids than an admiral. A taxi had pulled up, Herlihy and Bayer had climbed out and gone in. They held hands. I was envious. Every cop in the precinct had tried his luck with her and struck out. She laid brass. The next day I flashed my badge and asked about the couple. The apartment was in her name, the rent was high and it was a two-year lease. Bayer was married. Her husband was a schoolteacher. They lived in Queens. When I saw them in the precinct they were cool to each other and properly distanced. I began to notice her clothes, her jewelry. I'd thought the stones fake. Now I knew better. Herlihy was spending all his kickback on her. I'd not told anyone about their relationship. With Herlihy gone, she probably had a new rabbi. She'd made enough money to buy a town house.

I gave her five minutes, then followed. I opened the small gate and rang the bell. The door opened slowly, as if by itself, and I stepped in.

The gun shoved an inch below my ear hurt. I began to twist away.

'I've been waiting, sucker.' Bayer stepped back.

'Take the position.' She searched me expertly; the gun pressed hard into my back. When she finished I straightened. Bayer stood a few feet away. 'I've been expecting you for two years.'

The room was brown and brooding. A heavy shag rug covered the floor and the furniture was dark and antique. Heavy curtains hung over the windows. I sniffed: it had the peculiar odor of a woman alone. No mixed manly smells. One wall was covered with photographs of her with the famous: PCs, mayors, television stars. She needed proof she was real.

She gestured. I sat. She kept a solid armchair between us

and she remained standing, looking down. The gun was steady.

'You've a convicted felon,' she said conversationally. 'I could shoot you. No questions asked.'

'You that scared of me?'

'No.' But she flushed.

'How about a drink?'

'No. What do you want?'

'Herlihy.'

She laughed. 'Why ask me?'

'You were lovers.'

She looked malevolent. Her knuckles whitened. Only discipline kept her from shooting. 'Who the hell says so?'

'I do.' I shifted. The gun jerked up. I froze. I found it difficult sitting so still, but I kept my hands in view. At the moment there was little I could do. She was too distant. 'You had that nice little pad on East 63rd. Pretty expensive. You still got it?'

'No.' She shrugged. 'There's no law against a relationship.'

'Hell no. There is against conspiracy. You were taking your cut from Herlihy.'

'There's no proof.'

'Oh hell there is. I've just got to whisper your name to Charlie Houldey and he'll be in here like a rabbit down a hole checking your bank accounts, jewelry, furs, every goddamned thing going back to year dot.' I moved a hand to my pocket. The gun shook. 'Just a cigarette.' I took one and lit it. 'This place paid for?'

'Yes.'

'On a cop's salary? Herlihy was your rabbi. No one else knew that except me. You both put on a good act in front of us. He hated women in the Department and you acted as if you hated the macho son-of-a-bitch.'

'I still do.'

'But you laid him, often.' Close up there was a cutting edge in her eyes. She would press the trigger if needed and clear the mess later. 'I wrote it all down in prison and it's in safe keeping. I get chopped and a lot of people fall, including you. Prison isn't a good place for a cop. It's the nearest you get to hell, alive.'

She brushed her hair back. It was a soft feminine gesture and for a moment, her mouth partly open, breathing gently, she looked sensual. I knew if she didn't shoot she'd lay me. I saw the thought; the calculation of a woman with a good face and body. It was the coinage, debased though, yet still potent. She'd suckered Herlihy with the same act.

'Okay,' she said and sat down. She took the sofa across the room. The gun was carefully placed by her side as if it had no more use. She crossed her legs. I thought panty hose didn't make as good a sound as silk stockings. She had good legs. She shrugged prettily. It made her look warm and vulnerable. 'I don't know where Herlihy is. He quit and took off.'

'He retired gracefully. He got full pension and kiss on the ass from the commissioner.'

'You still hate him?'

'Guess. Okay, when did you last hear from him?'

'A couple of months back. He was in town and wanted to see me.'

'But you told him to drop dead.' Women like her knew when to kick a man! Especially when he was down.

'It was over for us,' she said sweetly. 'He's got religion and travels around preaching.'

'Which organization?'

She frowned as if trying to remember. I knew it was there. She was still calculating. I could remove Herlihy permanently.

'No name. His own.'

'Where is he?'

'You want me to do all your leg work?'

'Why not?'

'In New Jersey.' She picked up the gun and went to a small desk, scribbled on a piece of paper and handed it to me. She sat down again. 'He's scared of you.'

'Why?' She shook her head.

'Was he in town a couple of days back?'

'I don't know. Sometimes he rings me. I told him not to.'

She couldn't hide her disgust. He had been discarded, yet he returned to haunt her and she didn't like that. She wouldn't like many things.

'I got shot at.'

'He might have done that.'

'What's he drive?'

'I don't know,' she said. 'Any more questions? I've got to get ready.' She stood up. The gun was scooped up and held casually.

I stood. One of the faces with her in a photograph was familiar: Christine Breelander.

'Friends?'

'Yes. Now get out. Next time you come to my home, I'll gun you down. You're a known felon.'

'You're one hell of a tough lady. Who's your rabbi now?'

'I don't need one.' She gestured with the gun.

The cold air was welcoming.

'Where's your husband? The schoolteacher.'

'We split.'

'Poor bastard.'

I saw her knuckles whiten. Her lips compressed and turned down. She no longer looked very pretty. The mere movement of her mouth stripped away a layer of façade. I went out to my car and started it. I saw the curtains move as I pulled away from the kerb. It was a nice quiet street, no different from the one I'd lived on once. All the houses had their lights on, the curtains drawn, the glow of warmth behind the windows, the sounds of music, television, voices. A nice quiet street where nothing happened: kids grew up, families split, rage was suppressed inside business suits.

I drove south on the Garden State Parkway. It took a couple of hours before I turned off towards Point Pleasant and drove down the narrow road towards Mantoloking. It was a small, deserted town. During summer it would be crowded and boisterous, packed with the traffic of cars and people. At ten it was as still as the cold gray sea beyond the thin strip of beach. I ate dinner in a small but pleasant lobster restaurant. I had no choice. Everything else was closed. The waiter gave me directions to Herlihy's rented house.

It was not on the beach itself but by a jetty overlooking the expense of flat, silvery backwaters. Shadows crossed the moon and the water turned different shades of silver, giving an appearance of restless movement. It was cold and bleak and the small house was isolated from the others. I trudged around to the back and stepped softly on to the porch. A light was on in one room. I peered. Herlihy was alone. There was a small altar covered with a white cloth, a cross and a painting. Herlihy was kneeling in prayer.

The door was not locked. It wasn't any warmer inside. The house felt as cold as a tomb. I slammed the door shut. Herlihy started but did not turn or rise. His fervor only increased. He was sweating too.

'She warn you?'

'Yes. I have been waiting.' He rose, holding his hands still in prayer and turned. He looked gaunt and wasted and he smelt bad. His dog collar was frayed and grubby and the dark overcoat looked dusty. His eyes shone with martyrdom, of sweet and self-inflicted anguish. He looked a man who should be grateful for a cruel and violent death. It would be his repayment. He should have been a missionary, sent to some strange and savage place. He made a sign of the cross.

'May the Lord bless you and keep you.'

'Thanks but it wasn't the Lord. It was the government.' I looked around. The room was sparsely furnished. On a table was a pile of books and a half-consumed steak. 'So you got religion, Captain?'

'Yes, my son. Truly you were like a son to me.'

'Listen, Paul, how long have we known each other?' Herlihy had whispered in the darkened car by Willis Avenue Bridge. Manhattan faced us, the cliffs of glass and concrete shining brilliantly.

'Years, Captain, years,' I replied.

'I've got you into my command – a special request.

115

You're the best goddamned detective I know. We're going places, Paul, way up to the top. And we're gonna get rich.'

'How, Captain?' I had asked sitting like a child listening to a loved parent.

'Easy. All we do is provide information. When a place is going to get raided, other things. We'll get paid for that, handsomely. It's dangerous but the money's great.'

'I don't mind the danger, Captain. That's why I became a cop. The money will help. All the others in?'

'Most are,' the captain said, smiling.

We shook hands, gripping hard the way good friends do when they've not seen each other for a long time.

'Thanks, Paul,' the captain said, as if it were I doing the favor. 'You've got to be careful.'

'Sure,' I said, thinking the captain meant we shouldn't get caught.

'I don't mean it that way, Paul. Careful, spending it. There's gonna be a lot so you got to think how to spend it, bit by bit, so no one gets suspicious. You know damn well that the way you catch a thief is to check out his spending habits. When he's blowing money around, you have him. So be careful. If you need advice, come to me.'

'What'll you be doing with it, Captain?' I asked, pleased with the conspiracy.

'Oh, I got plans.'

Dumb plans too it turned out. The stupid bastard spent it all on Bayer. Minks, diamonds, vacations, apartments, restaurants.

I hadn't known about her then. The captain climbed out of the car. We shook hands again. 'Say, Captain,' I asked, 'what would've happened if I'd said "no way"?'

'I would've transferred you out.'

'Why are you scared of me, Captain?' I couldn't get to shake the habit, even for this bastard.

He looked surprised. 'Because I betrayed you. I thought you knew.'

'You?' I was elated. 'Harry didn't tip them!'

'Harry. What's he got to do with it?' He looked contrite. 'It was me. I couldn't help it. Oh Jesus.' He wept. 'I was blackmailed, Paul, I swear it was not of my own doing. Someone found out and threatened to spill everything. The price was you.'

'Me. Who?'

'I don't know, I swear. I got a note – stencilled – no prints. It spelled out what I'd been doing and said I was to set you up. I had no choice.' He began to babble away. 'I was weak then. The Lord was not with me. I had shunned the Lord out of greed and lust and he could not guide my footsteps. My weakness betrayed you, Paul. I have prayed to the Lord ever since then for guidance and he has led me away from the evils of flesh and wealth. He visited me in the night. He came, Paul, truly, like a light out of the heavens. He spoke to me, Paul. He told me to leave the comforts of my family, the path of the sinner, and take up his cause. I should go out, he said, and spread the word. It was difficult, Paul. The path has been stony. I was afraid but I am persevering.' He gasped for breath. And appeared to glow from his insanity.

Herlihy kept talking. I shifted across the room and checked the other door. It was locked. I kept my distance from the man. I'd seen insanity burst into unexpected violence.

'I followed you out of prison on Christmas Eve. I waited outside the hotel but I didn't have the courage to tell you what I had done.' He sighed. 'It feels better. I kept it inside for these years.'

'Screw you, Herlihy. You take a shot at me?'

'I have given up the path of violence.'

'You've no idea who sent the note?'

'None. I tried to check. Then I got another, warning me again. I had a good position. You understand. It was you or me.'

I sat in the car looking out on the black water. Herlihy had wanted my forgiveness; he'd prayed and clutched my feet. Hell. How could I? Thank God it wasn't Harry. I couldn't

ELEVEN

I MUST have fallen asleep for I came awake suddenly two hours later. I tried to remember what had disturbed me. I heard the late-night traffic outside and the sigh of cooling radiators. I stared at the low ceiling.

I couldn't relax. Somewhere in my mind was the sound that had taken time to penetrate my consciousness. I lay still for five minutes, then heard it again. The squeak of a shoe. I crossed to the window and took my gun from the ledge. It was cold but reassuring. I checked it and moved to the door softly. I flicked the catch and opened it, then wished I hadn't. I saw the gun and braced myself. The fist was shaking. The sleeve was expensive suede, pale brown. The face was young, delicate, the mouth was full and round and weak. There was an attempt at a moustache but only a faint dark stain of hair. The youth's eyes were brown, bulging with courage that could be drained, but so hyped it could also pull the trigger. A gold chain hung around his neck and he wore a black silk shirt. He cut a pretty figure, if it hadn't been for the automatic.

'Who the hell are you?'

'You keep away from Yolande. She's mine. I'll kill you next time.' The gun trembled and he was making a huge effort not to pull the trigger. It only needed a sudden movement to scare him.

'You love him?'

'Her.' He sniffed. His nostrils were flared, reddened at the edges the way a gun would be after firing. He took out a Kleenex and wiped his nose. A drizzler. He was on coke.

'Yeah. Her.' I had used the 'him' deliberately. 'I'm not taking her away from you. I like real pussy.'

'What the fuck do you know about real pussy, man? They're cunts, that's what they are. Stinking, smelly cunts. They're always using you, trying to break your balls, that's what they are, man. Ball breakers. That's all they want to do. When they've broken you, they chuck you out. A woman like Yolande is for real. She don't do mean things, man. She wants to be loved and looked after. She knows how to please a man more than any of those cunts strutting down the streets. Cheap bitches. Whores, that's what they are. A buck for a fuck. That's what I paid them, a buck. They don't know how to love. They only love themselves. I love Yolande, she loves me. We know each other's needs, we need each other. I don't want some mother fucker like you coming in and trying to take her away from me. I came here to blow you away, man.'

So he didn't like women. I didn't argue. The gun steadied as if those words strengthened his resolve. He would only kill if he was truly afraid, afraid of being hurt, his face damaged.

'Yeah. You like it your way. I like it mine. If you love Yolande that much, you should have known I was the one that helped to get her operation. She tell you that?'

'Yeah,' he said reluctantly. 'But you coming back and asking her questions, man, she's getting worried and nervous.'

'I am sorry to have caused that trouble.' I smiled. It was mean, too full of teeth. 'Why don't we stop pointing guns at each other? I just wanted to find out about her connection – Nick Silver. He got chopped.'

'He deserved what he got.'

He lowered the gun. His resolve waned. He seemed a sleep-walker awakened in strange surroundings. The fantasy, the anger of love that had so possessed him moments ago, giving him the power nearly to kill a man, had vanished; drained away long ago with the effects of the coke. I took his gun. He was harmless now, until the next time he was charged with coke and love. I felt sorry for Yolande. This was what she loved and wanted love from. It had a price. A hit. Maybe too: silks, suedes and gold chains. Yet no doubt they understood the nature of their relationship better than more conventional couples.

I pushed him down in a chair. Near enough, I smelt the perfume. Halston with a dab of Worth. A strange mix, too sweet. I stepped back.

'What's your name?'

'Peter . . . Doe.'

'Your real name?'

'David Alban.'

'You've done time?' When Alban didn't answer I pushed the gun gently against his neck under the ear.

'Yeah. Two years for robbery. That was some time back. I haven't done anything since, I swear.'

'Sure. You knew Harry?'

'How does one know a cop? You meet 'em, period. Some you like, some you don't, but it doesn't make a hell of a difference to them.'

'And Harry? You liked him? Maybe you didn't?'

'Not much.' He turned, a flutter of panic, as if those words struck a distant chord. 'I had nothing to do with his murder.'

'You alibi'd? I bet you are.'

'I don't know. When did it happen?' The gun remained on his neck, harder. When I didn't reply he began to perspire. Faint pricks of moisture which gradually swelled and then slid, gathered others and fell, staining the shirt. 'I swear, I didn't have anything to do with his killing. You don't have to like a guy but you don't kill him.'

'Yeah?' I pushed harder and Alban twisted with the pistol.

'It's not a good enough reason any more. Killing a guy because you dislike him. At one time we killed for a bit of food and then because we hated someone or got told we got to hate someone, so we went out and chopped him down. Now you kill someone because it's that hour of the day. Maybe you didn't like the shape of his face, maybe he was looking happy, maybe he didn't see you when he should've noticed you. Hell, you don't need reasons any more for killing a guy, Alban, you know that.' I stepped back and measured him. He wasn't small but he wasn't big either. Yolande was maybe an inch smaller.

'You know anyone called Angel?'

Alban considered. 'No. Who's she? It's a pretty name.'

'No one who would've liked you. Where were you Christmas Eve?'

'What time?'

'Just give me a rundown on the major events in that day.'

Alban squinted in thought and moved his head. 'I can't think with that in me, please.' I eased the pressure but let it rest on his neck. 'I can't think of anything in particular. It was a usual day. I got up, had something to eat, went out to get myself a bag, rapped . . . ' He tapered off. His life was dreary and repetitious and talking of it made him aware of the fact. 'In the evening, I hung out with Yolande, maybe a friend dropped by. She's got a better memory than I have, she'll tell you what I did. She always asks me to tell her. Sometimes I don't exactly remember and she gets jealous as hell because she thinks I'm seeing another woman.'

'A transvestite? Woman?'

'A real woman, I told you, man.' He flared briefly, like a match, then flickered out.

'I'll check that out with Yolande. Now maybe you can remember something else. This Nick Silver made a connection at a party on the East Side and Yolande supplied half a K of coke to a person unknown. I want the address of that party.'

'I can't remember.'

I slapped him, not hard. 'I'm tired. Get that memory working.'

'I don't know. Yolande knows. I swear. I remember she was given the address and we caught a cab into Manhattan. She told me there was going to be good coke there.' He sniffled in disgust. 'It was bad stuff. You know, the guy didn't know what he had bought. Some Puerto Rican garbage.'

'Get up.' I yanked him upright and jammed the gun in his side. 'We're going out.'

'Where?'

'Your boyfriend. Yolande told me you knew where that party was. I swear I don't know why you mutha fuckers lie. It's found out sooner or later and then someone gets hurt real bad.

'It's her, not me, I swear.'

I pushed him out of the door in disgust. Love had ended in the interests of survival, in the interests of minimizing pain and blame. His face was too pretty to get damaged: beat up on Yolande. It would give him pleasure then, a feeling of invulnerability because he was not being hurt. Then, he would comfort Yolande.

We got in the car. I kept the gun on my lap, scanning the streets. It was nearing dawn and the streets were empty. Night was a time when even doormen hid. We took the elevator up in silence and I prodded Alban out in front of me.

Alban raised his hand to knock.

'Use your key.'

We stepped into darkness. Softly, the murmur of television. I thought, when the world ends television will continue into eternity, feeding on the entrails of reruns.

Alban switched on the light. 'Yolande.' No one replied. He called again. His voice was frail in the silence, its timbre muted. I pushed him out of the way. The living room was empty. Nothing had been disturbed. I still winced at the decor. I tried the bedroom door. It was locked.

'Got the key?'

'No. Sometimes she gets real mad at me and locks me out.'

I knocked.

'Yolande darling. It's me.' He knocked again and we strained to listen for an answering sullen murmur. None came. The sweetness of deodorizers, perfumes and after-shave, deep under like fear in the blackness, gave me a head-ache. I stepped back. It was a shoddy door. I kicked. Once, twice. The lock and wood splintered. I put my shoulder to the door and it flew open.

'Oh my God,' Yolande moaned hysterically, trying to sit up.

I shoved him back down and gestured Alban over to the bed. He perched primly at the foot, avoiding Yolande's glare.

'Okay, now you tell me where the party was?'

'What party?'

'Yolande!' I slapped him hard. At dawn I get upset easily.

'He knows.'

'She knows.'

We could've played games all day. You get tired too of slapping people. You want to punch them out. They fell silent, staring at me.

'Tell me about Nick Silver.'

'What's to tell? He free-lanced. Ask your mob friends. He bought from them too.'

Homicides have more dead ends than a wheel has spokes. I used a pillow for a silencer and fired Alban's gun into the mattress. They wrinkled their noses at the cordite and watched me dig the bullet out. I emptied Alban's gun and dropped the bullets with the one I'd dug out into my pocket before tossing it back to him.

It was the morning of New Year's Eve. I would be glad when we slid into another year. This hadn't been a good one. I drove to the forensic lab. It was in the same building as the ME's office. I hoped someone could do me a favor. I wandered around the familiar corridors, poking my head into small laboratories. I recognized no one until I reached the last door. It was an office and a thin black man sat behind the desk. I didn't recognize him at first. Detective

John Dekker had thinned; his suit appeared a couple of sizes too large and his face had the gentle, patient air of a man who knew he was dying. We'd worked Vice together a long way back.

'They got me pushing papers,' Dekker said as I sat down. 'Good to see you.' The question of my past, like his own, remained unspoken. Dekker had a high forehead, neatly combed graying hair, a long face. It was when I looked closer that I saw in the brown eyes the shadows of the pain.

'What is it?'

'Cancer,' Dekker said. He lit a cigarette, smiling tiredly. 'Too late to stop this. How was it?'

'Bad.' I saw Dekker eye the scar. 'Washington Clay was in with me.'

'A bad mutha. What can I do for you?'

'You have access to the lab?'

'Yeah. They'll do a favor.' He took the two bullets. One that had been shot into my shirt, the other from Alban's gun.

'Run a ballistic test on them. Maybe they match, something or the other.'

'Like what?'

'Try Harry's.'

'I'm sorry about him. He was a great guy. Give me a day or two.'

'Thanks, John.'

'Any time.' We shook hands. 'Maybe we can have a drink some time.'

'Why don't we.'

There was a telephone booth on the corner and I tried a private number. When it was answered I identified myself.

'I need a favor.'

'Yes.' The voice was polite and noncommittal.

'I want some information on a pusher called Nick Silver. He was chopped a few weeks back but he had some important contacts on the Upper East Side.'

'So what do you want exactly?'

'The address where he made a contact to sell half a K of coke.'

'I'll call you back.'

I gave the number and waited by the phone. An hour was nothing. Cops, like prisoners, get used to waiting. They wait in corridors outside courts, wait for young ADAs, wait for witnesses, wait for perps, wait for bookings. They wait in the heat, the cold, the rain, the snow. They wait in cars, on benches, on their feet. Sometimes we think, sometimes empty-minded; sometimes watchful, depending on why we wait.

The phone rang.

'Scott?'

'Yes.'

'We'll try to get you the address you want. It's a big favor. We need one too. On the fifth, 9 p.m., be at Joe's restaurant on Greenwich.'

The phone went dead. It was a command.

It took an hour to drive to Chatsworth. I took the ramp and turned at the traffic light. The streets were quiet, littered with tricycles, toys, roaming dogs. There was a feeling of comfort; soft, cosy, pampered. I knew the life: weekends in the yard, swimming, cook-outs, neighbors for dinner, a few cocktails. Snow covered the ground.

My house looked like the others. Sparkling windows, newly repainted, repairs all done, the air-conditioners covered. I studied everything meticulously, paying attention to the new fixing of the drainpipe, the double-glazed windows, a new paneling in the garage. Lauren had a good handyman. I didn't want to intrude immediately. I was unsure of my welcome. I imagined she would be polite, constrained, unsure once again how to treat me. The children would be curious, staring up at me, trying to recall their father. Lauren's darting glances: sharp, surgical, already defensive.

I walked around the house down the narrow pathway. I pushed the gate open and stepped past the bush I'd planted. It had grown into tangled hair. Lauren saw me through the kitchen window and at first there was a fleeting warmth, then the swift mask of defense. Our emotion towards each other remained as tangled as the bush.

The kitchen was warm and shone with affection. It was twice the size of the cell I'd lived in.

'It's not quite New Year's Eve and here I am.'

She laughed: 'That's a change.'

'I'm trying to but it's rough.'

'It is for me, too. What is the etiquette for a woman whose husband has just been released from prison? Does she behave as if nothing happened? Or what? I just don't know.' She seemed on the verge of tears but when I went to comfort, she backed away.

'I don't either.'

'We've got to give ourselves the time to get used to each other and see how we feel. That's if we want that.'

'I do.'

She remained silent. I pecked her cheek as she turned away and smelt her hair: shampoo fresh and delicately perfumed. I wanted to touch it but couldn't. Her nose was straight, slender and the nostrils flared, hinting sensuality. She had a gingham soul. In spite of the children, physically she'd changed little and could still turn over my heart.

She poured out coffee, glanced quickly, then concentrated on her task too hard. I wished then for the power to read her mind.

It wasn't difficult to remember when we'd first loved each other deeply. It was not that long ago; yet I imagined it had happened at a different time, when we were children. No, when she was a child. I had never been one. I felt I'd been full-grown all my life. All cops were like that.

We'd met when the firm she'd been working for years back had been burgled. She had expected the detective to be a shabby down at heel man, smoking stale cigars and wearing frayed clothes. I had strode in: elegantly suited, polished shoes, clean-shaven. Everything about me reflected style. She didn't know then that detectives deliberately dressed splendidly to ensure they were recognized on the streets as 'The Man'. It was an image we cherished, this expensive show of prosperity which, at that time, I didn't have. I'd been young then. A third-grade detective; my gold shield still shiny. After the questioning I'd returned to her desk to ask for a date. Curiosity, I guess, had made her say yes.

'The girls are downstairs. Or would you like to open your presents first?'

'I should open them with the kids.'

She thought of accompanying me, then decided to remain. At some time I would have to be alone with them.

The living room had not changed much. Underfoot was the forty bucks a square yard carpet, wall to wall, on the shelf the $11,000 stereo system, the furniture was imported European, and the artifacts, bought with cash, from East Side antique stores. Paintings, crystal, old pistols, silver decanters. No house in town had a more expensive interior. A pine Christmas tree stood in one corner. My study was smaller. It was wood-paneled. The paneling had been taken from an old Bronx apartment they were tearing down, and moved intact. There was a small wood-burning fireplace and shelves of books. In one corner were the framed citations: bravery, clippings of my exploits, certificates of promotion, medals, photographs.

I went down the steps softly. Sandy played with her toys; Paula lay on the couch reading. They'd grown. They were like miniature adults now, no longer children. Paula looked like Lauren. She had the same legs, the same slant in her face with the shadowed eyes, as if she were drowsing. Sandy resembled me more.

'Hi.'

Sandy reacted immediately. She squealed, jumped, ran and flung herself at me. It was the spontaneity of a child not yet doubting or questioning her emotions. She smothered me with her arms and wet kisses that smelt of candy. Paula marked her page and came over. I put out an arm and she too came into my embrace. While Sandy laughed, Paula wept softly.

'We were expecting you on Christmas Day,' she said.

'I'm sorry. I was delayed. You're as beautiful as your mother. God, you've both grown so much.'

'We missed you, Daddy,' Sandy said.

'And I both of you.'

'Ohhh, you hurt yourself?' Sandy traced the scar with her finger.

'I got one too. See.' She bared her arm. A small, half-inch visible line remained.

I carried her over to the couch and sat with her on my lap. Paula sat by me, holding my hand like a shy girlfriend. I'd forgotten how difficult it could be at times to talk to children. I had a different kind of patience. A watchful, waiting one. Not one for quiet conversations. I tried, however, and in the answers and questions, caught up with some of their life. School, friends, games, cousins, grandparents, Christmas.

'You must come to school when it re-opens and meet my friends,' Paula said.

'And mine.'

'What did you tell them?'

'You were separated from Mom.' Paula smiled shyly. 'It wasn't a complete lie, was it?'

'No.'

Then her curiosity got the better of her. I was sure her mother had suggested they discuss the problem later.

'What was it like in prison?'

'Terrible. I hated it.'

'Then why did they send you?' Sandy asked. She tilted her head to watch me with a bird-like curiosity. She had my same steady gaze, unblinking. 'You are a policeman.'

'I was. I did something a policeman shouldn't do. We're like men of the cloth, a priest, I guess, but I failed in that.'

'You sinned.'

'Yes. I was punished.' Then I added, 'I was a bad cop.'

'Uncle Harry said you were a good one. You just did wrong. He called you a fallen angel.'

'He was being kind.' He always was.

'We miss him too, Daddy,' Paula consolingly patted me in that adult manner a child adopts. Intuitively she'd sensed my sorrow. 'Your Christmas presents are waiting. And, Sandy, don't blurt out what they are.'

We returned to the living room and the girls called their mother to witness the occasion. The ritual made me uncomfortable. They had conspired to forget my long absence for they dreamed of continuity in their lives and I was still a part of it. They would not let go. The forgiveness was too easily attained.

I opened Sandy's first. She had drawn the greeting card herself and bought the tie out of her pocket money. Paula was more sophisticated. She gave me a tie pin, an adornment I never wore. I embraced them gravely. Lauren gave me a watch. It was a slim, gold one with a black face. I hugged her, feeling her respond, and wanted to keep holding, but then she stiffened.

'We must talk,' she said softly.

'Yes.'

'Lunch, children.'

We ate in the kitchen. The sunlight streamed in, making the room glow as if we were all lit from within. I knew now it was a conspiracy, for they laughed and talked.

Most times, in those old days, mealtimes were quiet.

'I thought I'd call Sandra,' I said when I'd finished.

'Give her my love. There's a letter for you on the table.'

'And Mom said we could stay up and see the New Year in,' Paula said.

'I said you could stay up late. Not till midnight.'

'Daddy?' Paula appealed to me to arbitrate.

'Ten o'clock. Next year we'll make it midnight.'

'Aw hell,' she stomped downstairs to the basement, followed by her sister. For the first time Lauren and I smiled at each other.

I made the call, staring at the letter. I didn't like the look of it. The address was stencilled and it had been mailed on Christmas Eve.

'Hi, Sandra. Paul. What are you up to?'

'Packing. I'm going to take a vacation . . . once it's all over.'

'Sandra, will you do me a favor? Can you delay the funeral until I can clear Harry's name?'

'If you can. He'd like that; sò would I. How long?'

'Quite soon, I hope,' I lied. 'By the way, what happened to Harry's video-recorder?'

'What video? We never had one. Paul, will you help with the arrangements? I want to bury Harry here.'

'Sure. Which funeral parlor is he in?'

She gave me the address. I knew it. I'd seen a lot of bodies there. I didn't really want to see Harry's again.

'What's happened to Harry's files? He always kept copies of his cases.'

'I guess in the filing cabinet. You're welcome to them.'

We talked a bit more but then I had to say goodbye and face the letter. The note inside was brief and stabbed me – Ask your wife about John Croix. It was a question I was afraid to ask.

TWELVE

IN CANDLELIGHT, Lauren looked ephemeral. The flame fluttered over her face, forming valleys of shadow and light. The beauty, tantalizing, hidden, secretive. The eyes caught bright, sparkling, but withdrawn. She wore a severe dress, up to her collarbone, the hair brushed back and tied, make-up hinted. The innocence only attracted me more. I wore a suit, an open-necked shirt, a gold identity bracelet. It came from the old days. On my finger was a thick wedding band that still looked new. We sat in a booth, separate from the crowd. The restaurant was imitation Swiss with elaborate gold print menus and big numbers next to the dishes; the food was mediocre.

We had drunk champagne with the children and left a sitter to mind them.

'What are you going to do?' She leant towards me to be heard above the noise. She shrugged.

'I need to think. You did tell me I was free.'

'It's the least I can do.'

'So I gather. Just wave your hands and we all disappear. Very convenient.'

'It was meant not out of convenience to me. To you.' She stared at me in that hard manner the way women do when they rage.

'Who is John Croix?'

'That letter?'

'Yes. Anonymous.'

'My lover. He comforted me when I needed it. I was angry with you and I wanted to hurt you.'

'You love him?'

'I don't know. You love sometimes because they're there, and not for any other particular reason.'

'And conveniently he was there.'

'You weren't.'

She drank, snapped her fingers for another and we sat in silence until it came. Around us people were enjoying themselves. It was the wrong time to come out of prison.

'What would happen . . . what if we could make it work again?'

'When? This year, next year, some time . . . ? I don't like your life. Why don't you just forget being a cop. Be realistic. You're not one.'

'I know. But I can't just bury Harry and walk away.'

'He's your redemption, isn't he? By clearing his name you will have washed away your sin.'

'Aren't I allowed that one chance? I knew Harry better than anyone else on earth. I want him buried with honor. It was important to him.'

'And to you. Honor, loyalty. Harry always came between us alive; now, he haunts us dead.'

'He was my partner.'

'I know. Wives will never understand you love your partner more than you love us. Redeem yourself then – but for whom? The PD will never take you back.'

'For myself. I have one skill – and I want it to save me and Harry.'

We ate in silence. At 12.01, in the New Year, I paid the check and we left.

* * *

I spent New Year's Day looking for Paco Rodriguez. I tried his old haunts: the Methodist church, pool halls, bars, bodegas. Everyone had seen him around but couldn't tell where. His mother lived off Treemont. She was a crone, and she stared at me malevolently, still clutching her Bible. She had sat through Paco's trial in exactly the same attitude. The cops had been there before and received the same treatment: silence. New York's a good place to hide if you don't want to be found – ever.

By six I quit and headed for a bar. My feet ached and I was half frozen. I took my Red straight and stared at Christine Breelander reading the news as the fill-in anchor woman. She was smart and bright. A natural. It was showbiz with wisecracks. The news – what there was – slotted around their personalities like tinsel. Quite suddenly I felt as if she were staring straight at me. She knew I was watching. Her tone changed.

'Now our crime reporter, Mary Holt, has a follow-up story on the death of Detective Harry Margolis.'

Mary Holt wasn't as glamorous, but still very young. She stood in front of the 48th precinct. I knew what she'd say. Narcotics were found beside Harry's body. The Department had sat on the story as long as possible. I didn't want to watch now. I went back out into the cold evening. January 1st. Another fourteen days to go. I had to find Rodriguez before he found me.

The Lawrence Funeral Chapel was on Prospect Avenue at Boston. It stood in the middle of the block; its imposing false brick façade distinctive even in the night. It resembled a Madison Avenue bank. No neon signs, a dark somber door set in an archway, decorated with plastic laurel leaves and lit by the glow of carriage lamps on either side. The dark curtains were permanently drawn across the bay windows.

Like an all-night druggist Lawrence never closed. I pushed the bell. A solemn organ note vibrated from deep inside. The note was supposed to soothe the caller. It only filled me with gloom and foreboding – the final sound a man heard before passing from life. I heard steps, a lengthy pause and knew I was being looked at. Even funeral chapels were robbed. The door opened. A small, plump man with a neat thin line of hair on his top lip; flat hair, carefully spaced, lay on his skull. He wore a dark suit, a dark tie, black shoes and smelt as if he had been slid out of a mortuary drawer. He even exuded a formal chill.

I stepped in. There was a veiled resistance, a man only wanting to give an impression, yet not wishing to show defiance openly, should it bring down violence.

'Mr Lawrence in?'

'He is otherwise engaged.'

'Disengage him.'

In the reception hall were religious pictures on the walls, pamphlets on the side table and armchairs. The chandelier, tarnished and bulky, looked as if it had been stolen from a Transylvanian castle. The chapel had a similar fixture, except larger. It glowed coyly now, barely lighting the pews. Beyond lay darkness and shadow. The altar was an elaborate piece of marble and mahogany with a stained-glass window behind it. The window depicted a vague religious scene: sun, clouds, a hill, haloes. It could appeal to any religious group. In the Bronx there was every religious group. The lighting behind was artificial. There was an office under the window at the rear. The greeter was whispering to Lawrence, announcing my presence.

'Hallo Lawrence.'

'Mr Scott,' there was sepulchral delight, even though I hadn't uttered the magic words, 'no expense spared'. Lawrence resembled the greeter, with a more generous paunch. His vest was open for comfort and he hastily buttoned it, controlling the abandoned flesh. His hair was more sparse. It lay in strands only at the back and top. The front shone. His hand was cool, dry and dusty; had it rested in the same dust that consigned flesh and bone?

'I heard . . .'

'Yes, I'm out. Business looks good.'

'People get to eat, pay taxes and die,' he smiled at his witticism. His employee chuckled; a practiced sound, effortless. He would have made it in his sleep at the sound of a Lawrence saying. 'What can I do for you?'

'Mrs Margolis sent me. You got everything right? And give her a fat discount.'

Lawrence winced. At least it appeared he had. His mouth soured and his eyes crinkled. 'That's all you cops . . . ' He hesitated, then decided to allow the title to stand . . . 'ever want from me. Discount. I'm going broke.'

'We've given you enough business.' I lit a cigarette to rid my nostrils of that stale bitter smell that pervades a funeral home.

'You remember Detective Harry Margolis?'

'Certainly.' A visible shadow of sorrow passed over his face. A pained expression. 'I was deeply saddened to hear of his passing. The Lord . . .'

'Yes. Harry did you a few favors. Return them. Where is he?'

'Resting in the South Chapel.'

It was a bare room . . . the coffin was closed. I didn't open it.

'Anyone come to pay respects?'

Lawrence scrunched up his face and caressed the thin line of hair on his top lip. It was no thicker than a pencil mark and gave as much comfort. He finally nodded.

'Cops. I recognized some of them.'

'No one else?'

'Many others. Ordinary people come to say goodbye. He was liked. I have known many to leave our world without the comfort of relatives and friends. We bid the person goodbye and God bless. Sometimes that happens. Then Mr Pinto and I say a prayer for them and comfort them.'

He spoke as if the dead lived and possibly thanked him for his kindness before climbing into the crematorium. Or the grave. Lawrence sank his head down, the roll of fat spread over his collar and spilled down his shirtfront. An avalanche of flesh that threatened to fall and roll down his paunch. He glanced up from that posture of deep solemnity. I recognized the calculation that passed for thought.

'Who else?'

'What's it worth?'

'You don't get hurt.'

'A young man. I didn't like the look of him. He peered into Detective Margolis' face and smiled.'

'When?' I knew it had to be Paco Rodriguez.

'Yesterday.' His eyes still calculated. 'And then there was a TV crew. The woman said she was making a special on Harry.'

'Channel Three?'

'Yes. She interviewed some of the people, and also me.' He looked pleased. 'I made her do it outside so people could see my sign. It is always good for business.'

'I bet.'

I rang Christine and arranged to meet her at an uptown restaurant. It was a small Italian place created for fat expense accounts. She was already there, talking to the *maître d'*, and gave me her cheek to kiss. It made me feel slightly better.

'I see you're still working on the special.'

She raised her brow. 'Of course I am. I'm still hoping you'll change your mind.'

'I'm thinking about it. You going to include the narcotics angle?'

'Yes. It's a fact, isn't it? I can't disregard it. I'll get laughed out of the business.'

'It was planted. I'll prove it.'

'When?' I had no reply for that. 'I've got to tell it all, Paul. It's my duty as a journalist. Look, we all liked Harry. I saw the people who came to the funeral parlor, but I can't help it if it turns out he was crooked.'

'He wasn't.' I leaned over and held her hand. 'Can't you sort of film around it?'

'You trying to corrupt me?' She squeezed my hand. 'I'm sorry, Paul, I just can't.'

'When is it going to be broadcast?'

'After his funeral. It'll be the last shot. When is it?'

'Soon.' For how long I could hold that up, I had no idea. I had to clear him, but already I felt the pressures. Not only the Department thought him corrupt but he was on every

137

front page and TV screen, and in her special. It was the spike.

A couple of people stopped by our table.

'Should you be seen in public with me? An ex-con.'

'You're part of the story.' She laughed. 'Besides I'm rehabilitating you.'

'Why?'

'Let's say you're Kodachrome. Most men are monochrome. I can't figure you out as yet. You're rude, hard, unpalatable. Then suddenly gentle. You're more vulnerable than you think.'

'What's my weakness?'

'Love. You loved Harry. Your wife, the kids. Maybe, just to complicate, me. Or you need me.' She considered me quietly.

'Is it wise?'

'Loving is never wise,' she said. 'You end up hurt. What did you feel when Harry was killed?'

'Did? Do. I feel rage.'

'I guess I'd feel the same. How far have you got?'

'Far, but not far. Homicides are like that. You stare at the obvious but don't see it. There is one suspect. Paco Rodriguez.'

'He killed that kid. I covered the case.' She shuddered.

'Poor boy.'

'His father was killed too a couple of days ago. He swore he'd get me and Harry, but . . . '

'But?'

I shrugged. 'He's not bright. Sure he could have chopped Harry, but Harry wouldn't have let him get that close. His gun wasn't drawn.' I sat back, startled. 'For Christ's sake. It couldn't have been Rodriguez. Harry knew who hit him. We all forget that. We're all wasting our time looking for Rodriguez.'

I felt despair. How bleak the world appeared suddenly. The woman, the crowds, the lights, all died. I had made assumptions. On what? A date: January 15th. It had nothing to do with Rodriguez, except coincidence. What else? Convenience. You took the easiest slope. Rodriguez would have been an easy bust. This wasn't going to be easy. January 15th was my date. Not Harry's. All he'd given us was that scrawl: 44 se . . .

'Does talking help?'

I grunted.

'Paul . . . '

'I heard. Sometimes. When I got stuck before, I'd talk to Lauren. A homicide narrows your vision. You look at clues from one angle.'

'You talk to her about everything?'

'No. The horror is too much. She did crack one case. Harry and I caught a bad mutha once. A girl strangled and bitten . . . and other things. We had one suspect but he had a cast-iron alibi. He was in Bellevue. I was telling Lauren this and she said maybe he got out. We checked. The son-of-a-bitch had been let out for half a day to attend a funeral. You get locked in sometimes into a way of thinking. Sure we'd checked Bellevue first thing but they told us he'd been in. When we went back it turned out different. Their records were wrong.'

We had another drink. I needed it. 'Harry left one clue.'

She leant forward, frowning. 'What?'

'Off the record.'

'Of course.'

'He wrote 44 se . . . '

She waited: 'That all?'

'Yah. Except I don't know what it means?'

She continued frowning, puzzling it out. Finally she shook her head.

'Anything else?'

'I'm trying to break the narcotics angle. I have a CI who gave me a name. Except the name got chopped. So I've got . . . friends . . . helping.'

'Friends?'

I flattened my nose and bent my ear. 'They come in handy.' I didn't add that the favor they wanted in exchange worried me. I told her too about Captain Herlihy.

'I'm so glad he cleared that. It must be a great relief to you that Harry didn't betray you.'

'It was the best damned day of my life. Let's get out of here.'

It was freezing. The wind off the East River cut through our clothes and sliced to the bone in our faces. She kept her head bowed and snuggled deep into her fur collar, holding tightly to my hand.

'You won't mind. I'm feeling tired tonight. It was a long day.'

'No. Tomorrow?'

'I'm off for the weekend to my hideaway. I found it years ago. It looks on to a valley and I just lie around in jeans and a pullover and read books. I don't even have a TV there.'

'Where is it?'

'Far, far away. It's my Camelot.'

'Your what?'

'A place that doesn't exist. I'll take you there one day.'

'Where is it?'

She smiled secretively but didn't answer. 'I swear sometimes it's colder here than in Boston. I began my career there. First in radio, then in television, before I made the big apple. I wish it was summer.'

'You study there as well?'

'No, in Brown.' She whistled to a cab.

Her mouth tasted warm, moist and sweet as the last glass of wine. I turned back into the cold, feeling the loss of companionship. I had no place to go. My room was as barren as my cell and no comfort. I thought of Lauren and the warm house but it was unfair. My car had a ticket. You'd think in this weather the Brownies would want to keep their butts warm. Conscientious bastards.

I blew a dime and tried Dekker. He was just going off duty.

'It's Paul Scott. You got the ballistic results?'

'Paul.' He sounded surprised, as if he'd not heard of me before. Then he began to cough. I felt the rasp and pain down the wire. He fought for breath. 'Paul. I got good news and bad news.'

'The good.'

'Ballistics match one of the bullets with the same gun that killed Harry.'

'Which one?'

'The one that was fired. The other bullet we tested – doesn't match anything.'

'That the bad?'

'Hell, I've got worse. Don't tell me where you are. Don't mention to anyone you called me.' I heard him light a cigarette. I guess illness drives everyone crazy. 'You want to know who owns the gun that shot Harry?'

'Tell me.'

'You. Johnny Johnstone found the weapon. A .25 – your undercover gun. There's an APB out on you.'

THIRTEEN

I BOUGHT a pint of Red and slid into a transient hotel on 30th and Madison. Transient: no place to go, a sense of permanent displacement. The night clerk took the thirty, dropped the key on the desk, and didn't look up. The room smelt of recently buried pharaohs. It gave you bad breath just entering. The window was jammed, like my life. There was a glass in the tiny bathroom a roach wouldn't have drunk from.

I lay back and drank from the bottle. What did I have at the end of the day when normal men kiss their wives good night after a quick lay, turn over and fall into dreamless sleep? NYPD looking for me, period. The Shooter who chopped Harry was one and the same wanting to chop me, period. Who? Period. My mind sank into demented blankness. It's not answers – the truth – that drives men crazy. It's the questions: How many angels can dance on the head of a pin? When do we blow up the world?

I surfaced from the languor of Red. Half a bottle had passed. The Shooter was intelligent. He had been smarter than Harry. He was smarter than me, for the moment.

What moment? Out there in space a moment is eternity. It could be mine too. Harry knew the Shooter. Did I? Did I? Did I? My mind had an echo like an alcoholic the shakes. It couldn't help itself.

Harry and I. Our past? Which case? How long back? Seventeen years was a long time. The Shooter had patience. Time was of no consequence. A bad guy? Harry wouldn't have let him so near. Cops don't meet intelligent bad guys. Mostly dummies they lock up. The smart ones are never met. This one was smart. So we never met. Then why chop us? Harry found out something? He couldn't have. His gun would have been drawn. He found out too late.

The maid woke me. She was thin, bent, old. Her blue nylon uniform crackled with static. She muttered an apology and moved down the corridor still muttering. Some people talk to themselves to prove they live. I peered up the air shaft. I guessed it was noon. I saw a triangle of blue sky.

I showered and had lunch in the coffee shop downstairs. The food tasted as bad as the room smelt. My car had another ticket on it. I moved it before I got towed. I drove round the blocks aimlessly and finally stopped at a telephone.

'Get me Lieutenant Dwyer.'

'Who's calling?'

'Callaghan.' There are more Callaghans in the PD than you could shake a stick at.

'Yes.'

'It's Paul Scott.'

'Where are you?'

'At the end of the telephone, Lieut. I hear you put out an APB on me.'

'The chief did. Hold it.' He didn't bother to cover the mouthpiece.

'Hey, Sarge, pull those guys out from the stake-out on Scott's place. I got him on the line. Okay, Scott. Why don't you come in?'

'I don't want to get sweated by you for something I didn't do.'

'It's your gun.'

'Where did you find it?'

'Under some rubble across the street from where Harry died. You should know where you hid it.'

'Sure I do. Johnny gotten psychic now? He just knew which stone to look under?'

'He got tipped.'

'How?'

'I'll tell you when I see you, Scott.'

I watched a cruiser drift by. The patrolmen were slouched in their seats. I let the car pass and waited until it turned a corner. They may have made me.

'Harry didn't set me up, Lieut. Herlihy did. He told me. That removes the motive and no punk DA will press unless he's got a good motive. They all read Perry Mason in law school. Check Herlihy. I'll tell you where to find him.'

'We know where.'

I didn't like his sound. It was sharp, clipped. It gave out a warning. He didn't even breathe on the phone. He survived by osmosis.

'Where?'

'The Mantoloking morgue.'

'And I'm the suspect?'

'Nah. He ate his gun. Was he part of your ring?'

'Yes.' So he was dead. He'd paid. 'He was the boss.'

'I'll tell Charlie Houldey. He'll be looking for you pretty soon.'

I rang off, drove around and sat in traffic jams. I should have forgiven the poor bastard. I doubt whether it would have saved him. It would have removed one weight off his soul. My gun? What the hell had happened to it? I'd turned in my .38 with my shield. My undercover .25 I'd left locked in my desk drawer, I was sure. I rang Lauren at the office. She wasn't at her desk and I didn't leave a message. I rang my private number. I was to wait. I waited.

'Scott. We got what you want. Silver hung out with a rich crowd – TV stars, writers, showbiz socialites; he was their supplier.'

'Where?'

'Around. But mostly at parties thrown by a guy called

Anderson. He's got a town house: 17 East 93rd. You heard of him?'

'Yes.'

'He's got enough clout to shove you feet first down a rainpipe.'

'I thought you guys did that.'

'We don't like those kind of jokes, Scott. Be careful.' He nearly rang off in indignation. 'Don't forget tomorrow.'

It was a quiet street. In summer trees shaded it. Now they were stripped and shorn, like splintered pickets. The buildings were four and five storeys, deceptively anonymous, deceptively small. There was a consulate next door with a cop crouched in his sentry box. Number 17 was four-storeyed, a brownstone façade with a heavy black steel front door. It was flanked by cathedral-like windows, protected by bars. It looked an impenetrable building. I double-parked, mounted three steps and rang the bell. I heard nothing and waited. It took time. The distance was great. Finally I heard a muted step and the door swung open. The man was small and plump with neatly combed, fashionable hair. His face was heart-shaped, sallow-skinned and he wore aviator-type gold-rimmed glasses. His suit was dark and well cut and he wore it in the manner of a minor but powerful functionary. Beyond him I glimpsed a cavernous hall. A cut-glass chandelier hung from the ceiling and at the far end was a massive wood-carved fireplace. It looked more like a miniature cathedral. In between was an expanse of perfect white marble and a few velvet chairs for visitors. To the left was a marble staircase. The marble was darker in color, mellowed with age and use. It was a dozen feet wide with a marble bannister. To the right were arches, and beyond I caught the shimmer of placid blue water and smelt chlorine and damp bathing suits. A huge dog stalked over to the door. It had the same tawny coat as a lion.

'So you've looked. What do you want?' His hand rested on the dog's head. It was high enough to reach above his waist. They both gave the impression they had judged my position in the scheme of their world. I was no higher than the dog's head.

145

'I'd like to see Mr Anderson.'

'He's not in,' the man said.

'When will he be in?'

'Later.'

'Real helpful aren't you? Okay. When exactly can I get to see him?'

'Two, three . . . months. He's in Klosters. That's in Switzerland.'

'I also get geography lessons.'

'Sure. Then he goes to Cape Cod. That's in Massachusetts.'

'He leads a hard life.'

'Too hard. What do you want with him?' He examined me deliberately from head to toe. 'Cop, huh.' Then he reversed the examination. 'No shield. Otherwise you'd be blinding me with it.'

'Smart thinker.' The man stepped back and began to close the heavy door. I didn't put my foot out. The weight was enough to crush it. 'I haven't answered your question yet.'

'Maybe I lost interest in that.' But he stopped and remained waiting. Finally, 'What do you want with Mr Anderson?'

'I'm investigating a homicide.'

'And you just decided to pick on Mr Anderson. You were passing and the entrance looked interesting.'

I looked down at the dog, then back up to him. The man instinctively recoiled.

'Some day you got to step out of this palace and I'll be waiting to bounce you so hard into the sidewalk they'll need a jack hammer to break you loose.'

I spoke quietly in a passionless, almost uninterested voice. I made it sound not like a threat, not even a promise, but a fixed and scheduled event that would take place in a chosen place and time. I also conveyed that craziness only a cop can when he knows he has to intimidate, to reveal such a sense of destruction that his opponent thinks twice, thrice, before continuing his action.

'Okay,' the man said. 'How can Mr Anderson help in your investigation?'

'I'll tell him when I get to see him.' I took out my notebook. 'About seven months ago on May 8th he threw a party.' I appeared to read, and though my head was bent, I continued to watch the man. He remained impassive. 'There was a guest – a pusher called Nick Silver . . . '

I deliberately looked up and examined the great hall beyond the man's shoulder. I caught a glimpse of a woman. She was in shadow and I couldn't see any detail beyond the fall of silk trousers and feet encased in high heels. 'You remember him?'

'I have to check the book; Mr Anderson entertains a lot. But I certainly don't recall this . . . pusher. He doesn't entertain that kind of person.'

'He did. If you check your book you could refresh your memory. I'll wait. And don't shut the door.' The man hesitated, wanting to be rid of me but vividly remembering the violence he'd seen in my face.

He turned, saw the woman in the shadow and stiffened. When he turned back I saw the fading malevolence she had aroused in him.

'One moment.' He turned and began to walk back the length of the hall, keeping a good distance from the woman. I saw her gesture sharply and, as if fighting a powerful current, the man changed direction. They talked, softly; the man returned to the door. His face was impassive.

'Miss Carson will see you.'

I followed him. The dog sniffed my trousers. It was cool in the hall. Shreds of light came from the chandelier in a grotto which was parallel to the hall and ran the same length. Between the arches were large oil paintings; grotesque, demented, phantasmagorical. I could not absorb all the details. I would not have liked to live with any of them. To the right of the fireplace was a large window. It looked out on a courtyard, skirted by potted trees.

The woman stood at the window. She was slim, tiny and graceful. She wore a silk blouse and around her neck hung many gold chains, some with pendants. On one wrist was a gold watch, on the other a gold and diamond bracelet.

She looked ageless, unlined. Her blonde hair was pulled

147

so tightly back in a bun that it could have been a permanent facelift. She was beautiful, yet indefinably not. Blue eyes, a pert nose, distinctive cheek bones, a good mouth. Her eyes were hooded and her poise still, almost reptilian. If I touched I would feel no warmth, merely the chill of porcelain or a bloodless creature.

I sensed the man waiting behind me. She waved him away as if flicking dust. He walked slowly towards a door on the other side of the fireplace, opened it and glanced back. I saw the venom.

'Here, Saul,' he called the dog.

'Stay, Saul,' she said.

The dog, practiced in diplomacy, obeyed neither. It chose to lie by the steps.

'Who are you?'

'My name's Paul Scott.'

'I didn't ask your name.' She spoke with an unfamiliar accent, flattening her vowels to make them sound like 'i's.

'Well, you've got it . . . '

I had not thought it possible, yet I felt her chill increase. Her touch now would be fatal.

'You a policeman?' She emphasized her contempt.

'No. I'm investigating the homicide of one.'

'Who hired you?'

'I hired myself, lady. And I fire myself. I came to see Mr Anderson. When can I meet him? Jeeves there was vague on his dates.'

'He's away.'

'Who are you? The housekeeper?'

'Who told you that?' I visualized the hood spreading, poised to strike. Her fists were clenched so tight her nails must have pierced her palm.

'I took a wild guess.'

'I am Mr Anderson's fiancée,' she said. 'We have been together many years.'

'Some people like long engagements. When can I see him?'

'What is your authority?'

148

'None,' I said.

Quite suddenly she smiled. It was illusory. A woman like her was incapable of warmth or friendship. She was self-contained, hard, and the smile lay on the surface like peeled skin. She appeared to relax; the coils slackening but never so much that they could not be tightened.

'Maybe I can be of help?' She sat and gestured. I remained standing, looking down, and the coils tightened fractionally. The smile remained, even lighter on the surface. A whisper of breeze could blow it away.

'Do you remember a guy called Nick Silver?'

'Maybe.'

'He came to a party. What was the occasion?'

She shrugged: 'Business. That's the only reason Mr Anderson entertains. You know what he does?'

'Everything. TV stations, newspapers, baseball teams. He inherited nothing – a mere five million – and built it into a fortune.'

'It was three million. I met him when he was poor.' She said it mechanically, believing she continually had to defend her position and place in his life.

Bill Anderson came from one of the old, unknown, rich families. He came to public attention only when he started a personality magazine that had taken off. He'd branched into television, films, newspapers, gambling casinos. I had once seen him on television. He was a dark-haired, handsome man with a dissipated face and a clipped manner of talking. He always wore impeccably cut double-breasted suits and that dark hair looked as if it had been lowered on to his head. He was also a recluse, unlike those who appeared in his magazine weekly.

'Did you talk to Nick Silver?'

'I talk to everyone. Hello and goodbye. Mr Anderson never spends any time with them, unless they're an important client. I usually do all the entertaining. You can say it's kind of a PR exercise.'

'Did he meet Nick Silver?'

'No.'

'A big party and you can remember that?'

'I introduce him only to the people he needs to meet. Most others he doesn't want to. Or need to.'

'How many people were there?'

'Hundred. More or less.' She looked around, wanting me to encompass the size of her domain. A hundred wouldn't have even filled a corner.

'Did Silver come with anyone?'

'People come in bunches. Maybe.'

'Did he meet anyone here?'

'Mr Scott, there were a hundred people here. He must have met some of them.'

'Did he leave with anyone else?'

'I didn't see him leave.'

'Is it possible to have a guest list?'

'No.' She stood, arms crossed, cold. 'I've been patient enough.' She stepped around me, straight, unpliable, and began to walk to the distant steel door. I walked behind.

'How do I get to see Mr Anderson?'

'People like you don't.'

'People like me cause a lot of trouble, Miss Carson.'

She turned, smaller, yet giving an impression she was looking down on me.

'I doubt it.' We reached the door and she heaved it open.

'The cop who died was my partner. He was my only friend. I'm not going to give up easily just because Mr Anderson has a few connections.'

'He has many, Mr Scott.' She closed the door. She would have slammed it but it was too heavy for her.

Dusk: the air was perfumed with privilege. Chandeliered lights glowed from windows reflecting paneled rooms, expensive paintings, an emptiness of space and a quiet. Two women wearing furs strolled past me. The furs were carelessly worn like a daily cloth coat. I had joked once to Harry that all one needed was to cruise up Madison, between the 60s and 70s and grab the furs off the women promenading. We'd be millionaires in fifteen minutes.

I sat in the car, wrote notes and smoked a cigarette. I waited half an hour. The door opened and the man came out with two dogs. They looked exactly alike and stalked on either side of him. He carried a dainty pooper-scooper. I followed them on foot. They turned down 5th and crossed over. It was a daily routine. I sat on a bench. They strolled three blocks down, then turned and returned. The man saw me, hesitated, then came over. He sat and the dogs did too.

'How did you get on with Cobra Carson?'

'Not far.'

'That lady eats people alive. I've quit three times. But Mr Anderson always gets me back.' He lit a cigarette. 'I work for him, not her.'

'What's the difference?'

'She keeps off my back.'

'So I noticed. That's a long engagement they got.'

'He still hasn't divorced his wife. He has three kids by her. He's a great guy. That's why I keep coming back. One day . . . ' He sighed, believing such a day truly existed.

'You worked for him long?'

'Nearly fifteen years,' he said. He stared into space, trying not to imagine the gulf that separated their lives.

'What do you do for him?'

'Once a cop, always a cop! Chauffeur, other things if needed.' He turned to stare at me, then focused on the scar. In the fading light it didn't appear fierce or ugly. A mere streak on my neck. He shivered. It wasn't possible to tell if it was from cold or the thought of the pain inflicted in that scar. He looked a man who would avoid pain though he'd delight in inflicting it. 'He never met Nick Silver.'

'So you say.'

'I was with him. Carson spent a long time talking to Silver.' He laughed, without humor. 'They had things in common I guess.' He sounded obscene. 'When the party was over they all went out for a drink to Le Relais. On Madison.'

'What time did she return?'

'I don't know. I went home after the party. Mr Anderson didn't want anything. He began to work. He works at night mostly.'

'You'd like her out of the picture, wouldn't you?'

'Sure. But I'm telling you the truth. They all went out.'

151

'How many in the "they"?'

'Six, seven. Fashionable people. Rich. Useless.'

'You don't like the people that make your boss rich.'

'He doesn't either. That's why he doesn't go to his own parties. She loves them.'

'Any names?'

He became evasive. 'Just people.'

'No names?'

'No.' He stood up, stretched and his coat fell open. The gun butt peeped from his trouser band. 'I have a license for it.' He buttoned his jacket.

'You an ex-Viet?'

'Yah.'

I watched them fade into the dusk. He was a smooth operator: the type who pushed a pen in Saigon and ran crap games. Harry and I had spent that war as MPs down in Alabama. Sometimes it got dangerous.

I found a Hispanic barber to shave me. They're the only ones who use old-fashioned razors. I ate and checked into another transient. It looked and felt no different. People with no place and no one. They sat in the lounge looking at television as if it were the washer in a laundromat. Hell, who could tell the difference nowadays? Maybe a giant intellect with an IQ of ten.

I rang Lauren.

'Paul, what's happening?'

Women always begin conversations rhetorically.

'Why?'

'The cops are looking for you.'

'I know. When aren't they? Do you remember my undercover gun I used to carry when I was in narcotics? I think I locked it in my desk drawer.'

She hesitated. 'Yes. It was stolen.'

'When, for Christ's sake?'

'A year back. No, not that long. Eight months.'

'Why didn't you tell me?'

'What could you have done? Broken out and tracked down the villain?'

'What else?' She was itching to fight.

152

'Some money. Nothing else otherwise.'

'You tell the cops there?'

'I reported the burglary. They came, they looked, they went.' She softened. 'I'm sorry. I was worrying for you, Paul. Are you okay?'

'I'm fine. At least they'll have the robbery logged.'

Eight months. A long-time thinker this Shooter. Sets me up three years back, waits and sets me up again. In between, Harry. What the hell did we do together? We hurt someone real bad.

I knew they waited. They had commanded me to attend at a time and a place. I was half an hour late. I wore new clothes. It made me feel better, though the exhaustion showed in my face. My skin was more pallid, eyes darker and I moved like a man recovered from a long illness.

I stopped a block away from Joe's restaurant. It was in the east Village off Bleecker. The evening was crisp and cold and the streets were crowded. When I'd worked Manhattan South, I had liked the Village. It had been eccentric; full of harmless charm and extravagant people. In spite of the brightness of the shops and fast foods and theatres, I sensed the change. It lay too visibly on the surface and ran dark and deep. I saw the street now with a cop's eye: the men in pairs, the youths in doorways, the bars which only males frequented, the array of sexual violence displayed in shop windows, the edgy glances of people as they passed. The lights were no longer bright but tawdry, the buildings appeared shabbier, seedier, and had succumbed to the same neglect as the human spirit which once existed in the Village.

The restaurant was small, unobtrusive; it would not have been reviewed by *Gourmet*, nor frequented by strangers. It appeared empty. A couple sat at a table, a waiter leaned against the bar at the far end. He glanced at me and waited for me to sit. I went past him into the room at the rear. There was a party in progress. A dozen men and three or four women milled about. At the far end of the room was a bar and alongside it was a table laden with food.

'Hey look, it's Scott.' Peter Ventura was an elegant, urbane-looking man. He had a high forehead, a thin, almost

153

ascetic face. He appeared to smile too easily, though the smiles never touched his eyes. They reached only the crinkles. He was the brother of 'Three Fingers' Ventura, my protector in Lewisburg. Peter was 'One Finger' for no discernible reason. He embraced me. 'It's good to see you looking so well, Paul. I am glad you came.'

'I was told to.'

'It was an invitation. A drink?' A man fetched one.

'What are you celebrating?'

'The meeting of friends, old and new.' He took me around and introduced me to the men. The women were excluded. One or two I knew. We stopped and talked. I knew I had been summoned for a reason. I looked around and saw it. Across the room a man was looking at me. For a fraction of a second he stood poised for flight. The cigarette halfway to his mouth, the drink coming down. He was in his early thirties, fleshily handsome, sleek-haired, expensively dressed. He had a cherubic mouth and wore a gold watch and a heavy gold identity bracelet. As if nothing had occurred he began talking to his companion again. Detective Pete Rizzoli had been with me in Robbery.

Ventura took my arm. We moved leisurely, and inexorably, towards Rizzoli. There was jokes to be cracked, small talk made, bountiful hospitality to be practiced. Finally, we reached Rizzoli.

'Paul, you know your old friend, don't you?'

I studied Rizzoli. 'No. I don't remember. I'm Paul Scott.' I put out my hand.

Rizzoli shook it: 'Johnny Esposito.' He squeezed in gratitude, in warning. 'We met in Lewisburg, Paul.'

'I met lots of guys in Lewisburg.' We were watched carefully.

Ventura laughed. 'Sure you must have. Maybe you met Johnny outside, eh? Cops meet lots of people. You don't remember?'

'No.' I turned away. Ventura wasn't smiling. His eyes were cruel. I met his stare unsmilingly. 'Where do you think I met Johnny then?'

'Around?'

'I said "no",' I answered softly. Ventura didn't reply a while, lost in his calculations. Finally, he nodded.

'How about some food?'

'Sure. I'm a bad host. All I've fed you is booze.' We strolled over to the tables and a man gave me a plate.

'You sure you don't know that guy?'

'Sure, why?'

Ventura tapped his nose. 'He don't smell good. Like a cop. We checked his yellow sheet downtown. He's not a good guy. We checked to see if he was a cop. No file on anyone looking like him.'

'So, he's who he says he is.'

Rizzoli was under cover. Whoever ran him was good. A yellow sheet was natural; it was easy to make up and plant so it could be found. But Rizzoli's police records had been removed for added security. Men like Ventura could get access to anything and it had been a wise precaution. Except someone could have identified him. I felt for Rizzoli. He must have shat himself when he saw me walk in. He didn't expect favors from a crooked cop.

'So what's with this Nick Silver guy?'

'He pushed half a K of coke to someone. I'm trying to find out who.'

'Maybe we can help some more.' He soaked a piece of bread in the meat sauce and popped it in his mouth like a bon-bon. 'Depending on how you help us.'

He glanced back to Rizzoli. I didn't bother to turn. He watched me eat.

'Good?' Ventura asked. 'I told you so. I'd like to eat here more often, but it's dangerous to make anything a habit.' He sighed heavily. I grunted unsympathetically.

'Any idea who chopped him?'

'I don't know and who cares? He was just a pusher. I got more important things to do than figure out who got rid of a piece of garbage. All these Colombians and Cubans are making a man's life dangerous. They have no honor. No dignity. No loyalty. They are truly animals. That's what the cops should be worrying about.'

I had heard it before. I remembered a few years back

when I was in the 7th Homicide I'd investigated the death of one of his enforcers. Canteloupe was a brutal, hard man. He was the probe to test the family's strength in the South Bronx. In a small bar he met a violent end and the families knew they could not control the South American narcotics trade. A little Puerto Rican, ignorant of Canteloupe's terrible reputation, stuck a broken beer bottle in his throat.

Ventura leant forward, his face could not have been kinder. The eyes, however, remained hard with a hint of impatience. 'Look, Paul, as a good friend, you deserve to lead a good and peaceful life. Eat, sleep, screw, no money worries, go down to Miami for a vacation when you want, buy a new car. That's what life should be about. Make it easy on yourself. You got more to lose than anyone else, you know.'

'I've done that all my life and I ended up in prison.'

'Whose fault? You got caught but weren't you well looked after inside? We took care of you like you were one of the family. We will continue to do so.'

'If I remember?'

'Yes. No one does favors for nothing. You know that.' Two of his friends appeared at my elbow. I saw Rizzoli watching me.

'Maybe we can talk in private?'

'Why not?'

FOURTEEN

As I passed Rizzoli, I felt his scrutiny. Sweat broke on his top lip. There was no way I could reassure him. The poor bastard would have to sweat into an eternity. There was a room above, comfortably furnished with leather armchairs, a desk, heavy velvet curtains. I took out the envelope and tossed it to Ventura.

'What's this?'

'My graduation present. It's all there.' One of his men riffled the five grand and tossed it on the desk. He had sensitive fingertips. I was gently pushed down into a deep chair.

Ventura said: 'Give it back to him.' The envelope landed on my lap. 'Keep it.' He jerked a thumb to the door. 'You know Esposito, right? He's a cop.'

'Wrong.' The two friends came to stand either side of me. I felt very lonely. 'Never seen him in my life.'

The one on the left feinted. The friend on the right hit me hard on the side of the head. He nearly broke my neck. I saw spots large as tracer bullets honing in on me. I tried to stand. My feet got kicked away. The friend on the left took his shot.

I blacked out a minute or two. Ventura sat patiently. 'There's no cavalry going to come. You got no friends out there with badges. They think you're a shit. What the hell are they going to care what happens to you, Scott? You know Esposito?'

I tried to massage my temple. My hand was knocked down. If I could have stood I would have taken the hand off at the shoulder and beat him over the head.

'There are twenty-four thousand cops in this city, give or take five thousand depending on the city budget. I can't know all of them. I don't know him.'

'I'm a sensitive guy. I think you do.'

'Yeah?'

'Yeah.'

This time each friend took an arm and hauled them above my head and back. One held them. The other came round front. I kicked out. He sidestepped. He had lots of practise. He was also good and accurate. He began on my ribs and worked his way back and forth and then down. I couldn't breathe. Pain became finally a dull sort of distraction once it lost its bite. It was operating somewhere in the extremities of my body.

'You remember?' Ventura sounded faint. Maybe he was whispering.

'Sure I remember. He's a cop. You want me to say he's the Pope, I'll say he's the Pope. What the fuck do I care?'

'That's always the problem with pain,' Ventura said conversationally, I was still his dinner guest. 'You don't always get the truth. Only what is convenient to the person. Listen, I'm your friend.'

'I know. All my friends do this to me.'

'I was just asking questions. Okay, Esposito isn't a cop. I had to check, right?'

I sighed. It was probably sarcastic. I couldn't think of a conciliatory comment.

'Put his light out.'

The one behind me did.

The corridor was narrow. I could just fit. The walls scraped my shoulders, the door ahead came racing towards me like I was sliding down a telescope. I looked back for Harry, the two patrolmen. They weren't there. I was alone. I couldn't stop myself. The door flew open and the firing began. The guns were deafening but this time only Washington was firing, playing targets with me. No Harry.

I lay behind the garbage cans like a derelict. It was freezing. My body felt as if nails had been hammered through it. It took me a long time to stand. A careful operation. I was trying to maneuver through the pain but I kept knocking down the bins. The lights were blurred. The people too. They averted their faces and quickened their steps. Some crossed over. I touched my face, swollen and soft.

Walking was difficult. I was like a crab with four broken legs. If I could just get to my car it would be warm; a place to rest, to pass out. I found myself resting against a telephone booth. At least it sheltered my face from the cold wind. Dogs, cats, even humans, need comfort and shelter. Some place in which to curl up and heal. I dialed without thought. The phone rang and rang and I clung on grimly.

'Hello . . . who is it?' Lauren sounded sleepy and warm. Her voice was always husky.

'Paul . . . '

'Are you alright? Paul . . . are you okay?'

'I'm hurt.'

'Where are you?'

I looked around. They hadn't dumped me in a New Jersey saltmarsh with weights. 'I'm on Bleecker. I'll be in my car. White Chevvy. It's parked outside a place called . . . ' The lettering wouldn't stand still. 'Il Portico. A restaurant. It's closed. Everything is . . . '

'I'm leaving now.'

If I was still a cop, I would have dialed 911. How long? Five minutes. Every cop in the neighborhood would have responded to a 10-13. Listening to those sirens approaching was the sweetest sound a cop could hear.

I leant against cars and moved down towards mine. I felt in no hurry. The cold was an anesthetic. I made it and let myself slide slowly in. It wasn't much warmer inside. I started the engine, turned the heat on and lay back.

I couldn't have slept. I passed out. I came to and Lauren was standing by the open door bent over me. Her face was washed, her hair uncombed.

'Can you make it to my car?'

'Yes. Thanks.'

She helped me slide out and I leaned against her. We maneuvered between cars. It was warm as toast inside hers and smelling of domesticity: Kleenex, candy, bubble gum, groceries.

'A motel somewhere. Not home.'

She took off my tie. It was a kind gesture, quite useless. She wasn't sure where I hurt. Or how bad.

'We better go to a doctor.'

'Not yet. No bullet wounds. Just bruised ribs. How are the kids?'

'I called Sandra. She's sitting.'

She lit a cigarette for me and drove slowly. It didn't help. The Manhattan roads could have been a dried riverbed. I had difficulty smoking. I never thought I would. I couldn't suck but it smelt good. Normalcy could be returning slowly.

'You don't want to know what happened?'

'No.' She averted her face. 'God, no.'

She was frightened for me. It reminded her of the last time I was hurt and she'd kept vigil by my bedside. All cops' wives lived in fear. Their men went out daily, some returned in coffins or wounded and damaged. They grappled with beasts and monsters and returned home quiet, morose, edgy. We were like children in an evil garden, scared ourselves at times but enjoying the fear, the gush of adrenalin that made us walk so carefully, even on a family picnic. The streets were really our home: the bars, the gutters, the garbage, stagnant, filthy rooms we passed through daily, the violent, evil lives we touched and rubbed shoulders with. She could not understand our lives, no wife did. We told our stories as rousing adventures and only when one died did the adventures become nightmares that did not dissipate with awakening.

There was a motel a mile outside Chatsworth on a back country road. She went and checked us in, then helped me into the room. Nice and anonymous. We didn't talk as she helped me undress. She winced when she saw the bruises and the bullet scar. She knew it was new but kept grimly silent. I got into bed. It felt good to lie down, to fade from the world without outside force.

I woke and looked to the window. It was the kind of day on which you imagine nothing can ever go wrong. The past was too remote in the clear sunny day. The sky appeared washed after weathering a fierce storm and the air, I imagined, had that sweet, clean perfume of sap and fresh earth.

Lauren slept, dressed, in the other bed. Her mouth was partially open, pursed to kiss. She'd not changed in sleep. She always looked contented, enjoying rest. How often, as dawn came on those days, I'd watched her. I'd come off a late tour, unwind with a couple of drinks with Harry and by the time I reached home, the sky would be lightening. It was impossible to sleep. The mind was crowded with horror. I'd pull up a chair. Watching Lauren's tranquility was a comfort. And then the kids. I felt soothed by their innocence, faces a bit flushed, the sweetness of their bath and the delicate odor of perspiration. They smelt like Lauren.

She awakened, looked at me – with warmth? with concern? I couldn't tell. Then she stretched and sat up.

'How are you feeling?'

'Encased in armor. I creak when I move. Listen.' I lifted my arm. She shook her head, although I felt the bone creak.

'Old age,' she laughed. 'You should hear Mom and Pop. They sound as if they're made of metal in the morning.'

She rang home even as she spoke. Sandra answered. The kids were fine. The school bus was waiting outside and they wanted to talk. Lauren calmed their worries and made sure they'd eaten breakfast. Sandy asked where she was and Lauren said 'With Dad in a motel'. Then she glanced at me and smiled.

'Here, she wants to talk to you.'

'Hi, Sandy.'

'Daddy, what are you doing?'

'Lying down.'

She giggled: 'Is it a second honeymoon? I hope so. Mom did miss you. And of course we did too.' There was joy in her voice that couldn't be dismissed.

'Something like that. Give me Paula.'

She asked the same question but only echoing her sister. I echoed my answer. And gave her a loud goodbye kiss. Lauren and I looked at each other. Maybe we thought the same: the first time in my studio apartment. It had taken a month of dating to entice her back. A man never marries a woman he has had the first night. She makes him doubt too much. Lauren: I had no doubt by the time I took her to bed.

She went into the bathroom and when she came out she was nude. I still enjoyed looking at her, not with greed but with appreciation. She had a good body. Those long legs, firm breasts, flat stomach.

'Lie there and creak.'

She straddled me. She was hot and wet and gentle. I could not get enough into her. It was the loving familiarity. I knew her wants, she mine. We didn't speak, only kissed and caressed and, with long practise, climaxed together. She came to lie beside me, just resting an arm lightly on my chest and watching me smoke. For the first time in years, I no longer felt alone. That was her special quality.

'I love you. I wanted to say that before but I just wasn't sure that was what you wanted to hear from me. When you come out of prison, you feel no one really wants you.'

'I do. I love you too. It's been choking inside me and when you told me I could leave you, I felt so ill.' She kissed me. 'It's over. We'll make it work out somehow.'

We lay in contented silence and her hands stroked away all my anxiety.

She touched the bullet scar. 'What happened?'

'A reminder.'

'Of what?'

'I don't know as yet. The Shooter who put that in me had all the time in the world to take aim. And then to walk over and put one between my eyes.' She touched the bruises and I told her the reason.

'I'm glad you didn't let him down. What would they have done to him?'

'Chopped him.'

'It all sounds so simple. Solve the problem by killing.'

'For some people it is. Then their lives get complicated.'

'Whose doesn't? How many women have you slept with since our marriage. Slept? Huh?'

Her change of tack was sudden. I shrugged.

'I supposed I really don't want to know. Countless, no doubt. It's hard to keep track where a cop is. You aren't like other men. Their lives are scheduled and a woman knows where he is . . . most of the time. With a cop you don't. He could be on special assignment, on a stake-out, on overtime, on night shift, or getting laid.'

'Or hanging out in court. That's where we spend most of the time. And writing up reports.'

She sat up. 'You hungry? I'll get something from home.' I heard her washing and she came out dressed. I lay staring at the ceiling. It was a dull and depressing green.

'Today the sixth?'

'Seventh.' She lightly touched up her face.

'Seventh! What happened to the sixth?'

'You slept. I haven't been home for two days. I just couldn't leave you here by yourself. Why?'

'Nothing. Eight days to the fifteenth.'

'Harry's case?'

'Yeah. I keep going round in circles.'

'Why didn't that Shooter kill you?'

'I don't know. Maybe someone with a grudge. Maybe I was the wrong guy.' I made light of it and distracted her. 'What does 44 se . . . mean to you?'

'Nothing.' She shrugged into her overcoat. It was cloth, much cheaper than Christine Breelander's. I told her why I'd asked. She stood lost in thought.

'Se . . . ? A? Season? Seat? Sea? B? I can't think of anything. C? Sec . . . ant?'

'What's that?'

'A straight line intersecting a curve. It was a clue in my crossword puzzle. I never got it.'

'I didn't know you did crossword puzzles.'

'Sure. Every day on the train to work. C? Second . . . secede . . . secret. Forty-four secrets? You had so many. Maybe you numbered them.'

'Like jokes? No.'

'Sector? Secular . . . ' She went out of the door. 'I'll think about it.'

I smiled. Crossword puzzles. You live with people for years and don't see some things they do. Secant? Jesus, Harry wouldn't have known. Dying men don't write secant. Second. Seconds. Of what? Secret? I wish we had numbered them.

I creaked and sat up. It took me time to get to the bathroom. I filled the tub and sat in a foetal position. They made them the size of wombs. The hot water eased my aches. I heard the door open and slam. Lauren put her head in forty-five minutes later. She'd changed her clothes.

'Semester . . . semi-something . . . sense . . . ' She poured coffee from a flask and handed me a donut. I drank and ate. 'Sepal . . . '

'Don't tell me what that is.'

She laughed. It was filled with humor, the promise of spring. Hearing it felt more miraculous than the water. She bent and kissed me. I tried to grab her and she jumped back.

'I won't.'

There was a gentle, almost apologetic knock on the door. We looked at each other. She shrugged.

'The manager telling us not to wet the towels,' she said and went out.

It wasn't. The lieut and Johnny Johnstone hid her from view as they stared down at me. They noted the bruises noncommitally.

'Front tail,' the lieut said. He tossed me a towel and they stepped back into the bedroom.

Lauren shrank beside their bulk. They did not only fill space, they stole the air from the room.

'Professionals?'

'Muggers.' I dressed, watched by all three.

'Amateurs. Make them?'

'No.'

'Any charges you want made?'

'Make it a routine police investigation.'

'I'll do that.' He began to unwrap a cigar. Stopped. Then looked at Lauren. She nodded and he continued. There was some chivalry left. 'We sat on the house.'

'I guessed that. You want to cuff me? I'm telling you, you're just wasting time. I wouldn't have touched a hair on Harry's head. I loved the guy.'

'I know. Johnny, Mrs Scott . . . could you excuse us a moment?' He rose while Lauren left with Johnny. She looked at me with fear. I knew her thoughts. Just as we were returning to normal, I was to get swept back inside. The lieut studied the end of his cigar a while.

'Pete Rizzoli said to say thanks.'

'You running him.'

'No. A friend. Maybe that's why you got walked over?'

'Maybe. Your friend better pull him. They're getting suspicious.'

'I'll pass the word. Poor bastard. I feel sorry for him: sweating to death each time a new face walks in. Why didn't you tell them? They're your buddies.'

'I wasn't feeling friendly.' He stared incuriously. I saw the faint flicker of interest, quickly extinguished. 'I've got faults, Lieut. Betrayal isn't one of them.'

'I know. We picked up Rodriguez. He's clean on Harry.'

'Harry wouldn't have let that punk on the same block as him.'

The lieut nodded: 'He chopped Angel. Son-of-a-bitch. First the kid, then the father. He heard Angel was out to get him so he thought he'd finish him first. Animal.' He said it dispassionately. You reserved passion for those you loved only.

'What have you got on Harry's case?'

'Forty-fourth second.'

'Could be. We thought about that. Forty-fourth second of what?'

'A tape. There was a video in his room.'

'What tape?' The lieut looked pained, yet patient. 'There are a zillion tapes out there. *Star Wars*?'

'No. Someone showed him a tape on the day he died. What kind of watch did he wear that day?'

'I think it was a digital. So he timed the tape. He knew something was going to come up. He'd been told.'

'Yah. The Shooter had a gun on him and made him sit and watch it. Before he got chopped he had time to write the timing. The Shooter then packed up the video and walked out. No witnesses?'

'We canvassed up and down. None. It was Christmas Eve. People don't take note of ordinary things. Maybe it looked like a Christmas package, all pretty. What about the coke?'

'He wasn't dealing.'

'You can prove it?'

'My CI. Yolande says she was the supplier. She didn't ever see the face of the buyer, but a guy called Nick Silver made the connection. He's dead.'

'So if she didn't see the face . . . it could still be Harry.' He jerked his thumb up to the ceiling. 'They want definite proof. Not just your say-so. Or mine. You know he was clean, I know he was clean. They don't. You want me to pull in your CI?'

'She won't talk. I'll lean on her. Heavily. I've only got a week.'

'Why?'

'I got warned. The Shooter wants me too.'

'Why the hell didn't you tell me that before, for Christ's sake?'

'You wouldn't have listened. You were trying to nail me.'

He shrugged. That didn't bother him too much. You chase every lead. The air had turned murky with our smoke and it gave some character to the anonymity of the room.

'Well we're still checking his back cases but I can't see Harry letting any one connected come near him. Maybe we have two Shooters. One chopped Harry; the other you. There might not be a connection, Paul.'

'I feel it.' It sounded lame but he understood. Then I felt

doubt. Maybe there were two Shooters. The one after me had nothing to do with Harry. It was coincidence.

I watched him carefully tap the ash into the wastebin.

'Tell me about Sandra. Were she and Harry close?'

I shrugged: 'Not really. They'd drifted apart but I don't think he'd ever have divorced her. They grew up together and she's got no one.'

I knew what he was getting at, and then quite suddenly I remembered the scrape of sound when I'd visited her Christmas Day. What had it been? A whisper.

'You know how much Harry was insured for? Million and three-quarter is big numbers. He was killed on duty, remember.' He puffed and stared at his cigar. 'We ran a routine check. She said she was having lunch in a place called The Bistro in Chatsworth around the time Harry was chopped. No one remembers seeing her.' We let the silence lie, neither wanting to disturb it. If a cop could get his rocks off, so could his wife. 'We're going to talk to her some more.' He got up and strolled to the door.

'What about the warrant on me?'

'So I haven't seen you yet.'

FIFTEEN

TIME WAS precious – the hours and days running out – but I felt no sense of hurry. I wanted to remain with Lauren, immerse myself in her love. The kids had gone to school when we returned home and Sandra back to her place. I knew the lieut and Johnny would be there.

'Did Sandra have anyone?'

Lauren looked up warily from making our sandwiches. She shrugged in that womanly, defensive way.

'They went over to talk to her now. Her alibi didn't hold water.'

'I think she did. We get lonely too.' She put the plates down and I poured out wine. It was a celebration. 'I suspected but she didn't tell me anything. Why?'

'She picks up a million and three-quarter in insurance.'

She frowned, then finally shook her head. 'I don't think she would have done it.'

'Wives do it often.'

'Let's not talk about it any more. Remember, you've changed.'

It was pleasurable too in the house alone. After lunch we

went up and made love, reawakening all our lost memories. The times we courted, danced, were happy. We made no mention of the bad things. They had to be forgotten temporarily; a frail illusion but a necessity if we were to remain together.

She drove up with me to the city afterwards. We planned another honeymoon. Nowhere expensive; just alone. By the time we reached the Village it was late afternoon. I looked for my car. It wasn't where I'd left it and I hoped it had been stolen and not towed. Its disappearance was part of the illusion too. I dropped Lauren off at Penn and felt that familiar pang at our parting, as I watched her fade into the crowds. I had to say my goodbye to Christine and rang her. It couldn't be done over the phone. She wanted us to meet.

I ran uptown on Third Avenue. The traffic was slight and I reached the TV station only fifteen minutes late. Christine sheltered in the over-bright lobby and when I honked she came running out and slid into the car. We kissed lightly and with the sensitivity of all women she glanced and withdrew.

'You feel different.'

'I know. Let's go eat somewhere special.'

'That usually means we say goodbye.' She stared straight ahead of her. 'Lauren?'

'Yes. It was strange. I got beaten up.' She looked to see if the damage showed. 'Mostly in the body. Good pros. All I could think of was to reach out for Lauren. She came and helped me.'

'I was out of town.'

'I could lie and say I tried your number. I didn't. I would have liked to have called 911. A 10-13, but I knew they'd never come. I wasn't one of them any more. I was still Lauren's husband.'

She slid over and took my arm companionably. 'I'm glad. You were so lost when I first saw you in the hotel room. You had nothing. Harry was dead. Lauren uncertain.' She kissed me lightly. 'It's good to find someone special again, isn't it?'

'Yes. Except Harry will never be around.'

'No, he won't,' she said softly then added: 'Let's go eat.'

She chose a place on the Upper West Side, La Bocuse. It was on Columbus. The windows were steamed and it had a pretty decor. I was grateful it wasn't crowded. A pianist played classical music and it had an air of graciousness.

'How far have you got on Harry's case?'

'We think . . . '

'We?'

'The lieut, Lauren too. We think he meant the forty-fourth second of a tape he was being shown by the Shooter.'

'You forgiven?'

'No. Neither the lieut nor the PD will ever forgive. I'm a felon, period.' I looked out of the misty windows. The traffic flowed, dreamlike, downtown. 'The lieut wants to break this case and he'll use me until I become inconvenient.'

'How many detectives has he on the case?'

'Besides Johnny? It's a cop killing. Quite a few others but not as many as when the PD had homicide units. The advantages of using me are that I knew Harry better than anyone else. And that I can lean on a person without getting suspended for police brutality.'

'You enjoy that role?'

'No. If only people would tell the truth violence would be unnecessary. They won't. They don't. Not the first time. Maybe the second or the third. A cop bleeds for his information.'

We sat silent. It felt, not uncomfortable, but awkward. She'd withdrawn and stared at the pianist intently without hearing him. There were faint shades of exhaustion under her eyes. I thought it was because of our situation. It had begun in anger, softened, grown companionable, and then shifted back to this silence. It was my mistake. I presumed. It was fatal.

The food came. She toyed with her salmon and salad. Pecking at it, not nibbling.

'What'll you do when you find the perp?'

'Hand him over to the PD.'

'I don't believe you. You're not Harry. He would have done something like that. You? I think you'll kill him.'

170

'I think once I would have. Not now.' I chewed slowly on my lamb, sipping the wine. I was ravenous. Love-making always made me hungry. 'But it depends on the situation. If I have it under control, then he goes to the PD. If I don't . . . it's him or me.'

'Yes, I suppose it does depend who's in control.' She sighed and brushed the hair out of her eyes.

'Maybe the PD will beat me to the Shooter.'

'I doubt it,' she said drily. 'Otherwise they wouldn't be using you. They're going round in circles, like you.'

'I've stopped circling. I've got to find that tape.'

'What is it?'

'I don't know. But it exists somewhere. Harry saw it.'

'You will give me the story as an exclusive? Promise?'

'Promise. Always the reporter.'

'Always the cop. We broke it and if you give it to another channel, I'll kill you.' She laughed.

It broke her mood and she became cheerful. She finished her dinner and ordered dessert. She told me about a series of special assignments she was going to do. She was ambitious. A local channel wasn't enough. She had to break into national reporting. The webs: ABC, NBC, CBS. They were her Mecca.

'How was the weekend?'

'Restful. I love the country, especially in winter. It always seems as if it has been preserved in glass. You know, clear and clean and fragile. I have a huge window that overlooks the valley and I sit there for hours, just dreaming and staring.'

'I guess I'll never get to see it.'

'Why not? We can still be friends, can't we? Just because we were lovers, we don't have to end up as strangers. I hate that. I'm sure if you and Lauren had split, you would have remained friendly.'

'Yah. The kids are always there; thank God that's not going to happen now.'

'I'm glad for you.' She squeezed my hand. 'I tried to interview the lieutenant but he . . . ' She lowered her voice and growled: ' ''It's an on-going investigation and I can't comment.'' I've got about five, six minutes. I'm reserving most for you.'

'When it's over, you've got the exclusive.'

We bundled up and stepped out into the cold. The wind had picked up and it cut into our faces. As we strolled to the car, she tucked her arms in mine and leant against me. In another circumstance I would have taken her to bed. I wasn't in the mood now.

'I'll catch a cab.'

'No.'

On the ride down, avoiding our personal lives and the case, we talked about the Islanders. She was a fan and watched their games. The Rangers weren't worth the time. It looked like another year for the Stanley Cup. I mourned the demise of the Canadiens. They'd been a great team once, full of fire on the ice, and then swiftly they'd turned ordinary. The Islanders were hot. They'd won the cup three years running.

She kissed me on the mouth and I was grateful we would remain friends. I promised once more to give the exclusive and waited until she'd entered the security of her lobby before going back uptown.

My room felt unused and anonymous. Nothing had been touched. It no longer felt lonely though. I had memories. My gun was still where I'd left it after Houldey had searched and left: wrapped in a plastic bag in the toilet.

I figured the best time to catch Yolande was breakfast. He would be asleep still and not drifting. It took twenty knocks before the door finally opened.

'What the hell do you want?'

'Conversation.' I pushed. He resisted on impulse and then fell back. He was half dressed. I didn't look at him. In the gloom he looked unreal, something only half realized, half dreamed. 'Put some clothes on. I brought some coffee.'

'I don't want any fucking coffee. And I don't want any fucking conversation.'

'You got both. That's life. All bad breaks and you don't even have your make-up on. Get dressed.'

Sullenly he returned to the bedroom. I took the coffee

from the paper bag. I'd even bought him a donut. He returned wrapped in a silk negligé. He looked bad. His face was drawn and weary and the skin seemed separately asleep still: wrinkled and worn. He ignored the offerings and sat staring malevolently.

'Tell me all about Nick Silver's connection.'

'I told you.'

'I forgot. Tell it again. Sometimes you remember things better the second time around.'

'I don't remember better at dawn.' He turned brave, like a faucet. 'You know what time I got to bed? Six o'clock. And you come in here at eight, I can't think straight.'

'How're you going to keep your beauty if you get to bed at six? I'm told models always get to sleep by 8 p.m. Talk to me.'

He sat sullenly silent. Mouth clamped shut. I stood up.

'I told you everything. Nick made a connection. I delivered a half K of coke to that address.'

'All in one lump.'

'I told you. Four deliveries at a time. I passed it through the door.'

'The money got passed out. I saw nothing.'

'No curiosity?'

'In this business you learn not to get curious.'

I remained standing. His stare was fixed on my chest. Even if he knew he wasn't going to talk any more. I strolled into the bedroom. His lover lay curled up asleep. Mouth open, shivering. Even his dreams were coke-filled. Yolande stood by the door.

'What are you going to do?'

'Watch.'

He turned over. I slapped him hard. He came awake, bewildered and frightened, groping for Yolande's side of the bed.

'Don't. He doesn't know anything.' Yolande was by his side, cradling his lover. Soothing him. He snuffled and managed to make me standing by the side. He seemed to crawl deeper into his protector.

'What's he doing here?'

173

'Social visit. A breakfast meeting.' I tried to pull him free. Yolande held on. He whined and clung to her. It was like shaking off a leech. I put my gun to his head and pulled back the hammer. The click froze them, tears and all. Their faces didn't change expression.

'Now tell me more.'

'I swear I don't know.'

'What does he want?'

'He wants to know if I saw the buyer for that half K. I swear . . .'

'You'll be holding a corpse in one minute.'

'Hey, it's me you two are talking about.' He looked at Yolande, then peered cautiously at me. 'I saw the buyer.'

I eased the hammer down. Yolande pulled away from him. We both stared.

'I was jealous. I saw you go out twice with a bag, so the third time I followed. I thought you had a lover.'

'You know I love you.'

'That's what everyone says.' He looked mournful. 'I waited until you went in and followed. I saw you pass the bag and get the money. Then I hung around.'

'Why don't you ever trust me?'

'Because I'm never sure.'

'Talk about your insecurities later. Who did you see?'

'It was dark. A woman came out.'

'With the bag?'

'No. Empty-handed. I was on the far end of the corridor. She walked away and took the stairs down. I didn't see her face.'

'How was she dressed?'

'Jeans, jacket, wool cap. It was pulled down tight, so you couldn't see her hair even. It was the way she walked.'

'What else?'

'Nothing, man. I drifted around a bit and then came home.'

He watched me put the gun away. I wasn't sure he spoke the truth. What did Ventura comment? Pain doesn't necessarily bring out the truth.

'Okay. But if I find out you made it up just to keep from getting hurt, you better hide far and deep.'

I left them comforting each other. I phoned the lieut from a telephone box at the corner, watching the building. I told him where to pick up Yolande and her lover. They would prove Harry wasn't the buyer for the coke. It had been planted.

'You know anything about Harry's chick?'

'We didn't socialize. I'll ask Tony.' He covered the mouthpiece and I waited. 'He didn't either. Harry kept to himself after you got put away. He had a few chicks I gather, casual lays, but no one serious. I'll keep checking. I've sent Johnny around to pick up Yolande. Their statement will help but it won't clear Harry. The brass is going to ask the same question as I will: the chick was his front. She dealt, he kept clean. We need to find her, Paul.' He paused. I allowed the silence to build. 'You figure she's the Shooter?'

'Could be.' I saw the unmarked police car pull into the kerb and Johnny and Tony climb out. They looked up at the building and slowly strolled in. 'We put away a couple of women. But Harry still wouldn't have let them near him. Mary Wentworth. She killed her man. The other . . . I forget . . . You'll find the cases.'

'We will. Keep in touch. It's getting close to the fifteenth. You think the Shooter'll jump the date?'

'No. It's fixed. I figure Harry got chopped on Christmas Eve for a reason too. It was all planned out. Years back. The Shooter's got patience and good nerves. Lots of both.'

I rang off and waited. Fifteen minutes later Johnny came out, followed by Yolande and her lover, followed by Tony. The procession to the car went unnoticed. Neither of them were cuffed.

I called Lauren at the office. She answered happily.

'I'm missing you already. Where did you spend the night?'

'In my gloomy little room, thinking about you. We're making some progress on the case. There's a woman involved. But that's about all we know. How are the kids?'

'They send their love. You home for dinner?'

175

'Don't count on it. But I will get home. I've got to chase a few leads.'

'You had a call . . . the secretary of a Mr Anderson. He said to call on him. He would be available for the next day or two.'

'Thanks. I love you.'

I was expected. The steel door swung open and I stepped in. The chauffeur stood behind. Nothing had changed. The chandeliers still glittered on the water of the pool. A woman swam: with joyless, steady strokes, seemingly denying the pleasure of her body. She looked as if she'd been in the water all day and still had hours to go. I thought it was Carson. I couldn't tell. She lifted her face away from me. A dog lay by the pool; another approached, sniffed and returned to lie on the Persian carpet by the fireplace.

'I thought he was away?'

'He came back.'

I mounted the marble staircase, caressing the cool, silken stone balustrade. We came into a large reception room; it was the size of an ice rink. The carpet was pure white, as were the velvet drapes. At the opposite end was a massive granite fireplace. It looked European, gargoyles leaned outward, sneers on their misshapen faces. There was some furniture to sit on. The pieces looked forlorn, like benches in a deserted park. One wall, to my left, was ceiling to floor books, leather-bound, bought by the yard.

'Wait here. I'll see if Mr Anderson will see you now.'

Through an arched doorway I saw into another room. It was smaller but not dissimilar. An expanse of white with paneled walls. Beyond that, a closed door. To the left of the fireplace were three steps leading to a hall that ended in a doorway. The chauffeur went that route and I felt alone and stranded. Cast on an island, luxurious, opulent, yet barren of sustenance. I lit a cigarette. There was no ashtray. I used the fireplace; the logs were artistically arranged. The whole fireplace, looked at closer, appeared to lean outward dangerously. It was an ancient carving smoothed by many hands over the centuries. It must have weighed a ton or two and I knelt to see how it was supported. Two steel beams held it in place.

'It's from an old palace near Florence. The Medicis owned it once. They were Italian princes. It weighs one and a quarter tons and cost $125,000.'

Carson stopped by the door. 'And please don't smoke.' She was in a silk robe and her hair was wet. She left damp footprints on the carpet. She turned and entered the elevator and ascended. She had spoken mechanically, rehearsed like a tour guide in the wonders contained in the house.

It was an expensive piece of rock and I examined it once more. The work was delicate, yet powerful and obscene. I did not like the look of the gargoyles. Like the paintings in the main hall, they were torn from the same mad imagination and, though executed centuries apart, had been brought together by Anderson.

'He'll be with you shortly,' the chauffeur announced as he passed through to the staircase.

The room was a transient place, like an airport lounge. Despite its splendor it had an air of suspension, a leaden feel of eternal patience. Over the three-quarters of an hour other supplicants joined me. Four men, two women. They clutched briefcases, exactly the same: expensive, gold-clasped. They even resembled each other. They belonged to the same hierarchy for I noticed the deference one gave to the other. I found myself studied with open curiosity. I was not of their clan, not of that same ambitious mold. They had come prepared for the interminable waiting. Files, magazines, books soon hid their faces.

A secretary approached. She was brisk, cool and unhurried. I followed her up the stairs. The room I entered was as large as the one I'd left. The carpet was dark, as were the drapes and the walls, though paneled, contained no books. There was a large desk at one end of the room, below a wall-to-wall skylight.

Anderson was standing, studying a paper. He sipped, delicately, from a bottle of Tab. He was not a big man, though he gave the impression of size. His hair was too dark

177

for the weary lines around his eyes. His skin was too smooth and tight, its pallor white and porcelain. A man who seldom craved daylight. He was handsome with a kind of opulent indolence. He wore cream slacks and a black blazer. He looked freshly shaven and bathed.

'Mr Scott? I'm Peter Anderson.' His handshake was firm and he led me to two leather armchairs.

'Drink?'

'Scotch-on-the-rocks.'

The secretary withdrew. Anderson was silent, lost in a momentary dream. He also looked incalculably tired, as if rest, as pleasure would be to a preacher, was a sin. I did not break the silence. I studied the paintings on the walls. They looked expensive and were lit like investments, for their value rather than their intrinsic beauty. Some, I thought familiar. I could not name the artists. I presumed their worth from the surroundings. The secretary returned and placed the drink on the table between us. There were no ashtrays in this room either.

'I used to smoke,' Anderson said, 'four packs a day. I gave it up one day suddenly and now I can't stand the smell of cigarettes. They remind me of the lost pleasure.' He sipped his Tab indifferently. Even that gave no pleasure. He had imposed cruel disciplines on himself and took a sad satisfaction at the inflicted pain.

'Did you get that in prison?' He touched his neck lightly.

'Yes.'

'It's distracting.' He was suddenly petulant, as if I had brought in something unpleasant. 'You should get it fixed.'

'I can live with it.'

He was God and imposed his rule. The only vision he permitted was this opulent manor and the sky above. Probably he communicated to the Being. The scar unsettled him. He stared at it balefully.

I sipped the Scotch. It was smooth and expensive.

'How did you know I was inside?'

I always find out about people before I meet them.'

He tried to sip from his bottle and found it empty. He walked to the paneling behind the desk and opened a section. There was a small icebox stacked with Tabs. He returned with a full one.

'Have you ever met a truly evil man? Or woman?'

'Yes.'

'I don't mean bad guys. Killers, pushers, robbers. They are motivated by greed, by profit. Those aren't necessarily the wellsprings of evil, though they do cause, at times, irreparable harm, and at times an enormous amount of good. I mean true evil. We have a tendency in this society to attribute evil not so much to man – that would frighten us – but to spirits. Forces from beyond the grave, as some novelists and comic-book writers like to put it. And the evil even there is purely a destructive force. It kills a few people; the more beautiful the heroine, the more exciting is that force. But it isn't true evil.'

'I've known some bad guys who come pretty close to what you're trying to define. They kill, cause harm, not even for profit, just for the sheer pleasure.'

'Their own.'

'Yes. They'd blow away an old lady or a kid just to see them die.'

Anderson grunted, conceding a point. 'But you say they did it for their own pleasure. They achieved some joy from those executions. True evil is joyless. It is evangelical. It corrupts for the sake of corruption. I'm not saying I can define the true nature of evil. In the dictionary it is defined as a "bad force". That would be inadequate, wouldn't it?'

'Yes, if you believe evil exists purely for its own sake. Not for pleasure or even any human motive that we can understand. Then I presume it is more subtle. It searches for the weakness in a person, finds it and uses it to spread its force.' I glanced at him. 'You could be evil.'

'I suppose, to some, I am a force of evil. A communist would depict me as a force of evil and I him. But this is the semantics of politics, the rhetoric of opposing philosophies. Neither of us is truly evil.'

I was not surprised by the conversation. Men often rambled, skirting confessions, circling the kernel of their secret. I sifted and puzzled, trying to decipher Anderson. I had not been summoned for a discourse. Anderson spoke now of evil because he had touched it, been changed somehow. Enough for him to have thought deeply on the matter and to have struggled to define not merely its nature but the reason for its existence.

'Maybe if you look back historically it would help. Would Hitler have been truly evil?'

'Ah yes, our conventional label.' He pulled at his lower lip. 'He is the closest to us. His scars still remain on people on the earth; he has reached mythical proportions. He practiced genocide; but then so did other conquerors. Genghis Khan, Tamerlane, Alexander, the Caesars. There's an endless roll-call that includes the Soviets and the Chinese in recent times. Was it evil? Or dementia? The evil mind is a rational one. Not normal, rational. It reasons out its plan of action. As you just said, it finds the weakness of a man and exploits it. Your killers and criminals often function in moments of madness?'

'They do. The defense always claims insanity but it is a frequent insanity that is really sanity. They move from calm to violence in a split second without even a signal. That's the most dangerous moment for a cop. He has to judge when the man is going to reach that point of violent insanity. Then, to control it, we have to outdo that insanity. We have to show that we can get so insane that it would be dangerous to confront us. I suppose,' I added softly, 'that leaves us equally scarred as them.'

'You're straying.' Anderson spoke sharply, almost with a scholarly tone, dry and sepulchral. 'I suppose you're wondering why we have been discussing this subject?'

'Puzzled. You're wanting to make a point.'

'A point?' He pulled at his lip and let it snap back like a rubber band. 'No. Let's say curiosity. You were a cop – a hard profession – and then a criminal. A harder one. A strange species, Mr Scott. You were wanting information about a homicide. How can I help?'

As if on cue Miss Carson entered. She'd changed into slacks and shirt. The black silk shirt was open to her navel and gold chains hung in profusion. Her hair was pulled back tightly in that severe bun that made her eyes slant upwards, and her whole face appear to have a look of permanent surprise. Her beauty now had a marble quality, shiny, hard and impenetrable. She came to kiss Anderson. This distracted him and he clutched at her as if it were a role he had to play. Instead of sitting separately, she perched uncomfortably on the arm of his chair. His hand remained awkwardly around her waist.

'You know my fiancée?'

'Yes.' I took out my notebook. 'You had a party in May. I just wanted the guest list.'

'And what use will that be to you?'

'A man called Nick Silver made a connection at this party. An informant of mine supplied some narcotics to the person he met.'

'Do I need a lawyer on this matter?'

'No.'

'I'm sure cops always say no.'

'On the contrary. Otherwise the case gets thrown out. May I see the guest list, Mr Anderson?'

Silence. We heard the muted traffic at a distance. Their house was an oasis, cosseting its inhabitants from the grim reality of the streets. Carson stood, stiff from her awkward seating, and went over to a chair. She seemed impatient and glanced frequently at the expensive watch on her wrist. Anderson had none. The room also had no clock. Above, the sky was darkening with cloud, reinforcing the sense of detachment. 'I don't see why not.' He turned to her. 'Fetch it.'

I was surprised at her docile obedience. She went into the office and returned with a leather-bound book. Carefully she opened it to a page and handed it to me. I began copying names. You saw them on page six in the *Post*. They made inconsequential noises which were supposed to sound like the ten commandments. I stopped. 'Christine Breelander?'

Anderson shrugged. 'Why not? She's an employee of mine.'

'You own the channel?'

'I don't own channels, Mr Scott. I own a network. She's a bright, talented girl. She'll go far.'

I continued with the list and when I'd finished, I said, 'There's no Nick Silver.'

'He came with friends,' Carson said, too quickly.

'Who is this Nick Silver?' Anderson asked.

'A pusher. He was at this party. My sources are impeccable.' '

'I wouldn't have met him then.'

'Possibly.' I turned to Carson. 'He meet anyone specific on this list?'

'I can't remember.'

'How was he allowed in?' Anderson asked her.

'Friends of friends.'

'What friends? I can't have people like that here.'

'He turned up with a group. You know people always try to gate-crash your parties, darling.'

'Make sure he doesn't come again.'

'He won't.' I handed the book back to Carson. She shut it with a snap. 'Thank you, Mr Anderson.'

He nodded dismissively. He'd performed his duty, and I felt myself already forgotten.

'Did Nick Silver come with a woman?'

'I told you – I can't remember,' Carson snapped, then smiled in the same instant at Anderson. 'You know the way out?'

'I have a compass.'

SIXTEEN

CHRISTINE BREELANDER! It was a coincidence she'd been
at the party the night Nick Silver made his connection. Why
not? She worked for Anderson and he thought highly of her.
She also had a small measure of fame in this city; enough to
get her invited to any party. It was possible she had a more
convenient memory than Carson and remembered seeing
Nick Silver.

I rang her office. No one answered. I checked the time.
The news was over and she was on her way home. I tried her
home. Same response. I had to give her time to get back,
unless she was out for dinner. I thought of waiting at her
door but it had begun snowing lightly and the expressway
would turn dangerous if the snow continued for long. I rang
home to tell Lauren to keep dinner. On the eighth ring it was
picked up. No one spoke.

'Paula . . . Sandy . . . Call Mom. It's Daddy.'

The phone went dead. It must have been Sandy. She
would nod into the phone and replace the receiver. I tried
again. It was engaged. I gave up after fifteen minutes. She'd
not replaced the receiver.

By the time I reached the expressway it had begun

snowing heavily. The flakes drove across the road like a thick dark curtain and I crawled along, peering through the windscreen. It took a couple of hours to get home.

The porch light was on but the rest of the house was in darkness. I sat staring at it, thinking possibly that no light showed because the curtains were drawn so tight. The other houses threw patches of light on the screen of swirling snow. I opened the door. It was warm inside and I smelt dinner cooking. The house was in darkness. I hit the lights and called out: 'Lauren . . . Lauren.'

My voice echoed, no one replied. On the dining table were the remains of dinner. Four places had been set. Mine, at the head of the table, was clean. 'Sandy . . . Paula . . . '

I felt a chill. Cautiously I went from room to room, dreading what I would find. The silence was menacing and followed me. Nothing. Basement to attic was empty. I sat down: puzzled and afraid. Had there been bad news? Had she rushed to an emergency, taking the children? She may have left the kids with Sandra. I went over to the phone. The receiver lay on the table. It had been placed there deliberately. When I'd rung at seven-thirty someone had picked up. I stared at it a long time. I couldn't figure out anything. I looked around carefully. Nothing had been disturbed. There was no note, no message. Maybe she'd call. I used my handkerchief to replace the receiver. It was a reflex gesture. I wasn't sure what had occurred. I used the kitchen phone to ring Sandra.

'Sandra . . . Paul. You seen Lauren or the kids this evening?'

'No. I saw them yesterday. Why? Aren't they home?'

'I just got home. No one's here. I thought she may have had an emergency and dropped the kids off at your place.'

'I'm sorry, Paul, I haven't seen them.'

I rang Lauren's parents. Her mother answered. The chill of her voice froze my ear. I had shamed her personally. Nothing to do with Lauren. She hadn't seen Lauren or the kids either. She'd spoken to her that morning and suggested a divorce but . . . I thanked her.

I rang around all her friends. No one had seen her. I went

over to the neighbors. They'd not seen Lauren leave. They had no reason to look out of the window. I returned to the empty house. It seemed to have grown colder and I turned up the thermostat even though I knew it would not drive the cold from my body. Nor ease the pain in the pit of my stomach. Lauren and the kids had disappeared. There had to be an explanation. Simple, logical. I tried to be logical. My mind wouldn't function. It spun in circles.

She'd return. I waited an hour. The silence was oppressive. It closed in, pressing on my ears. This was a house of continual noise: kids, music, the television. It now felt abandoned, ghost-like. I moved from room to room. I didn't know what I was looking for. Some signs. I checked the front closet. Their overcoats had gone. It gave small comfort that they would be warm.

I rang the cops. A patrolman answered and I reported Lauren and the kids as missing. He wanted to know if we'd had an argument. I said no. He took down the details in that laborious police fashion. There was a moment of silence and another voice came on the line.

'Detective Paul Scott?'

'Yes. Ex.'

'This is Sergeant Hayes. Frank Hayes. I was with NYPD. Remember?'

I tried and failed. The name had no bell.

'I and my partner backed up on the Washington Clay collar. There was one hell of a lot of shooting. You got hit . . .'

'God . . . yes. How are you, Frank?'

'Great. I quit the PD. Too hectic. It's nice and quiet around here. Listen, Paul, I'll come over in fifteen minutes.' He paused a beat or two. 'I'm sorry about Harry, he was a real great guy.'

Hayes hadn't changed. He was a heavy, thickset man with a boy's face. His hair was still blond. We shook hands and he was pleased to see me. He made no mention of my fall. I'm sure he knew. He took down a fresh set of notes and prowled around. I followed as if I didn't know the job. It occupied me.

We returned to the kitchen. Both puzzled.

'Maybe she'll ring.'

'She hasn't yet.' I fixed myself a strong drink. He took a light one. 'And I had the car.'

'She called a cab then.' He rang the two cab companies in town. Neither had made a pick-up from my address.

'Listen, I'm sure she's okay.'

'Stop saying that. I can feel something's wrong.' He fell silent. I shouldn't have shouted. 'Hey, I'm sorry. You could be right. What happened to your partner?'

'Dick Peterson? He's down in Florida. Retired with twenty years. I couldn't take that kind of life. This job came up and I jumped on it. I used to see Harry now and then. Just to say hi.' We fell silent. He peered into his drink, as if to see the future. It was blank for me. 'That was some shoot-out. Were you scared?'

'You bet. He's a bad mutha.'

'I was glad you and Harry were up front and we were only the back-up. You know, when the shooting started, I tried to squeeze off a shot at Washington, but Harry was in the way. What was that kid's name? The one you blew away.'

'Charles Hyslop.'

'That's it. Some kind of revolutionary?'

'Yes.'

He finished his drink. I offered another, wanting him to remain. His company was better than this empty house. He radiated a calm which once I could also. If it was someone else suffering.

'They were gonna do some TV program on that shoot-out. You catch it?'

'Never heard about it.'

'I got interviewed . . . oh . . . a couple of years back. What happened? Who was there? Blow-by-blow of the events.'

'Yeah?' We walked to the door. I felt exhausted. 'Which channel?'

'Three, I think. The chick was a police reporter, Christine Breelander.'

I stopped. Her name had come up twice in one day. All in the way of work.

186

'What did she ask?'

'Who shot Hyslop. Who shot you. You know, the details.'

'And you told her I shot Hyslop?'

'Sure. You and Harry. I also told her the PD investigated and cleared you both. I gave evidence to them as well.'

'Two years back?'

'Around three. Funny. That happened when? Four and a half years back.'

'Yes.'

'Take care, Paul.' The snow was still heavy. 'I'll keep checking but if you hear from her call me. And I'll send someone around in the morning to check that phone for prints. You figure she got snatched?'

'What ese?' I'd not wanted to think about it. It had prowled the back of my mind. It didn't make much sense. Why snatch her? Ransom? None. 'There may be some prints you can lift.'

The silence was unwelcome. He seemed to have taken warmth with him. I sat and stared at the phone. I felt uneasy. Why would Christine Breelander ask questions nearly two years after the shooting? Okay, it was her job. She made a program. I wasn't sure how TV worked. They were weird at times. I rang her home number. I'd first ask her about Nick Silver. It rang and rang. No reply. It was past midnight.

I woke at dawn, stiff and tired. I'd fallen asleep on the couch. Tentatively, in a whisper, I called 'Lauren'. Then I shouted. The house remained empty. I felt sick and frightened. There was nothing to hold on to: no clues, no messages. At least that would give some comfort. I could work. I could put my skill to use. It lay useless like a blunt weapon.

I rang Sandra. She was still asleep and immediately asked whether I'd heard from Lauren.

'No. I want to come over to look at Harry's files. You still got them.'

'Sure. I'll make some coffee.'

I left two notes, written on foolscap paper. One on the

phone, the other stuck to the icebox. It was a forlorn, hope-less gesture. I felt like I was signposting the desert. Who would pass by here to read them? I prayed she would.

'You look terrible,' Sandra said as she opened the door.

'I feel it.' I took the coffee.

'What's happened?'

'I don't know. They just vanished. One moment they were there and then gone. I spoke to her this . . . yesterday morning. She was expecting me for dinner.'

'You both going to stay together?'

'We'd worked that one out.'

'You're lucky.' She seemed on the verge of tears. 'You know where his files are. I'll shower and fix breakfast.'

I went into Harry's den. I'd forgotten his efficiency. He kept copies of every case. They were filed by years in his cabinet. Even his notebooks were dated and stood in an impressive row. They were large leather-bound ledgers. He would take down statements and make notes and draw sketches of the crime scene. Harry could never draw. The bodies resembled chalk lines.

I flicked through the files. They were orderly. I picked up his last case. It was on the homicide of a transit cop. The man had been gunned down in a tavern in the Bronx at three in the morning. The gunmen had spoken three words only: 'Stick-up mutha fuckers.' The cop had pulled his gun, missed the gunmen and had been hit in the chest when they returned the fire. Harry had been the catcher. The file slowly unfolded the story of Cuban criminals who'd entered America when Castro opened Mariel Harbor. Out of one hundred and twenty-four thousand refugees, twenty-four thousand had been drained out of Castro's prisons. Two thousand of these fugitives were hit men. Harry had picked up this from a CI he codenamed 'Our man in Havana'. The CI led them to other informers; one who'd spent four years in a Cuban jail for fixing a soft-ball game. He told Harry about the 'bandidos' and how they identified each other by special tattooes. The tattoo was made between the thumb and index finger: three vertical lines was a stick-up man; two horizontal lines a drug dealer; two vertical lines a kidnapper;

a three-pronged pitchfork an enforcer; and an inverted cross a supplier of guns. A heart with '*madre*' was an executioner.

These 'bandidos' were the followers of a jail-house cult, Abaqua. It was African in origin and the god they worshipped was a thunder god called Chango. Occasionally Chango dressed as a woman. Mythologically, Chango was imprisoned and his mistress Oya brought Chango's crucible, hurled a thunderbolt at the prison and carried Chango to freedom.

Harry knew the streets well. He used them like a finely tuned instrument.

The 'bandidos' were scattered through the Bronx, Queens and Brooklyn. They were sheltered by priestesses called Madrinas, who appeared to have a prescription for all ailments. A gunshot wound was cured by chicory leaves and sugar; courage was given by eating the uncooked heart of a rooster washed down with holy water mixed with seven grains of pepper; and the police were evaded by wearing a necklace soaked in a special solution for seven days.

Against this piece of magic Harry and his partner, Don Diaz, used their own brand of magic: a gold shield. The Mariels, named after the Cuban harbor they had sailed from, were hard men. They killed, raped and robbed, without conscience. America was the land of the free for them and that meant they were free to commit the most terrible crimes. It was while Harry was questioning a suspect involved with a shooting that he got the lead on the cop killer.

The case ended with Harry bursting through the front door of a Queens' apartment and catching the killer watching television.

I was wasting time. I searched back over the years and found the Washington Clay file. I sat and read it to refresh my memory. It had begun one summer morning. A cop spotted a parked car with three men in it. He approached it and without warning the occupants of the vehicle had opened fire. The car had sped away, leaving a dying cop. His partner had taken a shot at the car but in that fading dawn light had not been able to make the plates. I couldn't blame him. His partner was dying. His description was vague: an off-white Chevvy, old model. Harry and I caught the case. We spent days canvassing the apartments on either side and finally came up with a teenage girl. She'd been looking out of the window the night before and had seen the man. She described Washington accurately and identified his picture from the sheaf we showed her. And then we'd walked the streets, using every CI we knew to find Washington. Three weeks passed before we got a second break. Harry's CI supplied an address in exchange for a suspended sentence. We picked up a warrant and went into the building, and that was when the shooting started.

Charles Hyslop – Caucasian, five foot nine, weight one hundred and sixty pounds, blond hair, blue eyes, aged twenty-five – died. His prints were with the FBI. He had been a radical, not a Weatherman but a small offshoot. He couldn't return to normality. We never discovered what he was doing with Washington. Washington refused to talk about him. He was a buddy, period. I hadn't believed him. They could have been planning a bank job to fund Hyslop's illusive revolution. He had been born in New Jersey, gone to a private school and begun an Arts degree in Brandeis. Then he'd dropped out.

I stared at the closed file a long time. All I could think was: So? Was there a connection? I couldn't see it. Why was Christine Breelander making a program two years after the event? It had had a minor notoriety at the time, but had long since been forgotten.

'Breakfast,' Sandra called. I hadn't eaten . . . it seemed for days, and swallowed quickly, suppressing the guilt of normalcy.

'You see the lieutenant?'

'Yes.' She looked nervous but met my stare. 'I was with a . . . friend. You don't hold that against me, do you, Paul? You know that Harry and I were drifting apart. But I wouldn't have harmed a hair on his head.'

'I don't hold it against you.' I held the file. 'May I keep this?'

'Sure. You find anything?'

'Not yet. There is something but I can't make the connection. You look and look but don't see the obvious. It's in this file somewhere but I can't figure it.'

'You sound like Harry. He would sit and read and reread a case if he wasn't making progress. Make notes, stay up all night.' She sighed and stared out of the kitchen window. The sky was dull. Not a pleasant day to remember you were alone and lonely.

I made a call home. No answer. The phone rang forlornly, echoing into an eternity. I called Sergeant Hayes. He was off-duty but the patrolman knew the case. They'd swept the town and found nothing. They'd put out a description of Lauren and the kids. The moment they heard anything they'd get in contact.

'Can you stay at our place just in case?'

'Sure,' Sandra said. 'It's better than sitting here.'

Christine Breelander still wasn't home. I hesitated a long time. I could sit and wait or keep working. Everything was connected, even though I didn't know how.

My mood had changed from the previous day. I felt a sense of despair and rage. And fear. They alternated. I pounded the wheel in frustration each time the traffic slowed on the expressway. I had caught the rush-hour traffic. We crawled. My mind and blood raced. I couldn't control the sense of urgency.

Control: Christine and I had spoken about control. If I controlled the situation? If I lost control? It had been a strange conversation. I calmed myself. I had to control the panic. It wasn't easy. The traffic drifted sluggishly like a metal river partly damned. The roads were still slippery from the snowstorm. A couple of cars had slewed off.

It wasn't much better in mid-Manhattan. Second and Third Avenues were grid-locked. I swung off and took the FDR South. The sense of driving to a destination calmed me.

Okay: Christine Breelander. She had been a police reporter, was now an anchor person. In the old days most cops knew her, the way they knew the other crime reporters. Maybe she was a cop freak? Some women are. It gives them a kick to be with cops. She knew Harry. Nothing wrong. She wanted an exclusive if I broke the case. Normal. What wasn't? I couldn't pin it down. Something afloat: coincidence.

I found myself outside her apartment building. I needed to proceed slowly. First about Nick Silver. Then the rest. I searched for her name on the buzzers. There was no Breelander. It wasn't unusual. I hit a few buttons. Someone squawked at me.

'Messenger.'

The door was buzzed and I took the elevator up. The corridor was quiet and empty. I rang her bell. Once. Twice. It was a Yale lock. I looked around, took a piece of plastic from my wallet and slipped it in. I'd lost practise. It took time and sweat but finally the door swung open. It was hot and stuffy inside. Everything was neat and tidy, including the skyline outside the window. I wasn't sure what I was looking for. Where was the mangy cat? I opened the closet. It was empty except for wire hangers. The cat too was gone. I checked the desk. There was a neat stack of mail. It wasn't addressed to Christine Breelander. Ms. Sally Bruton. This apartment number. There was a couple of months' mail: mostly junk. I picked up the books. Sally Bruton was the name in most. Christine Breelander never lived here. I figured it was a friend's. Or a sublet. I'd deliberately been brought here.

I rang her office.

'Christine Breelander's on vacation,' her office told me.

'When will she be back?'

'I'll check.' The woman went away and returned. 'Three weeks.'

'Do you have her home address?'

'I can't give you that information.'

I hadn't expected them to. I checked the phone book. She was unlisted. It was my mistake. She'd brought me here and I believed it to be her home. How could I think differently? She had behaved at ease, the cat had prowled, she had made dinner. The normality had been reassuring. Once. Now it felt malevolent. She'd brought me here for a reason.

She'd carefully planned this make-believe. It hadn't been done on the spur of the moment.

Why?

I sat there half an hour. Why? She wanted to fool me. Why? She didn't want me to see where she lived. Her real home revealed something I shouldn't know about Christine Breelander. What?

Our affair had been calculated. She had no emotion towards me. Not one of like, love, affection. A different kind. Frightening. She'd wanted to get to know me better for a reason, to discover my vulnerability. What would hurt me the most?

I thought of Lauren and the kids. I was hurting badly. Christine Breelander wouldn't have touched them. She was a famous woman. Millions saw her each night on television. That made her real and honest and straightforward. We believe the people we see daily reading our news because what they report is supposedly the truth, we assign to them the quality of personal honesty. Why should Christine be different from the rest of the city?

I called home and my heart lurched when the phone was picked up. I'd forgotten Sandra was sitting there.

'Any news.'

'Nothing,' she said. 'I tidied up the place. You want me to stay all day?'

'If it's okay.'

'Of course it is, Paul. I may just have to go out to see the priest about Harry's funeral. But I won't be long. By the way, there's a letter for you?'

'What kind?'

She went to fetch it. 'The address is sort of printed. But very neatly.'

'Like a stencil,' I whispered. I felt the dread approaching.

'Something like that.'

'Use a handkerchief to handle it, please. What's the postmark?'

'It was mailed in town yesterday.' She listened to my silence. My fear contaminated her. 'What is it, Paul?'

'Open it. Use the handkerchief.'

She put the phone down and I heard her moving around and paper tear. I held my breath. Then she moaned out aloud and I felt the sweat break out on my face and the palms of my hands.

'What is it, Sandra?' I shouted down the line.

SEVENTEEN

I REACHED the 48th in fifteen minutes flat. It was lunchtime and the squad room was deserted. I ran into the lieut's office. Sergeant Lester had his feet up, reading *Penthouse*. He raised a mild eyebrow.

'Where's the lieut?'

'Lunch.' He saw my face and the sweat. His feet came down abruptly. 'Urgent?'

'Yeah. Can you reach out for him?'

He picked up the red telephone. It was the radio transmitter.

'Lieutenant Dwyer, can you call in, over.' He repeated the message twice. The telephone remained silent a long time. 'He should be at Castle Harbor. He usually lunches there. 'I can ring . . . '

The phone rang and he picked up. 'Paul Scott's here, Lieutenant. Seems kinda urgent.'

'Yes, Paul?'

'The Shooter's got Lauren and the kids.'

'You sure?'

'Of course I'm sure. I got home last night and they were missing. I told the cops there. This morning I got a message in the mail.'

'What did it say?'

'It didn't say anything. It was a Polaroid of Lauren and the kids.' My hands perspired and I wiped them on my suit. They hadn't stopped since Sandra told me what was in the envelope. A family is a cop's only sanity. It is the reality, the sunny comfort he clings to when he leaves the streets. It is his protection against the nightmares that live and die daily in front of him. Without it he would drown in his own terror.

'It had been taken in the house. I guess the night before.' I took a deep breath. 'Their faces had been cut out. On the back was a date. Printed. Not stencilled. The fifteenth.' Both the sergeant and I glanced reflexively at the calendar. The eleventh.

'Like the one Harry had on him?'

'You didn't tell me he got one.'

'I don't have to tell you everything,' he snapped. 'Except it had a different number on the back. The twenty-fourth. I guess he didn't take it seriously.'

'Why should he have? We get threats the whole time.'

I remember the time Harry and I walked out to the car. It was raining. We climbed in and when Harry turned on the wipers they swept two small objects on to the road. We got out and searched for them in the gutter. We found two .38 bullets. One had Harry's name. The other mine. They were professionally etched. Immediately we crouched and peered around the car, down the street, into the gloom beneath the expressway. Then we looked up. Half the squad was leaning out of the windows. They all burst out laughing. Cops play weird jokes on each other.

'I got one too.'

'Now that you didn't tell me.'

'You didn't need to know.' I took a deep breath. 'I have a suspect.'

'Who?'

196

'Christine Breelander.'

Lester raised both eyebrows. His stare was unwinking. The lieut was silent a long time. He seemed to be gathering his wits.

'Breelander? Jesus, Paul, you gone crazy? I've known her four years. What's she got to do with all this?'

'There's a connection. I feel it.'

'Feel it? What are you, some kind of psychic? You know what happens if we accuse someone like her of homicide? My ass gets put in the sling. The PC breaks my chops. I get posted to Staten Island supervising grass-growing. Feel it? C'mon, Paul. You were a good detective once.' He stopped to calm down. 'I'm sorry about Lauren and the kids. What can we do?'

'Listen, Lieut. I'm not crazy. I've been trying to reach Breelander, she's on vacation.'

'So? They take vacations too.'

'She took me back to her apartment. It's not her place, but someone else's. I figure she didn't want me to see something. Then two: I find out she was at the same party as the pusher Nick Silver.' He remained silent while I quickly explained my interview with Anderson. 'Then three: She made a program on the Hyslop killing. She asked Frank Hayes a lot of questions.'

'So she's at a party. So were other people. And it's her job to cover police work. She's got to ask questions. Like we do.'

'Lieut, you said I was a good detective once. I was great. Detective work is part instinct. I know I'm right. I need to find out where she lives. I tried directory, they won't give me the time of day. You can get her address and a search warrant.'

'I'm not getting any warrant, Paul.' He sighed. 'I'd just begun on a steak with onions and a cold Martini. I'll be there in ten minutes. Get the sarge to reach out for Johnny. And Paul . . . you better be fucking right or I'll have you back inside so fast your feet won't touch the ground.'

I relayed the lieut's orders and added: 'Can you get Christine Breelander's address?'

'Those muthas give trouble sometimes. I've got a contact in the telephone company. I'll try him.'

I left him and went to the interrogation room. It was empty. I wanted peace and quiet. I opened the Hyslop file and once more began to read the case. I read slowly and carefully, as if I were just learning the language. Detail, Harry always said, study the details. I felt him leaning over my shoulder as he always did.

On the third reading I suddenly saw it. The numbers lit up like neon. They'd been there all these years: dormant and dangerous. How many times had Harry, the lieut, Johnny and I glanced at them and moved on?

'Where the hell's Scott?' I heard the lieut yell.

I went out. Big Irish cops who've had their lunches interrupted are dangerous creatures. He glared at me and marched into his office. He didn't bother to take off his jacket but sat down heavily and stared at me. Those gray chops looked frozen. I dropped the file on the desk. He didn't look down. It lay between his massive fists like a broken bird. Finally, he lowered his gaze.

'I've seen this before.'

I pointed carefully: 'Look at Charles Hyslop's d.o.b.'

'Twenty-fourth . . . December.' His head remained lowered. He spoke gently: 'Okay, we have a connection between the Shooter and Hyslop. Maybe. I don't see Christine Breelander in the picture.' He looked up.

'Maybe lovers?'

'Maybe Mom and Pop. Sarge!' He didn't shift his eyes from my face. 'Get an address for Christine Breelander.'

The sarge slid the paper over. It was on Central Park West. The Dakota.

'Oh hell, that's all we need. The Dakota.'

'She's rich,' the sarge said.

'Everyone living there is rich. And that means they got clout. And that means I've got my ass in a sling.'

'Well, you've always said position is everything.' The sarge met the lieut's glare blandly. 'Scott isn't a cop.' They both avoided each other's eyes. They seemed to be talking in

198

different rooms. Not quite hearing. 'He goes in. If he finds anything we get a warrant.'

'I didn't hear a thing,' the lieut said.

'I didn't say a thing,' the sarge said.

'And I was never here.' I turned to leave.

'While you're not here, we'll start checking Breelander.' He shrugged.

'Just in case. Start with where she was on the twenty-fourth, Sarge. Around the time of the shooting.'

'And check about a special she was supposed to be making about three years back. Before I went inside. It was on the Hyslop killing. She talked to my back-up patrolman, Frank Hayes. He's a sarge now out in Chatsworth. I also saw a picture of her and Bayer together.'

'What's that got to do with it?'

I hesitated. I could give up Bayer or give up on Lauren. This was a necessary betrayal.

'Bayer and the captain were in with me on the kickbacks. She took her cut from the captain. Someone knew everything about me from the start and used it to blackmail the captain into turning me in. It all started back then. Bayer could tell you that Christine Breelander asked a lot of questions about me.'

'Bayer. She's a tough one. She's not going to talk to me just because I ring up and say hallo.' He pulled at his earlobe. 'I'll get Charlie Houldey to talk to her. He's going to be very pleased.'

The Dakota looks like a medieval castle. It takes up a whole block between 72nd and 73rd. John Lennon died under its arched entranceway. It wouldn't be an easy building to penetrate. One doorman was huddled in the sentry box on the street. Two others sat in the office inside. I paced the opposite sidewalk, impatient and impervious to the cold. There was a moving-van parked at the side by the basement entrance. I walked over and peered in. It was half empty with furniture. I picked up a bedside table and carefully went down the slope. The door was open. The basement was cavernous. I punched the elevator button, loaded the table in and left it there when I got off on the sixth floor. I found myself in a long corridor, disappearing into the distance. Her apartment was 622 and it was at the rear. There were two locks on her door. One a dead bolt. I used the picks Sergeant Lester had lent me. He'd wiped them clean of his prints first and passed them to me with his head averted. It took over a minute to open the top lock. I used my plastic in the lower one.

It was a high-ceilinged, large apartment. The furnishings were modern, imitated from *House and Garden*. There were stretches of white carpet, a whole wall of books, a piano, and glass tables with art books. The kitchen was ultra-modern. It led into a dining room, which seated eight, and then into a corridor. I went softly down it. The walls had prints and paintings. The first door was her bedroom. Silk curtains hung down from the ceiling, forming a tent around the bed. The bed was raised a couple of feet off the floor.

On the dressing-table were silver-framed photographs. I took them to the light. One was a color shot of a middle-aged couple. They held fishing rods in their hands and looked quietly happy. The other one was of Christine – a head shot – taken from a magazine cover. She preserved her own fame.

I replaced them as the phone rang. I ignored it and searched the rest of the room. There was little else. She had an expensive taste in clothes.

The next room was her study and viewing room. There was a video-recorder next to the television set and a whole stack of tapes. I fitted one in and watched Christine Breelander leap on screen. She was reporting a robbery. The background looked like Boston. I timed it but it only ran to thirty seconds. I didn't rewind. I slipped it out and put in another. There looked to be around a hundred tapes: the span of her television career. It could take a whole day to go through them all and I wasn't even sure what I was looking for. Only the forty-fourth second.

The phone rang. This time it didn't stop until the twentieth ring. I ignored it and concentrated on the tapes. Each minute was being wasted as I fumbled methodically through her video files. Running them together, the years were compressed into minutes. I saw her mature. She grew better, sharper, more beautiful. Even in these precious seconds her intelligence was obvious. I'd not seen her often before. I'd watched Channel Five before I'd been sent up. They were not all crime reports. Some were on politics, social issues, funny fillers, off-beat stories. Cute stuff.

I held my watch – Lauren's Christmas gift – in my hand. Timing, timing, timing. Some ran for a minute. I saw nothing that would have made a man with a gun at his head scrawl '44 se . . . ' My eyes ached. I looked at the time. I'd been watching seconds, not minutes and hours. It was five-thirty. A day had nearly passed and I'd accomplished nothing. I was not even quite half through the stack.

I had tried in those hours to forget Lauren and the kids. I couldn't. They were lost and afraid: tied, locked-up, chained. I hoped and prayed they were not dead. The date was supposedly set for the fifteenth. People like the Shooter gave no guarantees.

I rang home. Sandra answered. There was still no sign of my family. The cops had come around, dusted the phone and taken the photograph to check for prints. I held out little hope. I was sure everything had been wiped clean.

I called the lieut. He came on the line immediately.

'What have you found?'

'Nothing . . . yet. I'm going through a batch of her video tapes. I'm only halfway through.'

'You better get out of there, Paul,' the lieut's voice was gentle. I heard the undertone of apology.

'Why? What's happened?'

'We checked her movements on the twenty-fourth for the time of the shooting.' He paused. I heard him draw breath. 'She's alibi'd.'

'Airtight?' My heart sank. It hurt too. I felt a profound loss at his words.

'Yeah. Seems to be. I spoke to her producer. A guy called . . . Dick Taylor. He said she was taping a special that day. They began at around noon and ran until four. He swears she was in the studio the whole time.'

I stared at the blank television screen. Breath had been driven from me. Alibi'd. What did it mean? The proven presence of a suspect at a different location at the exact time a crime took place. Unless you can with certainty prove they were not there, the case falls apart. She was seen in the studio. She could not have been shooting Harry.

'You there, Paul?' the lieut spoke. 'I'm sorry. We don't seem to be able to shake him.'

'Was he with her every minute?'

'He said they were taping. I guess she was there the whole time. Listen, I've sent Pat Shaughnessy and John Kane to Chatsworth to work with Sergeant Hayes. We're going to do everything we can to find Lauren and the kids.'

'They lift any prints from that photograph?'

'Clean.'

'Listen, Lieut. She has a brother. Maybe this guy Taylor knows where he lives. He could tell us where she is.'

'I'll try. What's his first name?'

'I don't know.' I heard his sigh of exasperation. 'I didn't think of asking her then.'

'Paul. We might be wasting time on her. The Shooter could be someone else. We still haven't tied her in with Hyslop.'

'I feel it . . .'

God, what if I was wrong. I doubted instinct suddenly. I may have confused it with hope. A straw to grab. Seconds, minutes, hours were hurtling by. Lauren and the children were receding from me into their graves. Sandy, Paula. I shivered with the fear they too must feel now. I only hoped they were all together. Lauren could comfort them. I knew in the rage of the moment, the threat to innocence, I would blow the Shooter away.

'I'll ask Johnny to check out her brother. He's still midtown in the studio. You want him to swing by and pick you up?'

'No. I'm going to do some more looking.'

Like an automaton I chose the next tape and slotted it in. I watched her again. She was becoming a part of my subconscious, an endlessly repeating role. The reporter. I stared at the other tapes. The one Harry had seen must have been important. It may not even have involved her reporting at all. If it was special where would she keep it? Not with these. She'd taken it up to the Bronx . . .

She's alibi'd, the lieut had said. Period.

I poured a straight Scotch at the bar. It was an elegant piece of furniture: marble and glass. She had every kind of liquor. I sat down and surveyed the room. Why hadn't she wanted me to see this place? I looked around a long time, studying every object. Nothing unusual or distinctive. A rich woman's apartment.

I fixed another drink. It was a thought: my presence was an act of violation. She didn't want me here. It was special, sacred to her. To have me look at her here would have been a desecration. Paul Scott, ex-con, killer of Charles Hyslop. Her body: it had been her coinage to discover more about me. She knew I was alone, vulnerable. Her comfort softened me, make me talk, to reveal a part of myself. What she had revealed was all calculated.

If it was calculated, I reasoned, it wasn't truthful. She couldn't hide her identity. It was too well known. What then? Her past. Her past with whom? Charles Hyslop. If I traced her life back, I'd find the connection. Once I had the connection, her alibi was faked. How, I had no idea. Taylor had lied.

I had no idea, either, what to do next. I could return to the tapes. It would take hours to complete them. I felt, instinctively again, the clue didn't lie in them. I sat up. What had I thought way back? An idea had slipped elusively through my mind and was lost in the darkness. A thought, a thought. Something that I had ignored. What? Painfully, slowly, I tried to trace back all the day's events. I came up blank. It was a thought. Not anything tangible.

The tapes. I had thought it might not necessarily be her reporting. What would be the story she showed Harry? The television coverage of the shoot-out with Washington Clay in which Hyslop died. I remembered the cameras and photographers. They'd heard the call over the police radio and arrived at the scene minutes later. I was on a stretcher, too dazed to raise a hand to shade my eyes from the glare of lights.

She'd not been a reporter in New York at the time. She'd shown Harry another reporter's tape. Where would she get the tape? From her own channel.

I began to reach for the phone when the silence was suddenly broken by a key fitting into the front door. I froze, one arm out, my fingertips just touching the telephone. The person tried the top lock first. I hadn't relocked it. The key didn't turn. I reached for my gun, flicked back the safety. The key slid into the bottom lock and the door swung open.

Christine Breelander stared at me in astonishment.

EIGHTEEN

A STREET is a cold place to be on as night falls. It was lonely too and I stood on the corner of 72nd and Central Park, bewildered. I looked back at the Dakota. It was warm, inviting, the sheen of wealth mantling those old walls. There was a telephone booth at the corner. The lieut sounded as weary as I felt.

'I'm going off-duty, Paul. You still inside her place?'

'No. On the street.' I breathed out. 'She walked back in.'

'Oh shit.'

Her astonishment had turned swiftly to anger at seeing me.

'What the hell are you doing here? How did you get in?' She dropped her groceries on a sofa and stood glaring at me.

'I thought you were on vacation.' A foolish remark. I hadn't overcome my shock. She was a suspect. Yet here she stood, staring me down.

'What the hell does that mean? I'm on vacation. That doesn't give you the right to break into my home. I'm going to call the police.'

She picked up the phone. I wrenched it from her and

slammed it back down. It cracked. I had had enough shit for the day.

'Where the hell have you been?'

'What are you, my jealous lover? Get out of here.'

'Where have you been?'

'Visiting friends. I'm allowed that, aren't I?'

'Who? I want their names.'

'I've no intention of telling you.' She looked around to verify her possessions. 'What is this anyway? An interrogation? You're not a cop any more. You're a felon. Get out.'

I stared at her. The rage appeared genuine. And yet I remembered her expression had moved from astonishment to anger. No fear. People always showed an instant of fear when they saw the unexpected in their home. This was New York. Fear was always present.

'Why weren't you afraid?'

'I recognized you.'

'You knew I was here?'

'No. You didn't tell me you had a key to my place. Or do you? That's breaking and entering.'

'You know all the right words.'

'I'm educated. I'm going to ask you for the last time. Get out.'

'Why did you take me to the other apartment?'

'Because I do have a possessive lover and I didn't want him to walk in on us. I was looking after Sally's apartment while she was away.' She walked to the door and opened it. A theatrical gesture. 'Now that I've answered all your questions . . . '

'You haven't.' I went over and closed the door. I shoved her down on the sofa.

'Tough con.'

'You bet. You knew Charles Hyslop, didn't you?'

'The kid you blew away?'

'Me and Harry.'

'Yes. Tough cops. I didn't know him.' She stared at me coldly. Beauty had melted. Her rage was raw. 'He was just a kid.'

'Old enough to carry a weapon and reach for it.'

'There was never any proof of that. What's all this about anyway?'

'Lauren and the kids have been taken by the Shooter.'

She didn't soften for a moment. Then, slowly, she did. It was like wax coming apart.

'I'm sorry.' Her anger returned. 'And what's that got to do with you in my place asking me questions?'

'I figured you might know something.'

'Me?' She laughed. 'I don't.'

I went out. She slammed the door so hard the explosion reverberated down the corridor. I heard people stir behind the safety of their doors. The side table was still in the elevator. I also still had my gun in my hand. I slipped it into my waistband.

'You ask her about Hyslop?' the lieut asked.

'Yes. She said she didn't know him. She was lying.'

'Why?'

'She called him a kid. He was twenty-four. That's a knowing adult.'

'Maybe. If you figure she's holding Lauren and the kids, what's she doing in her place?'

'She locked them up safe. They can't get out. She shows up and I'm supposed to think she's got nothing to do with it.'

'Paul, you figure she might not have anything to do with it. We're wasting time.'

'Goddamn it, I know. Sorry, Lieut.' I'd even run out of cigarettes.

'What about her brother? You know, there are no photographs of him in her place, but she always talked about him.'

'That's what Johnny found out. She talked about him, no one there ever met the guy.' I heard him scratching the stubble on his face.

'Okay, Paul, let's go your way for a day. Christine Breelander isn't going to tell you a damned thing now. Maybe Hyslop can. We'll start checking his background. Why don't you run over to his home? His family used to live in New Jersey. At 4284 Green Village Road, Madison. I'll put

a tail on Christine Breelander to see which way she jumps.'
He sighed dramatically. 'I must be crazy. If the chief ever
hears I'm working with a known felon, he'll have my badge
and gun.'

'Then why you listening to me, Lieut?'

'You were a mean mutha as a cop, Paul. But a good
detective. I said once before, I don't care too much what
happens to you, but I do care about Lauren and the
children. And I want Harry's Shooter. I don't care how, but
I want the son-of-a-bitch. You got any ideas where she
would be holding them?'

'I've been figuring that. She talked about a place she had
upstate. It overlooked a valley.'

'What else?'

'I'm trying to remember.'

'Upstate is one hell of a lot of territory. No name?'

I felt miserable. 'No. She just talked about it.'

'She talked a lot it seems and said nothing. I hope she laid
well?'

'Yeah.'

'Paul, you've got till . . . oh Christ. Nearly seven. We've
got guests for dinner and my wife's going to kill me. I've got
to go. Oh yeah. You've got until tomorrow evening. If we
don't make a connection between her and Hyslop, we better
start thinking up a storm.'

I went home. When you're tired and scared you can't
think straight. Thoughts get jittery. There was an unmarked
cop car parked outside my place. The lieut's two detectives
sat in the kitchen with Sandra, drinking coffee. I didn't
know either. They were both big but Kane was the
younger. They had no leads but their presence gave me
comfort. I wouldn't be alone immediately. The house was
painful and quiet would only heighten the sense of loss. The
detectives ran Sandra home and promised to be back early
the next day; just in case. Sandra hugged me. We both were
alone now. Her permanently. Me teetering on the same
edge of eternity. I lay on the coverlet. The moonlight frosted
the room. Objects glowed with a secret light. Lauren's
presence permeated the room. Her make-up, her clothes,

the odors of her perfume and powder, the delicacy of her taste. We had made love and lain together one afternoon which now seemed years back. In a summer that was fading memory.

It was a long drive to Madison. I left before dawn. The town and streets were empty. The banks of snow and darkness distorted the shape of everything. Turning them, in my imagination, gross and haunted. Even as a cop I'd never liked this time of day. It was the moment between death and living, the silence always menacing.

I had breakfast on the New Jersey Turnpike, and judged myself about halfway to Madison. The traffic was light my way and the small towns and rolling country slid past my window at seventy miles per hour. I hoped Smokey was tucked into a warm coffee shop. I had no badge to flash.

By noon, I reached Madison. The houses were far apart, the roads small and winding. I caught glimpses of the swamp to the west as I wound around looking for Green Village road. I hit it, turned west and followed it for four miles before finding the house.

Number 4284 stood well behind a high hedge. I turned into the drive. It was a big estate and the road wound through a snowdrift. In summer, trees would have shaded the mansion. Now they were stark and shorn. The house was a mock Tudor manor. Dark beams crisscrossed the walls, and the small, neat windows shone in the sunlight. I parked. No one noted my arrival. It felt deserted and the windows, now I was closer, were grimy. There were cracks too in the walls, paint had peeled, and the garden looked neglected. The snow gave it a façade of care. I honked. There was still no sign of life. I got out and rang the bell. The echo sank into the silence, leaving no wake. I peered in through a window. The furniture was covered with dust-sheets and I almost smelt the musk of decay. I swore in frustration. The Hyslops had left. I studied the window. It was divided into small panes. I could smash one and let myself in. Maybe I could find some evidence in the house. Where had they gone? What had happened to them?

'Who are you?'

I stepped back and peered up. A woman stared down at me.

'Mrs Hyslop?'

'Yes.' She had a soft beauty to her still. She looked in her late fifties, her hair was gray and her voice had a southern drawl. I imagined her in crinolines. She belonged to the past.

'May I talk to you.'

She nodded and withdrew. I went to the front door and heard her brisk steps down the stairs and across the hallway. When she stood in the doorway I saw a long, dim hall behind. She was tall and slim, dressed in a cashmere cardigan and wool skirt with a simple brooch on her breast.

'What about?'

'Your son, Charles Hyslop.'

Under the façade of care, I saw the melancholy rise to her face. It welled like a pool seeping into a hollow.

'He is dead.'

'I know that, Mrs Hyslop.' I gestured to enter. She didn't notice.

'Then why ask about him? He died a long time back.' She noted the scar, and she struggled with memory to place me.

'Who are you?'

'My name's Paul Scott and . . .'

'Detective.' Her voice chilled me. She'd not spoken any louder but the hate barbed that single word. 'Please get out of here. Leave my house, leave my property, leave me immediately. You destroyed my family, Mr Scott.'

She stepped back and shut the door. I heard the bolt slam in. She didn't move awhile, listening to me listening to her, then she crossed the floor and her steps receded. The house fell silent again.

I didn't blame her. I had killed her son. A mother didn't care whether he was good or bad. Only the manner of his death concerned and hurt her. And I was that manner. She nursed the hate as she would a child, all her life.

I returned to the car. 'You destroyed my family. Mr Scott.' How did one death constitute a family? Some other tragedy had occurred to her, related to her son's dying. Death does send ripples through life and shatter people. She was empty. Her neatness was brittle. She was a strong woman who held herself together and presented a genteel appearance to the world. Beneath was rot. Who else had died?

I started to turn the car and stopped suddenly. I had seen her face before. I couldn't remember where. It wasn't at the time of her son's death. There had been no pictures of his family either in the newspapers or in police files. She was familiar.

Of course. The photograph in Christine Breelander's bedroom. The man and woman. Her hair then had been ash-blonde. The gray and the lines in her face – she'd aged swiftly – had made her unrecognizable at first glance. I looked back at the house. I couldn't see any face in the windows. I felt she watched me. What had happened to her husband?

Madison wasn't a town. It was a village. A few houses clustered together. It had a couple of banks, a post office, a supermarket and a sheriff's office next to the fire station. The sheriff was a man in his fifties with clear blue eyes and a round paunch. He looked well contented with the comforts of his position. Not much work and lots of time to fish. The room reflected the man: a leather armchair, a few papers on his desk, a rack of pipes. Behind him was the holding cell. It was empty.

'I'm Sheriff Erikson. How can I help you?' He was affable.

'Paul Scott.'

He nodded and looked me over carefully. He gestured to a hard-back chair. I expected him to light up a pipe but he remained staring.

'I know. Mrs Hyslop rang me. She wants you arrested.'

'On what charge.'

'Hell, any charge I can dig up.' He shrugged. 'She wanted me to do that years back when Charlie was killed. What can I do for you?'

'Tell me something about Charles Hyslop.'

He brooded awhile: 'Charlie was a bit wild. Not troublesome but always up to mischief. The Hyslops are a good family. They've been here generations. Quite rich. They own property in Jersey City and other places. He had a good life but I guess Charlie wasn't satisfied with that. He wanted to change things, be a revolutionary. I lost touch with him when he went away to college. But when they were kids, I used to see them often.'

'They?'

'Yes. His closest friend was his kid sister. They'd fish together, shoot duck, hang out together. If you saw one, you were pretty sure the other wasn't far. They were really like twins, though Charlie was around eight years older than Christine . . . '

NINETEEN

IT WAS midnight by the time I reached the city. The 13th had gone, the 14th had begun. There were twenty-four hours left for the 15th. Not enough time. The lieutenant, Johnny and Sergeant Lester were waiting for me. The glare in the squad room hurt my tired eyes. Johnny pulled a bourbon pint out of a bottom drawer and fixed me a shot.

'We got your message. So you've made the connection?'

'Yes.' The bourbon hurt. 'Christine Breelander is Charles Hyslop's sister. They were a close-knit family. Very loving, warm, good people. Charles decides to drop out. He joined some kids to overthrow the government, and drifted into contact with Washington and friends. While the other kids grew up and straightened out, Charlie was still lost in the dream. When I shot him the family went to pieces. It was like dropping a pane of glass. His father began drinking heavily. He turned sad and angry. He died eight months after his son was killed. It was partly the booze but I gather from the sheriff it was also heartbreak. He loved his son. Mrs Hyslop is a strong woman. She tried to hold what remained together, but Christine left home to work in

213

Boston. I think from the moment her father died she began planning our killings. She wanted to hurt me and Harry as much as she possibly could. The way we'd broken her family. She was married to a reporter in Boston – Jack Breelander. But that didn't last too long and when they split she kept his name. I figure deliberately. Harry wouldn't have let her near him if her name was Hyslop. He never knew, I guess, until the last moment she was Christine Hyslop.'

The dead are lucky. They've quit. We remain alive and bleeding at their loss. It corrupts us, as the worms that corrupt the physical remains in the earth. Thoughts, emotions and pains nibble away at our beating hearts, hardening flesh and blood. Christine had to avenge her brother. She couldn't live without it. She was suffocated by her loss and the only escape was our death. Or Lauren's and the kids'. I was to be shattered the way she had been.

The sheriff had driven me to the cemetery later. The Hyslops had a special portion. They had a kind of aristocracy and a piece of the earth was reserved for all of them. Charles Hyslop lay beside his father. I understood, as I looked down at the headstone, why Christine had chosen January 15th. It was her father's date of birth. And my family's date of death.

'We picked up a tape,' the lieut said and took it from a drawer.

We went down the corridor to the interrogation room. He'd moved a television set and a video-recorder from another office. As he slipped in the tape, we checked our watches for the seconds. The reporter was Art Waters, a dapper black man with graying hair. He'd been a very familiar face around the precincts for years. I guess he'd retired and Christine had taken his place.

The report began with a close-up of him, the crowds, the street on which the shoot-out occurred. 'Police today close the case of the fatal shooting of a policeman three weeks ago. On June 23rd, around 9 p.m., Patrolman Luis Garcia approached a parked car in the Fordham section of the Bronx. While his horrified partner looked on, gunfire suddenly erupted from the car, fatally wounding Patrolman

Garcia. He died later in hospital. On confidential information, police raided apartment 405 in this building behind me. The suspect they were looking for was Washington Clay. Without any warning shooting broke out. A young white man, whose name the police have not yet disclosed, was killed immediately . . . '

The lieut stopped the tape. It was the forty-fourth second. The camera had panned up to a window. Charles Hyslop hung half in and half out. Death felt no shame. His face was covered with blood. My bullet had hit him in the head.

'That's what she showed Harry. It was the last thing he ever saw.'

'He should have written a name,' Johnny said quietly.

'With a gun at your head you don't think straight. She told him to watch for the forty-fourth second and he'd probably just jotted a note down.'

He pressed 'play'.

'One of the cops involved in the shoot-out was wounded. How badly, no one as yet knows. He is Detective Paul Scott . . . '

The stretcher was carrying me from the building. The crowds jostled to get a closer look. My eyes were closed. Harry held my hand. An ambulance man held the plasma bottle. The procession entered the ambulance and the sirens began . . .

'Johnny, you got the warrant?' the lieut stood up and slipped on his jacket. Johnny held it up. 'Let's pick her up.'

The sergeant remained behind. The lieut drove awhile in silence and then turned.

'You carrying a piece?' I didn't reply. 'For God's sake don't even let me see it.'

'What about her alibi?'

'It broke,' Johnny said. 'I went back and talked to a few more people. Taylor wasn't shielding her. He genuinely thought she was taping the whole time. But they had a break and she ran up to the Bronx and blew Harry away. No one saw her leave but one of the sound men saw her returning. She was carrying a parcel: a Christmas present. He offered to help her, as he said it looked heavy, but she refused. She told him she'd been up to the sixth floor but she had her coat on. He forgot about it until I questioned him.'

It wasn't only her brother's death that had warped Christine. She could have survived that, no matter how close they had been. Her father's death unbalanced her. Revenge is obsessive.

The lieut drove fast down the Westside Highway. In spite of the hour it was still busy with traffic, but the swirling red light cut past the cars. He turned off at 72nd Street and hit the siren at each traffic light. At the Dakota he pulled up at the entrance and peered around the street. The red light attracted the attention of the doorman. He watched but didn't approach. From across the street a man climbed out of a car and strolled over.

'Hi, Lieutenant. She's still in there as far as we know.'

The lieut grunted and we climbed out.

'You stay here, Paul.'

'I'm coming. She's got to tell me where she's holding Lauren.'

I followed them into the building. They walked unhurriedly. Once I too could stroll, controlling urgency. Now, I wanted to run. Another doorman stepped out of the room past the entrance.

'Christine Breelander?'

'She expecting you?' He studied us all. He knew.

'No.' The lieut flashed his badge. 'And try not to touch the phone.'

He shrugged and watched us drift through the courtyard. We took the elevator up. The lieut and Johnny touched their guns. I recognized the gesture. It was one of comfort. This wasn't a tenement but you were never sure. Sometimes the whole world was a tenement.

'We'll keep it quiet.'

The corridor was empty. The elevator doors closed behind us sounding unnaturally loud. We walked softly and carefully as if the ground was of glass. The lieut rang her doorbell and we all stood out of the line of fire. He rang again, then knocked. No reply. He rang. We waited.

A few minutes passed.

'Want me to open it?'

'Yeah.'

I picked the lock and used the plastic again. I was getting better with practise. I pushed the door open and stepped aside. The lights were on. The bag of groceries still sat on the sofa. My cigarette butts overflowed the ashtray. The apartment was empty.

'She didn't stay long.'

'Her mother's place? You said it was big and empty.'

'No. We would make that connection. The place upstate.'

'But you don't know where it is.' We went into her study. The desk had a filing cabinet next to it. 'We'll check her papers. There might be rent, receipts, letters. Something. Even an address if we're lucky.'

We each took a drawer. I had her bills. Credit cards, Con Ed, mortgage for this apartment, bank statements. I flicked through her check stubs. She wasn't efficient, but highly paid. One hundred and twenty-five grand was four times what a cop made. Most were unfilled. From the checks it wasn't possible to find any upstate payment. Johnny had her letters. Business, family, friends. The lieut was scanning idea files, articles, projects.

At the end of an hour it was nearly three in the morning; we looked at each other.

'Zilch.'

The lieut's eyes were bloodshot. Johnny's pouches under his eyes were even darker. I didn't want to look at my face. I felt drained and hopeless. We sat in silence in the living room. I took out my notebook and began rereading all my interviews. Harry's habit. When you come to a stop, go back. Always go back to see what you have missed. It is there. The other two watched me. I'd talked to so many people. Anderson, Carson, Angel, Captain Herlihy, Bayer, Christine, Mrs Diaz, the bodega owner . . .

I returned to Mrs Diaz. I read her answers carefully. Then I saw it. Harry had sent her a postcard of Niagara Falls. The postmark for the card had been Windham.

'Where's Windham, Lieut?'

'Upstate. Four, five hours' drive.'

'Any valleys around there?' Harry had visited her there.

'Should be. It's the Catskills.' He sat slumped awhile. 'Okay, let's go. We'll have to drive. It's too late to whistle up a plane.'

We stopped by the office and he made a call upstate. He woke the county sheriff and told him what he wanted done: find Christine Breelander's house but on no account approach it. We'd meet him in his office in a few hours.

We took spells with the driving. I slept first, lulled by the hum of wheels and the soft murmur of the men up front. I was shaken awake, still exhausted. I hadn't even dreamt. Just fallen down a warm, black hole. The lieut and I talked to keep me alert while I drove. Baseball, fishing, women, politics, sex, war stories. Anything to keep us both awake, to while away the solitude. We stopped for coffee, and by dawn we turned off the Interstate into the Catskills. The sheriff's office was a couple of miles down the road.

Sheriff King was thin and gaunt. He had an uncanny resemblance to a lizard coming out to sun. He examined us carefully and had coffee brought in by a patrolman.

'I think we found the house you want. It's not in Windham, but five miles out.' He looked accusingly at the lieut. He met a blank stare. 'I woke up all the real estate agents. They're mad at me. I didn't approach the place. I put up a road block on either end of the road. They can't be seen from the house.'

'That's good,' the lieut said. It pleased the sheriff. 'We'd like to observe the building without being seen.'

On the way out the lieut stroked the sheriff. It was his job to run interference for his detectives. Once the sheriff knew the facts he was on our side. Cops belong to the biggest private club in the world.

Windham was a small town deep into the Catskills. On the main street there was little: a supermarket, a hardware store, a bus depot, a gas station and garage and a couple of antique shops for the passing tourists. The houses themselves were scattered over a landscape of hills and valleys and narrow roads, hidden behind acres of farmland or else standing starkly by the roadside. We turned on to a small road. A police car blocked it and we maneuvered around. The woods were dark and bare, and the snow lay undisturbed except for the tracks of deer. On the hills we saw the ski trails and the chalets artfully blended in with the trees. The snow was blinding in the morning sunlight and here and there we saw a small figure gliding effortlessly down the slopes, like a drop of water down a beast's back.

The sheriff stopped before a rise and climbed out. There was a stand of trees to our right and we moved into its shadow and carefully climbed to the top.

'There.'

He pointed down. The land fell steeply from where we stood, then flattened briefly. A house stood by the side of a road. It was wood-framed, neat, with a lot of verandah space. At the back, overlooking a valley, with the hills hazy in the distance, was a glass-framed room. We could see a still figure.

'That's the house alright.' It fitted Christine's description.

The sheriff peered through his binoculars, then passed them to the lieut. He sucked in his breath and gave them to me. I focused on the figure in the glass room. It was Lauren. She sat on a chair, facing the valley. Apart from the chair, there wasn't a single other piece of furniture to be seen. I sharpened the focus. She looked so still. Then her head moved. On the floor beside her my two children lay on blankets.

'Sitting ducks,' the lieut whispered. Johnny took his turn with the glasses. 'We move. She shoots.'

'Where do you figure her to be?'

On the far side of the glass room were three old barns. They were black with age and looked as if they would fall apart. On the opposite side, about a quarter a mile down and parallel to us, was the edge of the forest. She had a clear shot into the room from either location.

'You guess.' He examined the room again. 'All glass. No hiding place when the shooting starts. Maybe she's inside.'

'I don't think so. She won't be able to see my approach.'

I watched Lauren with such longing. She sat straight,

unafraid. Once or twice she looked down at the girls. She eased her back and turned first towards the barns then the trees. She didn't know either where Christine waited.

'She a good shot?' the lieut asked.

'Yeah. She has a certificate.'

'At least she showed you something else. If only we could set up a protection on either side of Lauren.'

We drew back from the rise and squatted in the shadows. It was freezing but none of us noticed. I took out a cigarette.

'If anyone's watching, they'll see the smoke. In this air it hangs around,' the sheriff said.

'You get much traffic on this road in the day?'

'Not much. Some. The Jones farm is about five miles up. And it can be used as a short cut.'

I moved back down to the car. 'Think you can get a couple of farm trucks? High-backed.'

'Sure,' he said and they followed me.

It took him an hour to find the trucks. One was a grubby red, the other of uncertain color. They were both mud-splattered and one had a few bales of hay in the back. The lieut and I had changed into jeans and pullovers. We both wore skull-tight wool caps, pulled down low.

'Follow us up the rise, but don't show yourselves. When she cuts loose, you'll know where she is. Take her then. Alive, if you can.'

'If she's cutting loose,' the sheriff muttered. 'I sure as hell don't want any of my men killed just to take her alive.'

I drove first, the lieut followed with Johnny hidden in the back. Johnny had wanted to drive one, but as the sheriff pointed out, not many black faces were seen in the neighborhood. The cop cars followed.

I took a deep breath as I topped the rise and slowly rolled down the steep road. I watched the glass room. Christine could start shooting. The valley remained silent, except for the noise of our engines. As planned we stopped a quarter of a mile before the house in clear view of the barn and the stand of trees. We both got out and gesticulated in the direction we'd come.

'I hope to God she believes we're lost,' the lieut said.

'She hasn't opened up on Lauren yet.'

We looked around. The ground on either side of the road had no space to turn the trucks around. We got in. The only flat ground was in front of the house. We approached it slowly. I stopped on the far side near the barns. I peered at them and saw no movement at all. The gears meshed as I put them into first. Behind me the lieut was doing the same. It looked as if we were both turning around to go back the way we'd come.

We stopped a moment to change into reverse. We had to time it right. If one of us reached before the other, Lauren could be dead. And the children.

I caught a glimpse of the lieut's raised hand, and suddenly let in the clutch and jammed my foot down on the accelerator. The truck leaped forward and raced towards the rear of the building. I swung the wheel, and slammed the brake as I drew parallel to the glass wall of the room. The lieut did the same and the first bullet smashed into the side of his truck. She was in the woods.

I rolled out. Lauren looked in shock at me and began to move. I stopped her, and smashed in the glass with a tire lever.

'Get out fast.'

I ran in. Another bullet hit the roof, showering me with glass. A couple of pieces cut. I grabbed Sandy and Paula, ran back to the cover of the truck and shoved them underneath with Lauren.

'You okay?'

'I kept praying you'd come.' She leant against me.

'We knew you would, Daddy,' Sandy said. 'She's a crazy, isn't she?'

'Yeah.'

Christine kept firing but she had to aim high. The bullets smashed the top frames of glass one by one. From my view below the trucks I saw the sheriff's men slowly fanning out towards the stand of trees. A couple of them had rifles. They paused and fired. Moved, paused, fired.

Suddenly the valley felt silent.

CHAPTER TWENTY

THERE IS no good day to be buried. For the dead I guess they all look alike. For the living it helps to have the sun in your face and to watch the clouds scudding across a clear sky.

The gathering was impressive. The mayor stood bareheaded by the commissioner. Behind them was the brass. The sun glinted on their finery. The commissioner had spoken first. How many ways can you praise a brave cop? He called Harry a man of valor, a decorated and dedicated policeman killed in the line of duty. The mayor shot a political barb across the coffin. The one about brutality towards policemen. The guard of honor fired a volley into the air, and a bugler played Taps. Sandra, between me and Lauren, wept. Harry would have liked his funeral. He was lowered into the earth with the honor he had lived for all his life.

I watched the hard earth fall into the grave. I was glad I hadn't been the one to have killed Christine Hyslop. I couldn't have borne that much guilt. A brother and sister would have been too great a bloodstain. No one knew which bullet had killed her. They'd found her curled up in the snow behind a stump, cradling her rifle.

'She had lived with pain of her brother's death too long and was shattered by her father's death,' Lauren had said the night before. We'd put the girls to bed and she lay cradled in my arms. 'She told me you screwed well. It was her first remark.'

'You mad?'

'No. She said it to hurt me. I was determined not to let her. She'd come as we were finishing dinner. You don't expect a woman to point a gun at you and your children. She took a Polaroid of us and cut out our faces. She made me drive, with the girls beside me. She told me she'd killed Harry and why. I don't know. I felt sorry for her then. It must be terrible to lose someone you love.'

'I know.'

'When we got up there she locked us in the guest room. It had a small bathroom and the windows were barred. She'd decided to take us when you told her how much you loved us all.'

'Me and my big mouth.'

'It comforted me,' Lauren whispered.

'She'd set out to get you and Harry on the day her brother was killed. When she got to New York she became friendly with Bayer. She learnt all about you and Captain Herlihy, and wrote the notes to him. She told me we were going to die on the fifteenth. God, I was terrified. She was implacable. I wanted her to let the girls go – but she refused. You had to suffer. She left us for a day and came back very upset. She'd not expected you to find her connection in time. She knew then you'd find us. She said you were good. That's when she made me sit in that awful room – and wait for you to show up.'

The ceremony was over. The commissioner murmured to Sandra, then the mayor, then the inspector, then the captain. The lieut came last. He shook her hand, then after a brief glance away shook mine and followed the others. Position was everything.

I waited until they'd all left for their cars. The edge of a grave is a lonely place. You stare down into eternity. The coffin looked so alone and small.

'Take care of him, God. I loved him and he was my partner.'

I turned away and went home.